DOUGLAS SKELTON is an esta   en
books including *Glasgow's I*   *rt*.
He has appeared on a variety   es
as an expert on Glasgow crir   s'
for the Crime and Investigatio   ...Martin and Gary Kemp.
His 2005 book *Indian Peter* was later adapted for a BBC Scotland
radio documentary, which he presented. His first foray into crime
fiction was the acclaimed *Blood City*, which introduced Davie McCall.

By the same author:

Non-fiction

Blood on the Thistle
Frightener: The Glasgow Ice Cream wars (with Lisa Brownlie)
No Final Solution
A Time to Kill
Devil's Gallop
Deadlier than the Male
Bloody Valentine
Indian Peter
Scotland's Most Wanted
Dark Heart
Glasgow's Black Heart

Fiction

Blood City

Crow Bait

DOUGLAS SKELTON

Luath Press Limited
EDINBURGH
www.luath.co.uk

First published 2014

ISBN: 978-1-910021-29-3

The publishers acknowledge the support of

towards the publication of this volume.

The paper used in this book is recyclable. It is made from
low chlorine pulps produced in a low energy, low emissions manner
from renewable forests.

Printed and bound by
Bell & Bain Ltd., Glasgow

Typeset in 11 point Sabon
by 3btype.com

To *the memories of*
Edward Boyd and Roddie McMillan.
I never met them, but Daniel Pike showed
me that a crime thriller did not need to be
set in New York, LA *or London.*
Glasgow's mean streets would do just fine.

Acknowledgements

Thanks go to my 'Reading Posse' – Karin Stewart, Sandy Kilpatrick, Lucy Bryden and Alistair and Rachel Neil.

To Big Stephen Wilkie, Joe Jackson and John Carroll for keeping me right. If I've made errors, they're all mine.

To Elizabeth and Gary McLaughlin for their unflagging support in getting the books publicised (here's another one, guys – get cracking.) And Helena Morrow for keeping Canada supplied.

To Margaret, for keeping me fed while I struggled with the rigours of writing.

To Caron MacPherson and Michael J. Malone for their advice, Alex Gray for saying nice things, and Craig Robertson for the support.

To my editor, Louise Hutcheson, and the team at Luath for making real what always begins as some vague notion as I walk the dogs.

For certain background information on the drug scene in 1990, I am indebted to a series of articles in the Glasgow *Evening Times* during October of that year by Mike Hildrey and Ally McLaws.

And thanks are due to the Steele boys, Jim and Joe.

Prologue

THE BOY IS running across a field, the long grass around him sighing softly as a warm breeze whispers through its stalks. He is running, yet he moves slowly, like a film being played back at half-speed.

The boy is happy. It is a good day, the best day ever, and his young heart sings with its joy. They have taken him out of the city, away from the black buildings, away from the stench of the traffic, away from the constant roar of engines. A day in the country, where the sun didn't need to burn through varying levels of grime to warm the land. His first day in the country and he revels in the feel of the soft grass caressing his legs as he runs.

He can see them waiting for him at the far end of the field, the car his father has borrowed from his boss parked under trees behind them. They smile at him as he draws nearer and his father wraps his arm around his mother's waist. He gives the boy a friendly wave. It is a tender moment and the boy is sorry the day has to end.

But the air cools as the gap between them narrows and the field darkens as if a cloud has passed over the sun. The boy looks up, but the sun is still there, burning brightly in an unbroken blue sky. And yet, the day has shadowed and the grass has lost its colour. The green and sun-bleached yellow is gone, replaced by blacks and greys.

The boy stops and looks to his parents for an explanation, but they are no longer there. In their place is a dark patch, a deep red crying out amid the now muted surroundings, and the boy knows what has caused it.

'Dad, don't...' he hears himself say.

'Dad, please don't...' he murmurs as he backs away, fearful of what he might see in that pool of crimson. His mother, he now knows, is gone, never to return. But he also knows his father is there, somewhere in the red-stained darkness, waiting, watching.

So he backs away and he begins to turn, all the joy replaced by a deep-seated dread. He retreats, for all he wants to do now is get away from that corner of the field, and the sticky redness of the grass, so he turns to run, he turns to flee, he turns to hide.

But when he turns he finds his father looming over him, the poker raised above his head, the love he had once seen in the man's eyes gone and in its place something else, something the boy does not fully understand, but something he knows will haunt him for the rest of his life. Something deadly, something inhuman.

And then his father brings the poker swinging down...

* * *

Barlinnie Prison

One night in November, 1990

Davie McCall woke with a start and for a moment he was unsure of his surroundings. Then, slowly, the grey outline of his cell, what he had come to call his *peter*, began to take shape and the night-time sounds of the prison filtered through his dream-fogged brain: Old Sammy snoring softly in his bed; the hollow echo of a screw walking the gallery; the coughs and occasional cries of other inmates as they struggled with their own terrors.

He had not had the dream for years, but now it had returned. The field was real and he had run through it on just such a warm summer day when his mum and dad took him to the Campsie Hills to the north of Glasgow when he was eight. They had been happy then. They had been a family then. It ended seven years later.

Danny McCall vanished when Davie was fifteen.

But the son knew the father was still out there, somewhere.

He had seen him, just once, little more than a fleeting glimpse, a blink and he was gone. It had been ten years before outside a Glasgow courthouse, just as Davie was being led away. He could not be sure for it was just a flash, but the more he replayed it in his mind, the clearer the face became, as if someone had tweaked the focus. It became a face he knew as well as his own, for the son was the image of the father. It bore a smile on the lips yet there was a coldness in the blue eyes.

And then, just as Davie was pulled away, a wave. He had not registered it at the time but as the months passed and he replayed the scene in his mind, he became sure of it. A wave that said *I'm back*.

I

IT WAS A small room in a small flat and the glow of the electric fire stained the walls blood red. They used to call these one-roomed flats single ends, but that was before the estate agents moved in. Now they were studio apartments, to make them more attractive to the upwardly mobile. Not that the yuppies would be interested in this one. An enthusiastic salesman might call it a fixer upper, but really the only thing that would fix this place up was a canister of petrol and a match. It was run down, on its uppers. If this room had been a person, it would be homeless.

The wallpaper had been slapped on its walls back in the '70s, when garish was good. Bright orange broken up by black wavy lines and the light radiating from the three bar electric fire made it look like the flames of hell. The furniture – what there was of it – would have given items thrown on a rubbish skip delusions of grandeur: a lumpy, stained two-seater settee, a matching armchair, the back bleeding stuffing, an old kitchen table, two wooden chairs, one lying on its side. A standard lamp, the bulb smashed, also on the floor. An ironing board, open and standing, a man's shirt still hanging from the edge, the iron itself disconnected from the mains and discarded on the threadbare rug. There was a small kitchen area in the corner – a grime-encrusted cooker, a stained sink, a small fridge that looked incongruously new. The unmade single bed in the recess had clean, if rumpled linen, so someone was choosy about what they slept in.

It wasn't the decor that obsessed the men and women moving to and fro. It was the woman on her back behind the table. A heavy poker lay in a pool of blood beside her. There was more blood caked on the frayed carpet, spattered on the walls and streaked on the ceiling. The woman's face was a pulpy mass of battered tissue.

'For God's sake, will someone turn off that bloody fire,' Frank Donovan said. The heat was making him feel sick. A Scene of Crime technician reached out with a gloved hand to comply.

Donovan looked at the body and sighed. The wounds were so

ferocious that it was difficult to tell how old the victim was. They already knew she didn't live here – the flat had been rented to a man called John Keen one month before. Neighbours had never seen him and they had no idea who the woman was. Donovan would have someone check with the letting agent, see if they could pull a description of the guy who signed the lease.

A Detective Constable named Johnstone rifled through a handbag found beside the bed and removed a purse stuffed with five £10 notes and a Strathclyde University student matriculation card dated 1988 in the name of Virginia McTaggart. DC Johnstone handed the plastic card to Donovan, who studied the girl's face. She'd be twenty-three now, he calculated, dark-haired, pretty in an unassuming way. She wasn't pretty now, though. The bastard with the poker had seen to that.

He looked up from the card, back to the body, then scanned the room again. Something about this crime scene bothered him, as if a memory had been prodded but had not come fully to life.

'Frank.' Donovan looked up to Johnstone, who was holding out a handful of condoms. 'What do you think – working girl maybe?'

'Maybe,' said Donovan, looking back at the card. 'Get someone to check this card out with Strathclyde Uni. See what we can find out about her.'

Johnstone nodded and took the card back from Donovan. As the DC turned to the door he almost collided with Detective Superintendent Jack Bannatyne who, as ever, looked immaculate. Dark coat over a grey suit, crisp white shirt, muted red tie. Donovan, as usual, felt underdressed in his crumpled blue suit, lighter blue shirt and dark tie, all courtesy of messrs Marks and Spencer. Donovan was surprised to see his old boss here. He headed up Serious Crime now and a solitary murder up a close in Springburn wasn't usually something that blipped on their radar.

'Detective Sergeant Donovan,' said Bannatyne, formal as ever in front of the foot soldiers, as he studied the corpse at their feet. 'Bad one, this.'

'Yes, sir.'

'Battered with the poker?'

'That's what we think, at this stage. The PM will confirm.'

Bannatyne nodded, his eyes flicking around the room. 'Need a quick word. Can we step outside, away from this heat?' Donovan hesitated, unwilling to refuse a request from a superior but just as unhappy about leaving a crime scene. Bannatyne caught his hesitation. 'It's alright, Sergeant, I checked with your DI downstairs. He's happy to spare you for a minute.'

'Of course, sir,' said Donovan, wondering what brought him to this murder scene. He followed Bannatyne down the winding staircase to Keppochill Road. Blue lights flashed in the night from the variety of police vehicles angled at the kerb while technicians and officers, both plainclothes and uniformed, moved between them and the closemouth. Bannatyne led Donovan a few feet away from the hubbub for some semblance of privacy.

'Frank,' he said, keeping his voice low, formality dropped now that they couldn't be overheard. 'You'll've heard that Davie McCall is getting out in a couple of days?'

'Yes, sir.'

'I need a favour.'

'Okay, sir.' Donovan hoped he didn't sound guarded.

'I need you to make contact with him, once he's out.'

'With McCall, sir?'

'Yes. I think you have a...' Bannatyne searched for the correct word, 'connection with him.'

'Don't know about that, sir.'

'You saved his girlfriend from being shot that night. If you hadn't pulled her out of the way, Clem Boyle would've done her for sure. And you caught the bullet. He might think he owes you.'

Donovan resisted the impulse to touch the scar on his chest. 'Or he might think we're even because he chased Boyle and helped bring him down.'

'Maybe, but I'd like you to try anyway.'

Doubts aside, there was no way Donovan could refuse. They both knew it. 'What is it you need, sir?'

'You were involved in the Joe Klein investigation. You know there were questions.'

Joe Klein, the gangster they called Joe the Tailor, shot in his own home ten years before. The case was officially unsolved. 'Yes, sir. But no evidence. As far as we know, it was Jazz Sinclair.'

'He wasn't capable of doing an old hand like Joe.'

Donovan shrugged. 'Everybody gets lucky sometimes.'

'Frank, someone else was there. I know it. I need you to find out what McCall thinks, what he knows. What he's going to do about it. Joe was like a father to him and I don't need him coming out like some lone avenger.'

'That the only reason, sir?'

Bannatyne looked away briefly, then gave Donovan a long stare. 'I feel responsible.'

Donovan frowned. 'For Joe's death?'

'Yes. I told Johnny Jones that it was Joe who had put us on to him – remember we visited Jones in his flat that night?' Donovan nodded. Jones had been credited with kick-starting the big time heroin market in Glasgow, back in 1980. He was shot later that year. Another unsolved killing. There was a lot of that about that year, Donovan recalled. Bannatyne went on, 'I thought I was being clever but I think all it did was piss Jones off. He sent Jazz in that night but the boy wasn't up to it. Someone else finished the job, I feel it in my water. I owe it to Joe to find out who.'

Donovan shifted from one foot to the other. He felt he was out of line in saying what he was about to say, but he was going to say it anyway. 'Joe was a crook, sir. What do you care about him?'

Bannatyne gave him another of his long, hard looks then nodded, as if giving Donovan retrospective permission to ask the question. 'He wasn't a bad guy, not compared to what we have now – drug dealers, scumbags, thugs in shellsuits attacking innocent people. He had rules, he had standards. God help me for saying this, but he even had morals, of a sort. We'll never see his like again.'

Donovan nodded, understanding now. Bannatyne was old-fashioned, too. Tough, sometimes pulled strokes, but always basically honest and with a distinct lack of respect for desk-bound authority figures who had forgotten what police work was all about. There would have been mutual respect between him and Joe the Tailor, even though they were on opposite sides of the fence.

'I'll see McCall as soon as I can, sir. I'll let you know what he says, if anything. But if I remember rightly, he doesn't say much.'

Bannatyne nodded. 'All we can do is try, Frank. I appreciate it.' The DCI inclined his head towards the second floor window of the flat they'd just left. 'You got a victim ID?'

'Virginia McTaggart. Could be a tart, we're not sure. It's not her flat, so maybe her customer brought her back here. Flat's rented out to a John Keen.'

Bannatyne thought about this. 'Want me to ask Jimmy Knight to speak to his touts? He's got a few who work The Drag – maybe they know this lassie?'

Donovan knew that Jimmy Knight had a number of informers among the prostitutes who worked 'The Drag', the grid of streets between Anderston Cross and Sauchiehall Street. He had often walked the rain-swept area with Knight in search of information. Donovan knew that Knight extracted more than intelligence from some of the girls, the big cop being physically unable to keep it in his pants. Normally he wouldn't want Knight anywhere near an investigation, good and intuitive detective though he was, but as Bannatyne had asked, it would be churlish to refuse.

'That'd be a good idea, sir, thanks.'

Bannatyne patted him on the arm and walked to his car. Donovan made his way back to the murder room, his mind on Davie McCall. He had thought about the young man often over the past ten years, each memory accompanied by the dull ache in his chest where the bullet had caught him.

Davie McCall.

He was eighteen when he went in. He'd be a man now. He'd had a difficult time in prison, Donovan had heard, though jail was never easy. Donovan wondered how much it had changed him.

2

AROUND HIM THE night sounds of the prison continued. He had grown used to the coughs and the murmurs and the footsteps. He had even found comfort in them, just as he had in the routines of prison life.

When the judge sentenced Davie McCall, he showed no emotion. It stung that he had been sent away on perjured evidence, even if he'd actually committed the warehouse robbery, but four years inside didn't worry him. He could handle it. He had never been jailed before, never been to Borstal. Earlier that year he had spent his first night in a police cell following a square-go in Duke Street, but that hadn't exactly prepared him for life in the Big House. His mind, though, was filled with thoughts of his father's sudden reappearance, and he wandered through the induction process in a fog. He was aware of orders being barked by stern-faced prison officers, providing his personal details, being given a prison number as well as a striped shirt and jeans, showering then a quick medical – *bend over*, *cough*, head raked for lice, and questions designed to assess if he was a suicide risk.

There was no question of non-compliance, he and the rest of the prisoners were herded from one point to the next, making Davie think of the cattle in the slaughterhouse on Duke Street he used to pass on his night-time walks. He was a meat eater, but he always dreaded coming so close to that grey building with its sharp angles and its sense of death. None of the men here were destined for death, no matter how heinous their crime, but they were little more than cattle all the same. That was how prison worked – routine, order, discipline.

Then he was put in one of the dog boxes.

The tiny compartments, little more than a cupboard with a single bench at the back, were a way-station for prisoners while paperwork was being processed. It was only a few square feet and would have been claustrophobic enough if he was the only one in it, but there were two other guys already waiting when the prison officer ordered Davie inside and slammed the door shut. He pressed himself against the door and looked at his new companions wedged side by side on a narrow bench, their shoulders pressed hard against the walls on either side. He had never felt this before, this sensation of the walls closing in on him, and it was a tense two hour wait until they were taken out. Davie had never felt relief like it.

Barlinnie had five wings, each called a hall. Davie's new home was in 'B' Hall and the cell he shared on the second gallery with one other inmate – a petty thief called Tom from East Kilbride – was larger than the dog box at least. However, it was still no suite at the Waldorf, with two slop buckets in the corner that reeked continually of stale urine and shit and a single, slatted window so high up the wall that all he could see through it were ribbons of cold, grey Glasgow sky. His cellmate, his co-pilot as they called them in the jail, was an okay guy, if a bit dodgy, and Davie resolved to keep a close eye on whatever he had, but he generally kept himself to himself, which suited Davie.

Davie resolved to get through his sentence as easily as he could. He would give the screws no trouble, he would be a model prisoner and get out to resume his life. To get back to Audrey.

They had met on a night out in the West End when he had stepped in on her attempted rape by the same young guy who would later kill Joe the Tailor. Davie had taken a beating that night, but it had been worth it. He met Audrey. Audrey, who had almost died because of him but who still cared for him. Gorgeous Audrey, the straight arrow who didn't give a toss about his past and who saw something in him that he didn't know was there. Although he didn't like her seeing him in prison clothes and being ordered around by the screws, she insisted on visiting him as often as she could. She believed he could change and because she believed it, so did he. All he had to do was get through his sentence.

Rab visited two or three times in the early months, but Davie could tell the big fellow was uncomfortable. Rab knew he could leave the visitors room and do what he wanted on the outside, but still Davie could see a thin line of sweat beading on his permanent five o'clock shadow and, even though he tried to hide it, his nervousness was palpable. Eventually, the big guy stopped coming altogether, though he wrote now and again and sent messages via Bobby Newman. One year into his sentence, it was Bobby who told him that Rab was getting married, to a girl from Northern Ireland called Bernadette. She had been staying with relatives in Ruchazie and Rab met her at a party.

'Shoulda seen him, Davie, arse over tip he went, love at first sight,' Bobby said, his voice low so that others in the visiting room couldn't overhear them talking about Big Rab McClymont's personal business. Rab was a major player in The Life now, thanks to working with Luca Vizzini, Joe's old friend and business partner.

Davie smiled, 'Can't imagine Rab being married.' He was not as successful with women as Bobby, who merely had to look in a girl's direction to have her tumbling into bed, but Rab did all right. Now he was about to be married and, Bobby assured him, strictly a one gal guy. Whatever this girl Bernadette had, it was potent.

The match was further testament to the ecumenical nature of their training from Joe the Tailor, for Bernadette was Roman Catholic. Her family back home were far from pleased that she was marrying a Prod.

'They're pretty heavy back in Belfast,' Bobby had said. 'Don't know if they're IRA or anything like that, but they're a tough bunch. But Bernadette, she's not taken any shit from them. She just told them she was marrying Rab and if they didn't like it, they could go take a flying fuck to themselves. Maybe no those exact words, mind you, but that was certainly the sentiment.'

Bobby also brought news of Abe, the plucky wee mongrel dog Davie had rescued from an abusive owner. Joe had always said they must never accept cruelty to women, children or animals, and Davie had taken it to heart. It brought him Audrey and it brought him Abe. When he was sent down, he asked Rab to take care of the wee dog, but in his heart he knew the big guy was not an animal person. To be fair to Rab, he tried, but eventually Abe was rehomed with a young couple in Easterhouse. Bobby Newman had checked them out and he knew the dog was going to a good life. The girl was pregnant and they believed a child should be brought up around animals, which was good. Bobby said he looked in every now and then and Abe was happy, which pleased Davie.

So the months passed and Davie's release date grew closer as he settled into the routine of being locked down, slopping out, working making concrete slabs, in the cobblers or the laundry, lunch, exercise, work, teatime, lock-down, recreation, supper and lock down. Then the next day it all started again – slopping out, work, meal breaks, exercise, lock down. Every day the same. Every day being yelled at by grim-faced prison officers. Every day hearing the alarm bells go off somewhere and seeing the officers running to contain some trouble, for Barlinnie was full of violent men and the violence within them must boil over. Davie McCall had violence in him, he knew that, but he fought hard to keep it bottled up. And he succeeded.

Until Donald Harris came along.

3

AUDREY FRASER WATCHED the illuminated numbers count down to the ground floor. She was alone in the lift of the *Daily Record* high rise at Anderston Quay, heading out to interview a drug addict. It was bog-standard stuff, the horrors of addiction laid bare as the sub-heading would no doubt have it, and she wasn't particularly looking forward to it. There had been a time when she would have given her eye-teeth and one or two of her internal organs for a chance at doing such a piece, but she'd been green and hungry then. Now she was ripe and well-fed, thank you very much. But the interview was part of a larger series about the drug trade in Glasgow and the West of Scotland, and necessary, if she was to give the full picture.

The lift doors opened on the second floor and Audrey smiled

as she saw the reed-thin frame of Barclay Forbes. She had known Barc since those green and hungry days as a young reporter on the *Evening Times*. Barc had proved to be a good friend over the years, teaching her everything he knew about crime reporting. And his knowledge was extensive.

Barc returned her smile and said, 'Going down, hen?'

'Buy me dinner first, big boy,' she said.

He shook his head solemnly as he stepped into the lift and punched the button marked 'G', even though it was already lit. 'Sex on the brain, you.'

Audrey's smile broadened. 'What brings you to the dark side?'

Barc had worked for years with the *Glasgow Herald* and *Evening Times*, a broadsheet and tabloid respectively owned by a rival publisher. 'Retired man now,' said Barc, his voice still bearing the roughness of decades of smoking, though he'd given up two years before. Audrey was glad of that, she had nagged him long enough, and in the end he had given in. 'I can go anywhere I want. The *Sunday Mail*'s serialising the book, needed me in to do a wee bit of editing.'

In the year since he'd retired, Barc had been writing his memoirs, stories of Glasgow crime from the 1950s onwards. He said it looked like a trilogy as the first one only came up to the mid-'60s.

Audrey said, 'Hope they're paying mega bucks for the rights.'

'Bloody right they are. No that I'll see much of it, right enough, once the publisher takes their chunk.'

'Shouldn't have taken such a big advance then, greedy sod.'

The lift came to a halt and the doors slid open. Barc gave her a sideways glance as they walked out. 'Who's side you on?'

She laughed as they headed for the exit onto Anderston Quay, where Audrey knew a black cab was waiting. Even though she knew he'd given up, she still half-expected him to light up as soon as he was in the open. He didn't look right without a fag hanging from his lips.

'You want a lift?' she asked.

'Where you headed?'

'Gorbals, interview with a junkie.'

He nodded. 'Nice people you mix with.'

'Present company excepted?'

A smile. 'No necessarily.'

'Anyway, you taught me everything I know.'

'And don't you forget it.' His eyes flicked to the taxi idling at the kerb. 'Nah, thanks for the offer, hen – I'm headed up the West End. I'm keeping company with a lady of independent means in Kelvingrove now.'

Audrey gave him a leer. 'Keeping company? That what you young folks are calling it now?'

Barc shot her a stern look. 'Behave yourself, hen, no everything's about sex. You're no seeing this junkie alone, are you?'

'No, meeting a snapper there.'

'Good,' Barc nodded, satisfied. Audrey smiled again, glad that he was still looking out for her. He turned away and she was about to step down to the waiting taxi when he swung back and moved close to her again.

'I hear that guy you used to see is getting out tomorrow,' he said, quietly. She halted in her tracks.

'Davie?'

'You didn't know?'

She shook her head. It was just like Barc to know something like that. That's what made him the best, even now. 'Well, I hope he behaves himself.'

'Boys like him, they don't know any better.'

'I don't know, Barc, I always told you Davie was different.'

'That why a four year stretch turned into ten years then? 'Cos he knew better, 'cos he was different?'

She looked down at the ground. 'I'm not sure what happened there.'

'He reverted to type, that's what happened. You know it, hen – that's why you ended it.'

'I know,' she said, feeling guilty about the way she had handled things, but something in her voice made the old reporter's nose twitch.

Barc stared at her, his eyes narrowing as he tried to read her. 'Stay away from him, Audrey.' *Audrey, not hen.* That meant he was serious.

'Barc, don't worry – I'm over all that, believe me.' She kept her voice light and airy, holding up her left hand and wiggling her fingers. 'Respectable married lady, remember?'

He looked at the ring on her finger and nodded. 'Aye, married maybe. No sure about the respectable…'

He walked away and she watched him go. *Davie McCall.* She hadn't thought of him for a long time. That hadn't been an easy trick to pull off.

* * *

The man called the top flat of the high rise 'The Crow's Nest', even though the tower block didn't quite scrape the sky as much as others in the city. The Gorbals used to be known as Hell's Hundred Acres, a tag Audrey always thought unfair. But then, she'd never seen the place when the dark tenement was king. Back in the '60s, these flats had been hailed as the future, but now they were slated for demolition, though no-one knew when that would happen. From what she had seen, it was not before time. Audrey and Big George Gillan, the photographer, had passed a number of boarded up doorways as they walked to this one, the architect's dream crumbling into a damp, crime-ridden hellhole.

If it hadn't been for the man sprawled on the couch under the window, the flat would have looked derelict. There was no carpet on the floor and the ratty old armchair in which she sat was ripped and stained with who knew what. She knew she was going to have her trousers cleaned immediately. Or burned, which may be wiser. Big George leaned against a wall smoking a cigarette, refusing to sit on anything in the flat. His camera dangled around his neck, and he'd already snapped off a number of shots of the sallow-faced addict. Every now and then, she heard the click of the shutter as another angle appealed. He'd taken maybe twenty shots but only one would be used, the addict's face blanked out. Big George could have left any time but he opted to stay, being old school, and there was no way he was leaving a lassie alone with a junkie crook.

Through the grime-encrusted windows overlooking Queen Elizabeth Square she could see the city lying under a sky that looked as if it had been smeared by an oily rag. A gas fire hissed in the wall but the flat still felt cold, thanks to damp walls. There was nothing else in the room apart from the armchair, its neighbour in the corner, and the couch. No coffee table, no telly, no pictures, ornaments or mementos, unless you counted the two or three brown-tinged cigarette filters that lay on the floorboards under the window. She stared at the red-haired man opposite her, unable to shake off the feeling she'd seen him before. He was smoking a thin roll-up, but it was unfiltered. He had other uses for the items on the floor. Even without the usual detritus of habitation, this place had an unlived feel about it. Audrey wondered if it was his home or if it was some kind of Giro drop used by a handful of people.

He told them they should call him 'Jinky'. Used to be a footballer, he said, a good one. Could jink about with the ball. He'd been jinking about when they first arrived, always in movement and even when he sat, his leg bounced around. If it was nervous leg syndrome, Audrey thought, it was heading for a breakdown. They had talked for a while, but his needs grew too strong and eventually he excused himself and vanished into another room. Big George had raised his eyebrows at her. They both knew what he was doing. Tenner bag into a spoon, heated with a lighter, drawn into the syringe through the filter tip, then into a vein – probably his groin, given the years he'd been mainlining. The residue in the filter tip would be saved for a rainy day. He was more relaxed when he came back, but Audrey knew she was on the clock now. Pretty soon he'd be drifting into a deep sleep, and when he awoke he'd feel the need to jag up once more.

He spoke as if his jaw was stiff, like so many junkies, his voice coming from somewhere at the back of his throat. He spoke about his life, how he'd come from a good family here in the Gorbals but he'd joined a gang, drifted into crime, done time in the Bar-L, then Greenock, for assault with a deadly weapon. When he got out in 1984 he'd started using heroin, got hooked, and now here he was.

Still saw his wee maw around the streets, down the shops, but she didn't want to know him. Ashamed of him, so she was. Couldn't blame her, he said.

'Why don't you kick it?' Audrey asked, but she knew the answer before he shook his head sadly.

'Naw, darlin, no easy, that. Tried once, went to one of they addiction service places, Alban House, then did a spell at a rehab unit over in Cardross. It was fuckin hard goin so it was, pardon my language. Almost made it, too, but as soon as I came back here I was right back on the stuff. It's like bein in love, know what I mean? It's all you can think of, all you want, and when you're away from it you can't wait to get back.'

Audrey scribbled this down. It was a good line and she wondered if he'd read it somewhere. 'Where do you get your stuff?'

'Ach, all over, darlin. Here, there. You cannae go nowhere in Glasgow, darlin, without trippin over a dealer. Used to be there was a polis on every corner, or a pub, now it's a dealer. There's a couple work the Gorbals here, just down at the shops, fuckin yards away from the polis station, pardon my language. It's nuts, darlin, pure nuts. They're there puntin tenner bags and jellies and that and the polis are sittin in their wee office drinkin coffee and eatin dough-nuts, you know?'

She nodded. It was a tale told and retold across the city. Gorbals, Saracen, Possil, Blackhill. The police couldn't stem the flow of drugs on the streets, so it often seemed they tried to ignore it. She had even heard that senior officers had long ago decided they couldn't stop the trade, so they decided to control it by 'licensing' dealers to operate in return for information when it was needed. It was almost an urban legend, but Audrey had never found anyone to corroborate it. She wished she could – what a story that would make. Her husband wouldn't be happy, though. He was seldom happy with what she wrote. But then, he wouldn't, being a plainclothes cop.

'Anyway, darlin,' Jinky said, his voice sad, 'I suppose it's what I deserve. I've no been a good person, you know what I'm sayin? My maw would die if she knew all the things I'd done.'

'Like what?'

His face crinkled. 'Ach, robbin folk, hurtin folk. See my prison stretch? Was for usin a knife on a fella. Carved him up bad, so I did.'

'Why'd you do it?'

He stopped and considered her question, his eyes dull and life-less. 'Fucked if I know, pardon my language, darlin. I think I was paid to do it. I did that back then, got paid to hurt folk. There was a Tally man around here who used to get me to scare folk who didn't pay their debts on time. Known for it, so I was. Even in the jail.'

'In Barlinnie?'

'Aye, used to do people in there for fags and chocolate and stuff, you know? See if it was now, I'd be doin it for a hit.'

Audrey doubted that. He didn't look capable of hurting anyone now. He must've been a powerful enough bloke in his day, but the drugs had eaten him away. The tenner bag he'd jagged up in the other room was taking effect now. His head was beginning to droop, his speech slowing.

'There was this one bloke, though. I was told to give him a right going over, do him in if I could. It was nothing to me...'

Audrey suddenly became interested. Now here was a story. 'You were to kill him?'

'Aye. I'd be protected, they said. I'd get away with it, they said.'

'Who's they?'

He didn't answer, his chin sliding towards his chest, the forgotten cigarette still burning between his fingers.

'Jinky!' Audrey said, her voice sharp. His head snapped up and he focussed on her once more. 'Who's they?'

'The guy that wanted me to do it, right bastard he was. We all hated him. But he came to me one day and he gave me this Bar-L Special...'

'What's a Bar-L Special?'

'Plastic toothbrush with two razor blades melted into it. Carves a right deep double wound, so it does. And he gave me a fork, sharpened to a point. I was to stripe this guy and plunge him. If I couldn't kill him I was to put him out of action.'

'Out of action?'

'Cripple him...'

'What happened?'

He was drifting again so Audrey clapped her hands and yelled his name. His head raised but his eyes were glazing. She knew she didn't have long. 'What happened?' She asked again.

He thought about the question. 'The boy gave me a right doin, so he did. Never even got as much as a punch in. Like a fuckin machine he was, pardon my language. Pounded me like a piece of mince.'

Audrey felt her blood freeze. 'Who was this boy?'

Jinky paused, dredging up the name. 'I should remember it, so I should. Bastard put me out cold. I got transferred after that, away from Bar-L.'

'Try to remember...' Audrey was leaning forward now. At first she had simply sensed a great story, but this was all sounding very familiar. She felt her nerves tingling and she was no longer taking notes. She studied Jinky's face, trying hard to see the features of the burly, hard-faced convict she'd seen years ago across a court-room in the sallow cadaver before her. The addict's eyelids began to flutter again, the hit really taking hold. 'Jinky,' she said, 'this is important – what was the name of the person who beat you up?'

'A legend, so he was, but I didn't know that at the time...' His words were really slurred now, his voice barely a whisper. Audrey leaned forward to hear them.

'Jinky,' she pressed, 'was it Davie McCall? Was the boy you were sent to hurt called Davie McCall?'

He nodded, his head drooping. 'Fuckin legend he was, pardon my language...'

4

THE MORE DAVIE thought about it over the years, the more he was certain Harris had been hired to cripple him, or kill him. He'd never met him before, they had no priors, while the use of two weapons meant this was to be no casual striping. He looked down at the semi-conscious inmate and held his hands up to study them. There was no tremble. He wasn't even breathing heavily. As ever, he wondered at how calm he had remained throughout. He felt the cold rage that nestled within him lessen and return to wherever it came from. A sound like a faint wind that had risen in his ears began to still and finally died.

A prison officer appeared at the end of the corridor and took in the scene, his eyes flitting from Harris on the deck to Davie standing over him. Lomas, had to be. He had sent Davie to this deserted corridor, after all, had set him up for Harris to pounce. Davie could tell from the look on the screw's face that this was not the way it was meant to be.

'Stand back, McCall!' He yelled, but Davie didn't move. Lomas was a bastard, but he was a plucky one. He stepped forward, his body tensed for a fight. 'Back, ya fucker, and face the wall!'

Davie thought about taking him on but knew it would be a mistake. He stepped away from Harris and pressed himself against the wall, hands above his head. He heard Lomas take a tentative step towards the prisoner on the floor and say, 'Fuck!' Then Davie felt a sharp pain as the prison officer rammed a clenched fist into his kidneys.

'Don't you fucking move,' Lomas hissed. Davie tried not to give him the satisfaction of showing pain but the officer knew exactly where to hit because a fire was burning through his back. He shot a glare over his shoulder as Lomas stooped to retrieve the Bar-L Special from the floor and slipped it into his tunic. Davie glanced back to where the fork had landed and saw that had been pocketed too. 'I told you not to move, fucker,' said Lomas as he landed another blow, and this time Davie went down, his hand clutching the small of his back. Through the pain he fired a defiant look at the prison officer, who merely smirked. As a cadre of officers steamed up the corridor towards them, Davie kept his eyes on Lomas, trying to figure out why he wanted him damaged. Or dead. Two red-faced screws manhandled him against the wall, one pressing his face against the brick, the other pinning his arms behind his back and slapping a set of manacles on his wrists. Once subdued, he was hauled off to segregation.

Davie didn't really mind being in the Digger, even though the cramped little cell was even less comfortable than the one up on the gallery. Being in solitary got him away from his cell-mate's snoring and gave him time to think. He was lucky, too, for he only received one visit by the batter squad, sometimes known as the mufti squad. There were different levels of mufti – two-man, three-man, four-man and so on. Officially they did not exist. Davie had heard of them but had never actually witnessed an attack. Now he saw one first-hand. They came in during his first night in the Digger, the three-man team surging through the door of his peter like a black wave. Fists, feet and at least one baton rained down on him before he could move, all of them body hits. He understood what it was about – as far as they were concerned he had broken the rules and had to be taught a lesson. The prisoners came from a brutal world and they understood brutality, so punishment was swift and hard and physical. In prison, it's survival of the hardest, and some of the screws had to be the hardest boys on the block. Davie understood it, but he did not accept it. He knew it was an abuse of power, knew it was just the kind of behaviour that would backfire some day on the system. However, he did not fight back, even though he felt cold rage steal over him as they beat him, felt the power to retaliate pulsing through his body. But something told him that if he let whatever was inside him take over again, it would only make matters worse. So for the first time he brought it under control and he let them beat him, let them show off how powerful they were, and within a few minutes it was over. As he lay in his cot that night, his body throbbing in agony, he thought of Audrey and imagined her cool hands soothing his bruises and somehow he felt better.

His time alone allowed the bruises and contusions to heal and also gave him the opportunity to think about why Harris had been sent after him. Davie had gone out of his way not to cause any trouble or get in anyone's face. Violence was commonplace in the jail, but Davie didn't think it was anyone on the inside. But who? The only two people he could think of who had ever wanted him dead were both lying cold themselves – Johnny Jones had been found shot and Clem Boyle had been taken out by cops. A striping in the jail could be bought for a few packets of tobacco, a killing for not much more. So who hired Harris? Who had enough pull to get the boy to risk a life sentence? Not only that, a screw had set him up. Who the hell was behind it?

Then his father's smiling face and that little wave came into his mind, as it had many times before. The little wave that said *I'm back*. Davie became convinced that Danny McCall was at the root of this attack, that he wanted his son to leave prison in a wheelchair or in a box. Danny McCall saw his boy as a threat. The thought made Davie smile in the dark solitude of the Digger. It was a grim, determined little smile, and if Danny McCall had been able to see it he would have been fearful.

Harris's attack did not result in Davie's death or crippling, but it did lead to an extension of his sentence.

Lomas, the prison officer, lied in court, claiming that he saw Davie attack with no provocation. He also claimed Davie had taken a swing at him, which explained the visit by the muftis. The court, naturally, swallowed everything he said – screws, like cops, being paragons of virtue in the eyes of Scottish juries. Davie denied it but who the hell would believe a convict? He was given another eight years for the assault. He felt his heart sink as the judge handed the sentence down and his body was numb as the guards on either side of him led him to the cells below the court. He had only been months away from early release and then this happened. He had been defending himself but he was the one who was going down and Harris was being treated like a bloody victim.

Another eight years. He wasn't sure he could handle that. He had been a model prisoner, but the system had turned on him. As he travelled back in the prison van, Davie McCall decided he would show them what vicious was all about.

5

JIMMY KNIGHT LAID the two plastic bags of groceries on the small formica table in the tiny kitchen of the flat. He'd bought them earlier that afternoon, knowing he was coming to see her that night. Jack Bannatyne had asked him to tap his touts for info on the dead girl and Mary was best one he had. Even if she was dying of the virus.

'You're good to me, Mister Knight,' she said.

He didn't answer. He'd had a patchy relationship with the woman at best, but ever since she'd been diagnosed as HIV Positive, he'd felt sorry for her. He still held an assault charge over her head, but truth was that wasn't much of a threat after all this time. She didn't work the streets now, but she still had contacts among the working girls so he used her whenever he could. Naturally, there were no more freebies. The virus put paid to all that. But there was another reason that he kept coming back. He actually liked her.

'It's no free, Mary,' he said as he began to put the food away in cupboards. He knew where everything went. He'd done it often enough. Even so, he didn't like the cow-like way she looked at him now. He brought her food whenever he could, but it was just to keep her as healthy as possible for as long as possible. She still looked okay, thinner certainly, and she still dyed her hair a deep auburn, but he knew she was dying by inches. *She'll peg out sooner or later*, he told himself, *but until then I'll use her*. He may have liked her, but Jimmy Knight didn't do sentiment. He planned to have that put on his tombstone.

'What have you got for me?'

He'd asked her earlier to listen to the jungle drums about the Virginia McTaggart murder. Her face turned solemn. Without her make-up, and thin as she was now, he could see the scars of teenage acne clearly. That's what had given her the street name of Plooky Mary. She was the neds' favourite tart and that had made her invaluable to Knight over the years. It was amazing what a ned will say when he's doing the business.

'Ginny was a poor soul. A nice lassie, didn't deserve that.'

'She didn't live out Springburn way, did she?'

'No, she dossed up Maryhill Road. Lived with another girl, Patsy something or other, cannae mind.'

Knight nodded. He knew the Baird Street team had already found her address and spoken to her flatmate, another tart. She knew nothing, it seemed. 'Did she have any regulars?'

'Christ, Mister Knight, we've all got regulars, you should know that. You was one of mine...'

'Aye, but did she speak of any? She wouldn't go to a bloke's flat without knowing him, would she?'

Mary nodded. 'There was one, name of John.' She rolled her eyes at that. 'She talked to the lassies about him as if he was Prince Charming.'

'She say what he looked like?'

'Blue eyes, just. Older than her. That's all she ever said about him.' She slugged from her bottle again. Knight didn't know what was in it, but she knocked it back like water. 'Course, it could be a crawler, no this John at all.' Kerb crawler, a man in a car trawling the Drag for flesh. He'd pull up close by her corner, call her over, a deal made and she'd get in.

'Could be,' said Knight, but his copper's nose told him it was John, whoever the hell he was.

Mary saw the doubt on his face and nodded in agreement. 'But it's more likely this John guy. He'd phone her, arrange to meet somewhere, make it an all-nighter. I'll ask the lassies again, see if there's anything else they can remember.'

He had emptied both bags and now turned to face her. He took out his wallet and pulled out a £20 note. 'Gimme a call if you get anything more.' He laid the money on the table top. Mary looked at it and bit her lip.

'I feel bad taking your money, Mister Knight, after you buying me messages and all.'

'Don't feel bad. Just get me something I can use.'

'Aye, I'll do my best. But do you no want a wee something else, maybe?'

She set the bottle of medicine down and moved towards him, her head tilted in a way she thought might be sexy. 'I mean, I know we cannae shag but I can give you a hand job. No harm in that...'

He laid both hands on her shoulders, kept her at bay. There was a time when he'd've taken her up on her offer, hell, there was a time he'd've just told her she was going to give him a seeing to. But not now. 'You're all right, Mary. I'll pass.'

Her face fell. Knight wondered if the offer had been a way of boosting her self-esteem. Instead it had made her even more pitiful. He felt a wee bit sorry for her and he liked her but the idea of those diseased hands touching him gave him the boke.

6

IN THE DARKNESS, the photo of his mother held loosely in both hands, Davie thought about his meeting back in 1982 with the man they called The Colonel.

Davie had fumed in the prison van on the way back from court, having listened stonily as people lied about him. Two years before it had been security guards who Jimmy Knight had put up to perjury, now it was that bastard Lomas and Donald Harris. The inmates in the other cubicles seemed to sense his cold rage, for they were unnaturally quiet. He had been called an animal in that court room, even though he had only defended himself. They had painted him as some kind of monster. Okay, if that's what they wanted, that's what they'd get. He'd show them what a monster really was.

But they were way ahead of him.

As soon as he arrived back in Barlinnie, he was told the Governor wanted to see him. Until then, Davie had only glimpsed the screws' boss as he walked round 'B' Hall. He was a tall guy, his erect stance betraying his military background. He had a deep tan, suggesting long periods under foreign suns. You didn't get that colour in Glasgow. According to prison rumour he was ex-SAS and could kill with the flick of a finger. Davie didn't believe it but there was a power, a danger, that exuded from the man.

He was standing at a window behind his desk when Davie was shown into his office. He turned and motioned for him to sit down then told the two-man escort to leave them alone. There was no please or thank you, for this was a man used to giving orders and having them carried out with no questions asked. Davie sat in the wooden chair and wondered what the hell this was all about. He watched as he stepped away from the window and, still on his feet, flicked through a file on his desk. Davie guessed it was his prison record. They shared the room in silence for a full minute and Davie again noticed how straight and erect the guy was. No wonder they called him The Colonel.

The Colonel did not look up from the file as he said, 'Am I going to have trouble with you, McCall?'

When Davie didn't reply, the man's eyes raised sharply and bored into him. 'I asked you a question. I expect an answer.' Davie shrugged and the man sighed. 'I'll take that as a yes, then.'

He sat down in his big leather chair and studied Davie across the desk. Finally he said, 'What happened in that corridor, McCall?'

'Ask your screw,' said Davie.

'I'm asking you.'

'Doesn't matter what I say, you'll not believe me.'

'Try me.'

Davie held his gaze, trying to gauge what the man was after. 'Your man Lomas sent me to fetch a mop. Harris went for me with two blades and I took them off him.'

'No weapons were found.'

'Lomas took them.'

'Why would he do that?'

'Ask him.'

The Colonel did not reply. His face remained impassive as he glanced down at the file again. 'You'd not been in trouble with us until then. In fact, you were a model prisoner.'

Davie remained silent. He did not know where this was leading.

'So I'll ask you again – are we going to have trouble with you?'

'What do you think? I get another eight years in this shithole for defending myself...'

The Colonel's eyes narrowed and he gave Davie a hard gaze. 'Defending yourself? Harris has a broken nose, a dislocated shoulder and it's only by the grace of providence that you didn't fracture his skull.'

Davie stared straight back. 'Him or me, that's what it came down to.'

The man exhaled audibly through his nose and his mouth tightened. 'Mister Lomas has been transferred from this prison. Harris, too. I insisted on it.'

Davie's mind raced as he took this in. He believed the guy was trying to tell him that he knew what really happened in that corridor. He had no clue how the Colonel knew, and he doubted he would tell him if he asked, so he remained silent.

'I can't do anything about your sentence because it was handed down by the court and it's our job to carry it out. But I will make a deal with you – if you go back to the way you were before this happened, I can guarantee there will be no further trouble from the system. If, however, you decide to be a hard man, then we'll show you what hard really is. Do you understand?'

Davie simply stared at him, his face set in stone. 'Your batter squad has already had a go at me...'

Irritation flicked across the Colonel's face. 'There are no batter squads in this prison, McCall...'

Tell that to my bruises, mate.

'... and I will not stand for brutality on the part of my staff. If I hear of any such action, I will deal with the offenders decisively.' The firm jut of the man's jaw told Davie he meant what he said. But that didn't mean some of the screws wouldn't take matters into their own hands.

The Colonel sighed. 'McCall, the next eight years will be unpleasant, there's no getting away from it. Prison is not the holiday camp the press like to think it is. You called this place a shithole and that's exactly what it is. It's one hundred years old and constantly over-crowded with the scum of the streets. Have you seen *Star Wars*?'

Davie was surprised by the sudden change in tack and wondered where it was leading, but he nodded. The man opposite nodded back. 'My grandson is nuts about those films.'

Davie was still mystified as to what this had to with him, but he listened all the same. He had nothing better to do.

'There's a line in the first film, Alec Guinness says it, about this town, or space station whatever. He says you will never find a more wretched hive of scum and villainy. Whenever I hear that line I think of this prison. It's brutal and it's inhumane and sometimes it causes more problems than it cures. At its best it's a shithole, as you say. At its worse it can be hell on earth. It's up to you what end of that scale you serve out your time.'

Davie knew he was being warned off while at the same time being offered a lifeline. If he co-operated, word would be issued – no 'special treatment'. If he chose not to co-operate, some of the screws would consider it their duty to make him wish he had never been born, or at least that his father had finished the job back in that small Oatlands flat. The Colonel would not condone it, he would not sanction it, but it would happen all the same.

Davie nodded in agreement. 'Okay, I'll do it your way.'

Warmth crept into the Colonel's eyes then and there was the hint of a smile. 'Wise choice, son. Let's hope you and I have no cause for any further conversations of this type.' He pressed a button on his desk and Davie heard the door behind him open. The interview was obviously over.

As Davie stood up, the prison governor lifted an envelope from the file and threw it across the desk. A letter: Davie was not surprised that it had already been opened. As Davie caught it, he felt something hard inside, like cardboard.

'That came for you yesterday. She's a pretty woman...'

Davie's fingers tingled with shock as he slowly slid the photograph from the envelope. It was Mary McCall, his mother, in a shot taken on the day they went to the country. She was smiling straight at the camera because his dad had just said something funny. Davie felt something tighten in his gut as he stared at the snap, its faded colour raising old ghosts.

'There was no note with it, just the picture,' said the Colonel. 'Who sent it?'

Davie shook his head as if he didn't know. But he did know. He would have known instinctively even if he hadn't recognised the writing on the envelope.

Danny McCall was reminding his son they had unfinished business.

7

JACK BANNATYNE HAD been in and out of Luca's Café every few months since Joe's death, ostensibly to sample the scones, baked by Luca's wife. But Luca knew better. He knew the goddamned cop suspected who had really killed Joe the Tailor. He just couldn't prove it. The visits had stopped three years before, when he was promoted to Detective Chief Inspector and transferred to a station on the South Side. Then Luca heard he had stepped up another rung in the promotion ladder and had taken over the Serious Crime Squad, based in Strathclyde's Pitt Street headquarters. That was bad news.

It was bad enough that Luca couldn't shake off visions of Joe Klein, watching him, sometimes talking to him. Luca was not fanciful. He told himself it was no ghost, for ghosts didn't exist. The visions were merely manifestations of guilt. And he did feel guilty. He had killed many men over the years, but Joe had been different. Luca had to do it – Joe was getting in the way of business and if there was one thing Luca had learned during his years with the New York mob, it was that nothing gets in the way of business – but that didn't make him feel any better. So he grew used to seeing Joe sitting in his favourite booth in the Duke Street café and hearing his voice in his ear like a whisper on the wind.

But Bannatyne back in the picture was a pain in the ass. It forced Luca to be even more cautious in his dealings, more circumspect as Joe would've said, letting Big Rab McClymont take an ever more active role. Rab had someone on the inside who would let him know if eyes were turning in their direction. Occasionally an eager beaver would take it into his head to pay closer attention, but they were dealt with. If they were open to it, a deal was made and the cop walked away with some money in his pocket. If they were incorruptible, a body was given to them, an arrest, a sacrificial lamb, and the nosey cop went off to bigger and better things. Sometimes it was one of Rab's boys who were given up, but more often than not they steered the law towards someone working for one of the other crews. So Luca felt as safe as he could.

Then Jack Bannatyne came back and slid into his usual seat, as if he had been there only yesterday. He looked the same, but then it had only been three years. His hair was perhaps a touch greyer, his face carrying a few more lines, but his eyes were still bright and sharp. And missed very little.

'Inspector Bannatyne,' said Luca, his smile broad as he moved from the counter to greet the man.

'Detective Superintendent now, Luca,' reminded Bannatyne as he held out his hand. The two men shook like old friends.

'Ah, *si, si,*' said Luca, his free hand glancing against his forehead. 'I forget. So what brings you to Duke Street – long time, no see, eh?'

'Felt the need for one of your wife's fruit scones, Luca. And a cup of your special coffee.'

Luca nodded, knowing full well that the real reason was yet to come. 'Coming up.'

Enrico, the second-generation Italian who helped him in the kitchen, was washing up so Luca fetched the scone himself and poured the coffee from the pot he reserved for himself. His customers were happy with instant, but Luca liked his own special blend. So did Bannatyne. He carried the plate with two scones, two pats of butter and the coffee back to the table.

'Enjoy,' he said, and would have walked away had Bannatyne not touched him gently on the wrist.

'Sit a moment, Luca. We've not talked for so long.'

Luca shrugged and sat down opposite the detective, who had begun to butter one of the scones. Luca waited as Bannatyne carefully smeared every part of its surface, then took a bite.

'Perfection,' said the cop. 'Mrs Vizzini hasn't lost her touch.'

Luca inclined his head. 'I will pass on your good wishes.'

'Please do.'

It was amazing how quickly they had slipped into their old routine. Even their dialogue had settled into a familiar pattern that they had used so often before.

Then Bannatyne went off script. 'I hear Davie McCall's getting out tomorrow.'

Luca tried not to let his surprise show. He had known it was soon, but the following day? His mind feverishly worked out the date and he realised that the day had come without his realising. How could he have forgotten? 'That is good news,' he said.

Bannatyne nodded. 'Not for the person who killed Joe the Tailor.'

'It was that boy Jazz who murdered my friend.'

Bannatyne smiled. 'Luca, we've been over this before. We know Jazz didn't kill Joe the Tailor. And you know it, too.'

Luca sighed. 'You have me wrong. I am but a simple café owner…'

Bannatyne stopped chewing for a moment and gave Luca a hard stare. Then he swallowed the lump of scone and inclined his head. 'Of course you are. But just let me remind you that Davie McCall isn't like the rest of the neds. He was devoted to Joe and he's not stupid. He's going to know that a boy like Jazz couldn't get to the old man. No, Joe was killed by someone close to him. McCall will work that out, if he's not done so already. Plenty of time to think in the jail. And someone's tried a few times to have him killed, I hear. He's going to want to know who, I'll bet.'

Luca knew that what Bannatyne said was true. He had been relieved when Davie was sent down for the warehouse robbery. He knew about the attempts on Davie's life in prison, too. He could not deny that he was disappointed that none of them succeeded. He also knew that Davie was not the type to let sleeping dogs lie. He saw Bannatyne watching him closely but Luca was too experienced to let his thoughts reflect in his face. 'These things you say are true, but I'm glad Davie's getting out. We will all be glad to see him.'

Bannatyne nodded, not expecting anything else. 'Good. Because we don't want any unpleasantness to mar the peace of our great city, do we? Things have been relatively quiet these past few years. Let's hope they don't get out of hand.' Bannatyne finished his scone and drained his coffee. 'Always a pleasure, Luca.' He dropped some coins on the tabletop. 'That should cover what I owe. Plus tip.'

Luca scooped the money in his hand and nodded. They shook hands again and Bannatyne left with nothing further to say. Luca stood in the aisle looking thoughtfully at the money in his hand but not really seeing it. He must be getting old, missing the date of Davie's release. He hoped he wasn't slipping. That could be deadly.

When he looked up he saw the eyes of Joe Klein watching him from his booth.

8

TICK…

The clockwork routine of the little alarm counted the minutes. In prison, where inmates are allowed very few personal belongings, that cheap Made in Hong Kong timepiece was old Sammy's most prized possession, apart from his supply of fags. It was not the only sound in the cell, for the old man in the bottom bunk still snored softly and the cavernous halls of the Victorian jail continued to echo with various clangs. Davie could not sleep after the dream. He lay on his back, staring at the ceiling, listening to the night-time sounds as his mind roamed over his life in prison.

Tick…

Normally he slept well, even with the dreams, but not tonight.

For this was to be his last night inside. The following morning he would slop out for the last time, say goodbye to the few inmates he took anything to do with and then he would be processed and free.

It had been a long time coming.

Tick...

The old clock no longer worked as an alarm, but the single sound it did make told him that time was passing, albeit slowly. It always passed slowly in the jail, slower than he had thought possible. After ten years inside he was an old hand, even if he was only twenty-eight. Old Sammy in the bunk below had been locked up almost twice that time. He had killed a man back in the seventies, gunned him down during a payroll snatch that went wrong. He had been forty then, a handy guy to have around during a blag, certainly. But no gunman. He had tried to stop an accomplice from killing a security guard, but during the struggle the shotgun went off and blew away a chunk of the guy's chest. Sammy's accomplice was never caught and Sammy never grassed him up. Only Sammy's fingerprints were found on the weapon, which was dropped at the scene, and he went down for the murder. He was given Life with a minimum of twenty years and Sammy was bitter and angry about the deal he had been dealt so he took it out on the system. Eventually he settled down and was something of an elder statesman on the galleries.

Davie met him almost immediately after leaving the Governor's office back in 1982. He was transferred from 'B' Hall to 'A' Hall and given his new co-pilot. Although Davie had agreed to behave himself, the Colonel had decided not to take any chances and put him in with Sammy.

He was a tall man, a good foot taller than Davie, and his thick grey hair was swept back from his forehead in a wave you could surf on. The bristles on his jaw and chin were showing white but his face was remarkably smooth, only the tell-tale crow's feet at his eyes betraying his years. He gazed at Davie through narrowed eyes, as if he was sizing him up. Later Davie discovered that Sammy's eyesight was failing, but he was too vain to wear glasses. However, it was Sammy's first words he would never forget.

'So, son – I hear you're planning to be a fuckwit?'

Davie didn't know quite how to respond, but Sammy wasn't one to let it lie. 'Mug's game, that, take it from me. I've been there, done that, wore the fuckin t-shirt. Done it all, me – hunger strikes, dirty protests, flung my shit around like a fuckin baboon. Got me nowhere, except a series of kickings from the muftis and time added. But see now? Just do my time, get on with it.'

'You just gave in?' Davie couldn't help himself. He may have reached an agreement with the Colonel, but he hadn't yet decided if he would really stick to it.

Sammy smiled and the expression seemed to take years off his face. 'Naw, son. Prison's a force of nature and you can't win against a force of nature. But hey, it's up to you, son. You want to be a fuckwit, you go your own merry way. Me? I just hope they don't come to the wrong bed when they burst in, that's all. 'Cos see they screws out there? They think you're nothin more than animal and you need to be caged. They're no here to rehabilitate, they're here to keep you banged up because they and the outside world think that's what you deserve. And if you do what I think you're gonnae do, you'll prove them right. Don't do it, son. Prove them wrong and get the fuck out of here.'

As time went on, Sammy told him that he had decided to get that speech over with as soon as possible. He wasn't on the screws' side, far from it. He felt the prison system could be too dehumanising and when the shit hit the fan, he hoped he'd be there to see it. But all he wanted now was to finish his term and get out, get back to his family. He hadn't joined the system, not in his head, but merely played it at its own game, used it against itself. Protests just brought you solitary and that made time stretch, an hour banged up in segregation was like a day on the galleries, where inmates had access to recreation, to education, to work.

The screws treated Sammy differently from the other convicts. They knew what he was capable of and they knew he chose not to do it, not because he was beaten or bullied but because he had found another way. Sammy took no shit from any of the young scroats who passed through the hall. Davie once saw him deliver an open-handed slap to a young boy from Govan who stepped out of line. The boy's eyes burned and Davie was ready to pile in, but Sammy just stepped closer, thrust his chin into the boy's face and stared at him. That's all he did, just stared straight into the scroat's eyes, daring him to make another move. The boy backed down. A screw stood nearby and watched the whole thing. He would have done something had things got out of hand, but he knew the best course of action was to let Sammy deal with it.

It was Sammy who told him how to handle prison life, to focus on the little things and avoid thinking about the big picture. It's not one day at a time, it's one hour at a time, he said. Look forward to something every week – pie, beans and chips at teatime maybe, or the few hours a week out in the fresh air. Don't think about life outside, what you could be doing, because that will make it worse. The prison is your life, its routines your routines. Your peter is a dirty, stinking hole, but it's home, be it ever so humble. Slopping out is degrading and disgusting, but take comfort in the fact that while you're standing in line holding your chamber pot and then pouring it down the sluice, the screws are also subjected to the same stench and the sight of the shit getting tipped out.

Not thinking about life outside was made easier after Audrey stopped coming to see him.

Davie would never forget that final visit, shortly after his conviction for Harris. He knew what she was going to say before she said it. He could tell by her stiff features and the tension in her muscles as she walked towards the table. He knew what was about to happen and there was nothing he could do to stop it. Even if he wanted to.

'I can't do this, Davie,' she said as soon as she sat down. No beating about the bush. She'd probably been thinking about it for days. He didn't say anything. He knew she wasn't finished. 'I was in court. I heard what happened.'

That surprised him. He hadn't seen her there. But then he'd been so angry with the deal he was being dealt that nothing else mattered.

'I really thought you could change. I really did. But you can't, can you?'

He wanted to tell her that Harris had gone for him, that a screw called Lomas had put him up to it. He wanted to tell her that he had changed, that what he had done was purely in self-defence. But he didn't say anything. It wouldn't have made any difference. But still, he felt something inside wither and die. Even Audrey thought he was a monster.

After that he didn't send her any visitor passes and she didn't ask for them. He did not phone her. There were no letters. He saw her by-line in the *Evening Times* for a time, but then they stopped. For a while he wondered where she had gone, wondered what she was doing, wondered if she ever thought of him. Finally he tried not to think about her at all and he even managed it, at least during the daylight hours when there was something else to take up his attention: work, exercise, meals, routine. But he could not control his dreams. Audrey had represented the possibility of another life, and now that had been taken from him and his subconscious refused to let go. Some nights he would wake up thinking she was there with him, her voice soothing, her fragrance comforting, only to find Sammy's snores and the stink of the piss pots.

Davie followed Sammy's advice and kept his head down. There were three further attacks over the years – one witnessed by a screw who was able to state to the Colonel that McCall had reacted purely in self-defence. Even so, they put paid to any notion of early release. Another nobody knew about – Sammy arranged for the attacker to be removed without fuss until he came to, his bruises put down to slipping on a bar of soap. The screw asking the questions didn't believe a word of it, but he wasn't inclined to press further. Bars of soap were commonly left on floors in Barlinnie. Tripping and falling over in a peter was also prevalent. Prison can be a dangerous place for the accident prone.

None of the attackers would say who sent them. They were too scared. Although nobody was talking, Davie remained convinced that his father was behind the attacks. He still had questions, lots of questions, concerning Joe's death and how he had ended up in prison in the first place, but to get the answers he needed to be free. Even without the additional blemishes on his record, parole was out of the question as he would never admit to having attacked Donald Harris, and that was a prerequisite. He knew he would serve his full term.

But when he got out, he'd find the answers.

* * *

Audrey was at home watching TV when Les returned home from the backshift. She was ready for bed, sitting in the big, soft armchair she loved so much, legs tucked underneath her, wearing a t-shirt and a pair of tracksuit bottoms, sipping a mug of hot chocolate. It had been a habit to which her father had introduced her, hot chocolate before bed, and she'd never stopped it. Les thought it cute and girlish. She heard him drop his keys in the glass bowl on the table in the hallway of their flat and then he stepped into the living room. He was not surprised to see her still up. She always waited up for him: even when he was on nightshift she was generally already out of bed to greet him, unless he was late and she had to get to work.

He crossed the room, leaned in and kissed her on the mouth. It was a long kiss because she reached up with her free hand and cupped the nape of his neck, pulling him tighter against her. When they finally broke he straightened again and smiled. He asked, 'You done something wrong or are you just glad to see me?'

She smiled. 'Can't a girl kiss her husband hello?'

'I dunno. You don't normally kiss me like that when I get home. You been drinking?'

She gave him a stern look. 'You're taking all the romance out of this. You're not in an interview room now, Detective Constable Les Fraser.'

He raised an eyebrow. 'All the romance out of what?'

She laid the mug she was holding on the coffee table beside the armchair and stood up, stepping closer to her husband, looking into his face. He was very handsome, even when he was tired and unshaven. Brown hair, brown eyes, a kind smile showing strong, even teeth. He was slightly taller than her so she stood on her toes to reach him as she kissed him again, both hands framing his face, her tongue moving between his lips. His hands snaked round her waist and under her t-shirt to caress the flesh of her back and side.

'To what do I owe this pleasure?' He breathed.

'Don't look a gift horse in the mouth,' she said as she took his hand and led him to the bedroom.

Later, as he slept, she reflected on why she had been so intent on sex that night. She enjoyed it as much as the next woman, as long as the next woman wasn't some raving nympho. She particularly enjoyed it with Les but he was right, she did not often come on that strong. It wasn't uncommon for her to initiate proceedings when, as Les had pointed out, she had a drink in her. But tonight was different. Tonight she felt that she had to have him, had to be close to him, had to feel his hands on her and feel him inside her. She told herself she didn't know why. She told herself she just suddenly felt horny. She told herself she loved her husband and she wanted him. She told herself all that and some of it was even true.

But she knew what caused her need. Barc had raised memories. Jinky – Donald Harris – had planted them firmly in her mind. They had stayed with her for two days.

She knew she was going to see Davie again and didn't know what kind of feelings that might revive. Her seduction scene tonight was a means of reassuring herself that she not only still wanted Les, but that she needed him. Now she was satisfied. She loved Les. They had their ups and downs, their fights, fall-outs. He didn't like some of the stories she did and sometimes she didn't like the way he thought, but they overcame those differences and made a life. He was a kind man, a good man, a dependable man. He was the man she wanted to grow old with.

But as she drifted off to sleep, it was Davie's blue eyes she saw and his voice breathing her name that she heard.

9

DAVIE KNEW HE wouldn't sleep again that night, the dream had seen to that. He knew what had prompted it.

'I knew your faither, you know that?' Sammy had piped up that day as they walked round the exercise yard for the final time, each enjoying the weak sunlight.

The words always froze Davie's blood, especially now, when his mind automatically flicked first to that face in the crowd then the photograph of his mother. But Davie liked Sammy – more than that, he respected him. He respected the way he held himself, the way he dealt with people. The only other man Davie had known who held himself in the same way, who dealt with people in the same way, was Joe Klein. Even so, he felt a tightening in his chest at the mention of Danny McCall and he did not know how to respond.

'Didn't know whether I should tell you, after what happened, like. With your maw. Wrestled with it all these years, whether to tell you.'

Davie kept walking, staring intently at the backs of two other inmates ahead of them, just to give his eyes a focus. He was aware Sammy was studying him carefully, looking for signs of encouragement, but Davie could not let his expression betray his feelings. A small, childlike part of him desperately wanted the older man to tell him about his father, but another part wanted to hear nothing more. Finally, Sammy decided to press on. 'He wasn't always like that, the way he was at the end there. You know that, don't you?'

Davie gave a barely imperceptible nod. His dream of the day in the country was, in part, a reminder of the way Danny McCall used to be. There was another memory that Davie cherished: holidays on the Ayrshire coast, when Danny took them to a small house in Ballantrae. They were good times, happy times, bathed in Davie's mind with the warm glow of summer. Other people saw the violent side of Danny McCall's nature, for the work he did for Joe the Tailor was far from gentle, but in those days Mary McCall and Davie saw his loving side.

But that was then.

'He was a good man to have at your back, was Danny McCall. And a good friend. I see those qualities in you, son. Oh, he was hard, no doubt about it, and he did things that straight arrows just don't understand. But The Life is like that, you know, eh? Makes you do things you shouldn't, things you know are wrong, but you do them all the same. Take me, I knew I shouldn't've gone on that job with that bloke tooled up, but I did. Look what happened. It was my decision, nobody forced me, and a fella lost his life. And I ended up in here, away from my wife, away from my lassie. She was thirteen when I was banged up. Went off the rails a wee bit. She's got two kids of her own now, had the first when she was sixteen. I missed all that. I shouldn't have missed all that. Maybe her life wouldn't have turned out that way if I'd been there, you know? I couldn't accept it at first, which is why I was a fuckwit in here, but eventually I realised that it was all my own fault, you know? Danny, your da, chose The Life, chose to work for Joe Klein, chose to do the things he did. Nobody forced him.'

They walked in silence for a few moments and Davie sensed Sammy was struggling with himself over going further. Then...

'And he loved your maw. Never seen a guy more loved up...'

Davie could contain himself no longer. 'He killed her, Sammy.'

Sammy sighed. 'Aye, he did. And it was terrible, we all thought so. I was inside by that time, but I read about it and guys talked about it. But see, here's what I'm saying, or trying to say anyway – it wasn't really him...'

'It was the drink,' said Davie, dully.

'Aye, maybe. But something more, I think. Something else, deep inside him. I don't know what you'd call it – rage, depression, evil maybe, I don't know. I'd see it come over him, like something taking control, you know? A darkness. Don't get me wrong, whatever it was came in handy in his work, 'cos that's what set him apart from the other hard men, the chib men, the gun men. And the more it took over, the stronger it got. See, when I knew your dad, he never drank, never touched a drop. Maybe a beer now and then, he wasn't fuckin temperance, but the hard stuff wasn't for him. So, what I think is, he drank to keep whatever it was inside him down, you know what I'm saying? Shit, it's no like he was possessed or anything like that...'

But Davie thought differently. He had seen something inhuman in Danny McCall's eyes the night he had beaten his mother to death. Something cold. Something not quite right. He was drunk, it seemed he had been drunk every night for weeks, but it wasn't just the liquor. Something had taken hold of him that night and possession is as good a word as any, even if he wasn't vomiting pea soup or spinning his head.

Sammy concluded, '... but I always knew there was something eating away at him. And the drink didn't keep it down, didn't help at all, just made it worse. Fed it. So sure, it was your dad that did it, that killed your maw, but it wasn't really him, you know what I'm sayin? It was this dark thing that had finally taken over.'

Davie nodded. He agreed with Sammy, but it did not make him feel any better about it. 'So why you telling me this, Sammy?'

Sammy stopped and shook a cigarette from a packet of Benson and Hedges. He struck a match against the stone wall beside him and cupped the flame in his hands as he lit up. Davie waited as Sammy took a deep drag and blew a cloud of smoke upwards. The older man looked at him then blinked, and Davie knew that though some of this was difficult for *him* to listen to, it wasn't easy for Sammy to say either.

Sammy sucked at the cigarette once more. 'Because I've been talking to some people about you, son, people that knew you, or knew of you, on the outside. You're a good mate, a good man to have at your back, just like him. But you know what worries me? That you've got the dark thing inside you, too. I've spoken to boys that have seen you in action, son. They say that something happens to you, they saw it. And what they told me, I've seen, too. In your dad.'

'I'm not like him. I'll never be like him.'

'I hope you're right, Davie, I really do. That's why I'm saying this. You need to watch out for it. It's a sneaky bastard, this dark thing. You think it's your pal, but it's not. You think it's a handy tool, but it's not. It's like fuckin heroin: once it gets a hold of you, you're lost. Unless you're stronger than it is. So here's what I'm sayin. You're getting out tomorrow and like as not you'll go right back to your pals and The Life. And because you're Danny McCall's boy, they'll find a use for you, just like Joe Klein did... oh, I know he was an okay guy and he taught you all they rules an' that – don't hurt women, or animals, don't involve civilians – and they're all well and good but see, it's a different world out there now. Drugs have changed it. Used to be there was a focus to the violence, but now? Now anyone's fair game. And a boy like you, with what I think is inside you? They're going to want you, they're gonnae want what's inside you. And the more you tap into the darkness, the stronger it becomes. It happened to your dad, it can happen to you. Don't let it. You have a choice, son. You've already lost that lassie to it, that one I hear you muttering about in your sleep. Don't lose everything else.'

Sammy paused to let his words sink in, but he wasn't finished. 'When the devil comes knocking, you get two choices. You either let him in, or you tell that red-skinned, horned fucker to get the hell away.'

As Davie lay in his bunk on his last night inside, he thought about Sammy's words. He knew the world had changed in the ten years he had been away. But he had not. He was still Danny McCall's boy. And when the devil came knocking, he would have to deal with it.

IO

RAB MCCLYMONT pulled his thick coat tighter as he peered at the number on his pager's small screen. A stiff breeze flooded through the broken glass pane of the phone box and chilled his body. He hated the cold, always had. Some day, if he worked everything correctly, he'd take Bernadette and little Joe and any other kids they had by then to a land where it was warm and sunny. Even in November.

Cars roared past the box on Shettleston Road and further down he could see the Range Rover with two of his boys watching carefully. They didn't know who he was calling and they never would. Even Luca had no idea who Rab's connection was in Pitt Street. The only person who knew was Bernadette, for Rab told her almost everything. He and Knight had been using this system for years – pagers, registered in someone else's name, of course, used to relay the number of a clean public phone. When the little plastic box bleeped and a number flashed up on the screen, it meant one of them had something to pass on and the other had to reach another public phone to call the number in the display. Rab was confident the phones in his home and the one in Luca's café were clean – he paid a couple of British Telecom employees a hefty amount of cash to let him know if there was any undue interest in the lines. That wasn't enough for Knight, though – Rab had learned long ago that if there was one species more paranoid than drug dealers, it was bent cops.

'This better be fuckin good,' said Rab when he heard Knight pick up at the other end. 'Freezing my bollocks off in this box.'

'And good morning to you, mate,' said Knight.

Rab sighed. He was not a morning person. He didn't come fully awake until he had at least two cups of coffee. 'Spit it out, Knight.'

'Just thought I'd let you know Liam Mulvey's come into some cash.'

Rab said nothing as he processed the information. Liam Mulvey was a former Glasgow ned who moved to Ayrshire so his wife could be near her folks. He bought gear from Rab and punted it among the sheep and the associated shaggers down there in the country. And he owed Rab cash.

'How the fuck do'you know these things, Knight?'

'I could tell you, but then I'd have to kill you,' said Knight, and Rab knew he was only half joking. They'd had a working relation-ship for ten years now and Rab knew the big cop was capable of many things. However, he also knew that wasn't the only reason for the call. He wouldn't say that he could read the Black Knight like a book – that would be like trying to do Braille wearing a boxing glove – but he knew there was more to come.

'Your boy McCall's getting out today, I hear.'

'Aye,' Rab said, wondering where this was leading.

'Been a long time.'

'Aye.'

'He still not suss it was you who put him away?'

Rab fell silent again. So that's what this was – a wind up call. Knight knew that Rab's betrayal was a sore point, and he was never one to shy away from poking a wound. They had needed Davie McCall off the streets because he was a loose cannon in the wake of Joe the Tailor's death and that would have been bad for business. Rab had provided the basic information to have the boy jailed, pinning the leak on that sucker Mouthy Grant. Naturally, Mouthy had to go away, something Rab dealt with in his usual direct manner. The big man never agonised over Grant's death, but he suffered pangs of conscience over grassing his mate McCall. And, truth be told, he was a little afraid Davie would work it all out. The only other person who knew the truth was Bernadette. The question was, why was Knight bringing it all up now? Was he just doing it for fun, or was he reminding Rab that he should continue to play ball, and pay up, or he'd drop a word in McCall's ear about who grassed him up?

'Be good to have him back, eh?' Knight said, filling the gap in the conversation. 'Handy boy to have around.'

'We finished here?' The irritation in Rab's voice was heavy.

'That's us, big man. You get somewhere warm, get yourself tucked in. Maybe a nice mug of cocoa and a tartan blankie.'

Rab dropped the phone back on its cradle without another word. Sometimes Knight really pissed him off.

11

FRANK DONOVAN WAS running.

He didn't like running.

He especially didn't like running with two pockets filled with change, having won a jackpot on the puggy in the pub when the shout came in. It had been his plan to take the cash down the road to the bookies, put it on a nag and maybe claw back some of his losses, but events overtook him. He'd been having some lunch before he started the back shift and a veteran DS in for his midday tightener had his radio with him. When Donovan heard the name of the scroat the lads were after, he simply grabbed the coins from the slot and shoved them in his pockets as he dashed out. Now it was jingling down there like Santa Claus coming to town. He'd also had a couple of beers, which didn't help matters, and as he pounded through the streets of Garthamlock he could feel it slopping around his guts.

The scroat he and another handful of officers were chasing was named Mo Morris. Mo for Maurice. Maurice Morris – how the hell did the poor bastard end up with that? His dad was a tea-leaf, currently doing time in Her Majesty's Hotel Barlinnie, and wee Mo was a hopped-up wee shite with sticky fingers and a liking for relieving old people of their pensions. Donovan could see Mo haring down the street. He was a short-arse and short-arses could really move when they wanted to. They'd been looking for him for two weeks, ever since an old lady in Carntyne had been battered in her flat and her money nicked. That's all the scroat got, that week's pension and the old dear was still in a coma. Wee Mo was nippy on his feet but not too quick in the head, because he'd left his fingerprints all over the place. Even so, he'd managed to avoid being lifted, moving from place to place. The flat in Porchester Street was tenanted by a cousin and it had already been turned over, so Donovan assumed Mo had moved in only recently. But he must've been spotted by a concerned citizen who dialled 999. Unfortunately, he'd seen the uniforms heading into the close and skyed the pitch out the back window, jumping down onto the roof of some bin shelters, then away across the back court. The uniforms blew it in and, as Mo Morris was top of the Most Wanted list, any cop not involved in something else piled into the East End scheme, Frank Donovan among them.

Now here he was, on his tod, legging it down Balveny Street, jingle bells playing in his trouser pockets, trying to catch up with the fleet-footed wee bastard up ahead. Or at least keep him in sight. As he puffed and gasped in his wake, Donovan couldn't help but think of the *Roadrunner* cartoons. Mo was the Roadrunner, which made him Wile. E. Coyote. Any minute now an anvil with the Acme trademark would land on his head. That might actually be welcome because, truth be told, he was feeling none-too-clever. The beer slopping around his guts was making him feel decidedly seedy, and those bloody ten pence pieces were banging and rubbing against his thighs as if he had testicles like an elephant.

Mo veered into Findochty Street, but Donovan kept after him. Donovan knew he couldn't keep this pace up much longer – there was a pain in his chest now, which was worrying. He was only in his mid-thirties, for God's sake – too young for a heart attack. He hoped it was just wind. He fumbled in the inside pocket of his jacket, pulled out his radio, flicked the 'Send' switch and held it close to his mouth as he ran.

'DS Donovan...' His breath wheezed with the words, '... in pursuit of suspect Mo Morris on Findochty Street. Need assistance... over.'

'Units in vicinity,' a voice crackled back, 'stay with suspect. Over.'

Stay with suspect? Easy for you to say, mate, sitting in a control room and issuing bloody instructions into a microphone. Probably even got a nice cup of tea and a Jaffa Cake beside you. *And I know units are in the vicinity*, he thought, *just not my immediate vicinity, and that's where I need them because my legs are about to give up the ghost and this pain in my chest is really beginning to worry me.*

But he kept on going, the radio clutched in his right hand,

struggling to keep Mo's white t-shirt in his sights, that damned change rattling around like a miser's wet dream. He saw Mo glance over his shoulder and Donovan hoped that was a sign he was flagging. No such luck, for the wee man actually picked up his pace when he saw he was still hanging on behind him. Donovan felt the hope sink in his chest, swallowed up by the agony spreading across his ribs. *That's it*, he promised himself, *no more Scotch Pies at lunchtime.*

But that glance back proved to be Mo's undoing, because he failed to notice the dark-coloured Vauxhall zoom out of Craigievar Street and come to a halt just ahead of him. The driver's door opened and a large man shot out, moving faster than his size might suggest. Donovan knew who it was and knew him to be a fit sod. Mo turned forward again only to run right into the swing of an extendable baton. Donovan winced when he heard the weapon crack against Mo's chest. *That'll leave a welt,* he thought. Mo went down hard on his back and Donovan slowed to a halt, bending forward with his hands on his knees as he struggled to catch his breath. And not to throw up. He looked up into the grinning face of Detective Sergeant Jimmy Knight. He never thought he'd be glad to see that face...

'Frankie, boy!' said Knight, his voice booming down the street as he retracted the baton. 'I think you need to be getting to a gym. Disgraceful state to be in.'

Donovan didn't have the breath in him for any sort of clever response, so with a shaking hand he raised two fingers at the big cop. Knight laughed. 'Witty as ever, Frankie boy.' He looked down at the young man beginning to stir at his feet. 'Heard there was a wee bit of excitement and I was passing. Thought I'd lend a hand. Who've we got here then?'

'Mo Morris,' said Donovan, swallowing hard, his chest pain receding now.

'And what did Mister Morris do that he's exercised Strathclyde's finest this day?'

'Robbed an old biddy in Carntyne. Left her for dead.'

'Really?' Knight looked at the prone young man with renewed interest. 'What did you go and do that for?' Mo didn't reply, prompting Knight to stamp his foot on his chest with some force. The young man cried out. 'I'm speaking to you, ya wee shitehawk. Why'd you hurt that old lady?'

'Didn't mean to,' wailed Mo. 'Just happened.'

Knight bent down, grabbed the little man by a handful of hair and dragged him to his feet. There was a wicked gleam in Knight's eye that Donovan had seen before, but he wasn't about to let anything happen here. 'Jimmy,' he warned, 'take it easy. We're in the street here.'

Knight ignored him and peered into Mo's eyes. The big cop's face was impassive, but Donovan knew that meant nothing. Donovan looked around, saw no-one, but that didn't mean eyes weren't upon them.

'Just happened? Just happened? Pounding a little old lady until she passes out doesn't *just happen*, does it?'

Mo made the mistake of not responding and Knight shook him by the hair.

'Does it, you pile of steaming shit? Does it?'

'No!' yelled Mo, crying now.

'No, it does not.' Knight glanced at Donovan and went on, 'Know what, Frank, we should start beating on this guy, see what *just happens*. What do you think? Want first go?'

'Jimmy,' said Donovan again, 'we're in the street.'

'We could say he resisted arrest. I'll even let him take a poke at me, just to make it look good. Or if he's no man enough you can do it, Frankie boy. You'd like that, eh?'

Donovan couldn't deny he would like the chance to lay one on Knight, but this wasn't the time or the place. 'Jimmy, just cuff him and we'll take him in.'

'Oh, I'll cuff him alright. Cuff him about the ears.' Knight was staring into Mo's face once more. The young man was weeping openly now, saying he was sorry over and over again and even Donovan began to pity him, but Knight remained expressionless.

He looked at Mo as if he was some sort of curious specimen, his head tilted to one side, his dark eyes probing every feature of the boy's face. Then Knight sneered and with a flick of his arm propelled the little man towards Donovan.

'Take him, Frankie boy. He's no worth the paperwork.'

Donovan trapped Morris before he could do another runner, pinned his hands behind his back then snapped the handcuffs on. Two uniforms came steaming along the road towards them, hats in their hand as they ran. *Better late than never*. Knight climbed back into his car and slipped on his seatbelt. He lit up a cigarillo and blew smoke through the open window as Donovan handed the young man over to the boys in blue.

'Glad I bumped into you. Got some news, Frankie boy,' Knight said as the uniforms led the still weeping Morris away. Donovan waited as Knight took a long draw on the small cigar and exhaled another cloud of smoke. Knight was a Detective Sergeant, just like him, but he had a knack for making Donovan feel like an inferior. And now that he was with the Serious Crime Squad he was even worse. 'Got some info on your dead tart.'

Jimmy Knight, sensitive as ever. 'Okay.'

'Seems she was pretty active, but she only had one regular. Bloke named John…'

'John Keen was the guy who rented the flat she was found in.' That was all Donovan knew about the guy, his name. No-one had seen him in the close, the arrangements had been made with the letting agent by phone and post, with the cash for the deposit and the first month's rent delivered by a young girl who didn't leave a name. Christ, could've been Virginia, for all Donovan knew. And no-one had heard anything on the night of the murder – the flat next door was empty, the one upstairs inhabited by an old spinster who was hard of hearing, while the couple downstairs had been out cold all night after a two-day bender. Donovan couldn't shake off the feeling that this guy Keen had chosen the site carefully. And that meant he'd been planning the murder.

Knight blew smoke into the air. 'That'll be him, then. None of the other lassies saw him too clearly – he used to pick her up in a car – but one did meet him, briefly.'

'Can she describe him?'

'No much to go on. Glasgow accent, dark hair, flecked with grey, average height, good-looking, which begs the question why he needed to go with tarts.'

Donovan thought, *you should know*, but he kept it to himself. 'Maybe he had special demands.'

'Aye, maybe. He also had blue eyes. That's what she remembers most, his blue eyes.'

Donovan thought about this. There was something about the murder scene that had sparked a memory, but no matter how much he stretched for it, it remained just out of reach. 'It's not much, is it?'

'More than you had five minutes ago.'

That was true. 'Where'd you get all this?'

'Plooky Mary, so it's dependable.'

'You still running her as a tout?'

'Aye, don't know how long for, right enough. She's got the virus.'

'AIDS?'

'Aye.' Knight didn't sound terribly upset, even though he'd been using the girl as an informant for years. 'Stupid cow started using heroin a while back, shared needles with her junkie pals. She didn't listen to John Hurt on those telly ads when he told her not to die of ignorance.'

'You're all heart, Jimmy,' said Donovan.

'Cry me a river, Frankie Boy. She was only a tout, for fuck's sake.'

Donovan was neither shocked nor surprised by Knight's callous attitude. He had always known Jimmy Knight doesn't do senti-ment. Knight flicked the ignition and jammed his cigarillo between his teeth. 'I hear that Davie McCall's getting out today,' he said.

'Heard that too,' said Donovan.

Knight stared at him for a second and Donovan had the impres-sion he was waiting for him to say something else. Perhaps the big cop had heard that Gentleman Jack had asked him to make contact and expected to be kept in the loop. Donovan remained silent, so

Knight nodded and said, 'Got a feeling in my pish that we're in for some interesting times again, Frankie boy.'

Donovan shrugged and began to walk back to where he had abandoned his car when he'd spotted wee Mo. He heard Knight's car pull away and he watched it move past him. He thought about the murder room, he thought about blue-eyed John Keen, he thought about Davie McCall.

He couldn't shake off the feeling that it was all linked.

12

IT FELT STRANGE being out.

Davie didn't think freedom would have affected him so much.

It began when the big door slammed closed behind him and he was outside Barlinnie Prison for the first time in ten years. He was a free man. It was the same air he'd breathed in the exercise yard, but today it seemed fresher, sweeter. He stood still for a second to listen to the birds singing in the trees. He had heard them from the yard, too, but this morning their song sounded cheerier, as if they were glad to see him.

The screws had taken their own sweet time processing his release papers, a move Davie put down to a final show of authority. He should have been through the door in the big gate to the right of public reception earlier in the day, but bureaucracy would not be hurried. He sat around, his impatience growing, but refused to let them see it. He knew it had to end eventually so he sat calmly in the processing area and waited it out.

It was Bobby's blond hair that Davie saw first, then the smile as wide as the Clyde. Bobby had been a good-looking bastard when they were young, and he had improved with the years. The hair was shorter now than it had been ten years before, but he still looked like a young Robert Redford. He was standing beside the small car park to Davie's right. The larger car park to his left was already filled with vehicles.

'Thought you'd maybe banjoe'd somebody and they were keeping you in,' said Bobby as he shook Davie's hand.

'Crossed my mind, Bobby,' said Davie. 'Controlled myself though.'

'Had to move the motor about ten times,' said Bobby, pointing the way to a double-parked Blue Montego. Then he clapped Davie on the back. 'So – how does it feel to be a free man at last?'

'Good,' said Davie, but it was an understatement. Ten years was a long time and he still expected the harsh bellow of a screw telling him to get back into the gallery, to get a move on, to move his skinny arse before he put a boot to it. He wondered how long he would feel that way.

He breathed in a lungful of the cold November air before he settled into the passenger seat and strapped on the seatbelt. Even that felt unusual.

'Aye, you'll find a lot of things have changed in the old town,' said Bobby as he backed out of the space. 'City of Culture and all that this year. Sinatra played Ibrox, you know that? Joe woulda loved that.'

Bobby fell silent for a few moments and Davie felt his friend regretting his mention of Joe Klein. Davie nodded, letting him know it was fine. 'Aye, opera and ballet for masses,' Bobby went on. 'You didn't see Pavarotti out in the schemes, though. Some streets, the only culture they've got is what's growin on the bottom of their dirty dishes.'

Bobby steered the car down the drive away from the prison and Davie looked in the side mirror to see its grey bulk diminish. He never wanted to go inside again and he vowed he never would. Rab was right – losing your liberty is hellish, and Davie fully understood why even a visit gave him cold sweats.

'Course, the schemes are changing, right enough,' Bobby went on. 'Gettin done up an' that, you'll no recognise some of them, Davie, neither you will.'

Bobby halted the car at the bottom of the drive and said, 'So, where first? Better warn you, Rab's got a wee welcome arranged for you back in the Sword Street flat. Some of the guys, some burds. I wasn't supposed to tell you but I know you're no keen on that sort of thing.'

Bobby knew him well. The idea of a crowd of people slapping him on the back, welcoming him home, filled him with dread, but he knew he would have to endure it. Rab would have gone to a great deal of trouble, and Davie didn't want to offend his big mate. Saying that, he wanted to put the ordeal off as long as he possibly could.

Bobby was waiting, so Davie said simply, 'Abe.'

* * *

The street in Easterhouse had not been refurbished, although Davie saw quite a few which had. Bobby was right – the schemes were changing, but it was a slow process. The exterior of this four storey tenement was still blackened by thirty odd years of Glasgow weather, pollution and the ever-present threat of dampness. The young woman who opened the door to them was a cheerful blonde with an open, plump face and blue eyes that danced with good humour. Beyond her, Davie could see a clean, tidy living room that was freshly decorated and pleasantly furnished. However, as she saw first Bobby and then Davie, a shadow fell across her face that made him feel guilty.

'Bobby,' is all she said, but her tone told them she was wary.

'Ellen,' said Bobby, 'this is Davie.' She nodded politely but Davie knew she wasn't glad to meet him.

'You've come for Abe,' she said, her voice flat.

'Just to see him, that's all,' said Bobby. 'Davie's… just got back…'

'From the jail,' said Ellen, without judgement. 'I know who he is. I mind him from before.'

Davie remained perfectly still, though he was growing increasingly uncomfortable. He should never have come here – should have left well enough alone.

'Abe's no here,' she said. 'He's out wi' Darren and the wean.'

'Darren no working?'

A shake of the head. 'Day off. Going to see his maw later, it's her birthday.'

Ellen was still looking at Davie, her eyes curious. He wondered what she knew about him.

'Right, right,' said Bobby. 'Okay. Well. We just stopped by on the off-chance. Sorry to bother you, hen.'

She nodded and began to close the door, then she thought of something and she opened it again. 'He's a great wee dog, so he is.' She addressed this to Davie. 'The wean loves him to bits, Darren too. He's part of the family.'

Davie nodded, understanding that he was being warned off from taking the dog back. He turned and began to walk back down the stairs. Bobby, a bit embarrassed, thanked her again and followed him down. In the street, Davie stood for a moment, letting the weak sunshine play on his face. Bobby came out of the close behind him and said, 'Sorry about that, Davie. She's a nice lassie but... well...' Bobby ran out of words as Davie climbed into the car. He walked round the front and slid into the driver's seat. 'So, Sword Street now?'

Davie nodded and Bobby turned the ignition. Just as he was about to pull out, Davie reached out and touched his arm, staring through the windshield. Bobby followed his gaze and saw a lanky young man with thinning fair hair walking towards them holding the hand of a little girl of about nine. Abe trotted beside them, no lead, but confident and secure. The dog was obviously well cared for and happy, judging by the enthusiastic wag of his tail. He had aged, his muzzle coated with white hairs as if someone had rubbed castor sugar into them, and his pace slower than Davie remembered. He had been at least one year old when Davie rescued him, so that would make him around eleven now. His limbs may have been stiffer, but his tongue lolled from his mouth and as he looked up at the man and child, his eyes were bright.

Bobby had a hand on the door release, but Davie shook his head as he watched the father, daughter and dog near the closemouth. *So that was what a happy family looked like.* They passed the car, oblivious to the men inside, and he heard the little girl chattering happily and addressing comments to Abe, who wagged his tail even harder whenever his name was uttered. The three figures turned into the close and Davie watched them vanish inside, feeling something scratching at his throat and burning his eyes. He was not sure what love was anymore, but he knew he felt something for the wee mongrel. But he couldn't take the dog away from that home, where he was loved, where he was happy. He just couldn't.

And then, just as he was about to tell Bobby to pull away, Abe appeared again. He stood at the tenement doorway, staring straight at the car, his mouth closed now, his nose raised to sniff the air, his eyes almost quizzical as he found Davie's face. At first Davie thought the dog had not recognised him but then, slowly, the tail began to wag. He didn't move forward though, and Davie didn't want to get out. Neither man nor dog moved, they simply looked at one another, separated by the glass and ten years. Davie heard a man call Abe's name and the dog glanced over his shoulder back into the close, then turned to the car again. Davie felt the sting behind his eyes increase and he intuitively sensed the dog was looking for permission.

Go on, son, he thought. *Go home.*

Abe remained still. It was as if as if he didn't want to move, the bond he had formed with Davie back then still strong.

Please, Abe, Davie thought, *just go...*

The dog's bright brown eyes didn't move from Davie's face, though his ears twitched when he heard his name being called again from inside the building. He took a step forward, his tail swinging, and Davie was about to tell Bobby start the motor, to get him away from here. But Abe stopped and looked over his shoulder once more. Darren appeared at the closemouth and Davie heard him say, 'What you waiting for, pal? C'mon in the house.'

Abe turned to face Davie one last time and an understanding passed between them. He would always love Davie but he had a home now, a family, something Davie could not give him. Then the little dog turned and followed Darren into the close. Davie swallowed hard to dislodge the hard lump in his throat, part of him hoping that Abe would return. He didn't reappear. Davie kept his face averted from Bobby. He did not want him to see the tears welling in his eyes.

Goodbye, Abe, he thought. *Goodbye, pal.*

13

SWORD STREET HAD not changed since he left it ten years before. Different cars were parked outside the tenements and shop fronts that lined the left hand side, but the sandstone buildings looked exactly the same. No reason for them not to, he supposed, but after seeing the renovation work being carried out in the schemes, he perhaps expected change here too. As they climbed up to the second floor flat, they met a woman in her sixties coming down. She was dressed like a typical Glasgow pensioner – shapeless thin coat, patterned scarf on her head, shoes with low heels. She stopped on the landing and studied them as they approached.

'You have come home,' she said to Davie, her heavily lined face showing no warmth.

'I have, Mrs Mitchell,' said Davie, dredging the woman's name from the depths of his memory.

She nodded. 'Your friends, they are waiting.' Her voice still betrayed her Polish origins, though she had lived in Scotland since the late 1940s. She had married a Scot, had three children, yet never lost her accent. Hearing it reminded Davie of Joe. The woman lived in a flat that Joe had owned on the floor above. The old man had let her live there on a nominal rent and seeing her, hearing her accent, made Davie feel better somehow, as if Joe was still around calling the shots. The woman had looked askance at him and Rab, but always had a ready smile for Joe when he visited. She made her own *kielbasa*, a cheese bread for which he had a particular soft spot, and they would often sit together in her flat talking of the Mother Land.

'We'll keep the noise down, Mrs Mitchell,' said Davie. She had constantly complained of the noise they made. They were young then and unaware of the disturbance they could cause.

'No shooting, eh?' She said, and Davie knew she was referring to the night Clem Boyle had fired shots on the ground floor. A grim smile stretched his lips at the memory. 'No, Mrs Mitchell, no more shooting.'

She grunted, clearly not believing him, and carried on down the stone steps. Bobby grinned at Davie and said, 'Welcome home, eh?' Davie shrugged and took another step when he heard the woman's voice again.

'David,' she said, and he looked over the banister. She had stopped midway down the next flight and was staring back at him. 'Mister Joseph Klein, he was a good man.'

'Yes, he was, Mrs Mitchell.'

She nodded, as if satisfied that he agreed. 'I miss him a great deal.'

Davie sighed. 'So do I, Mrs Mitchell. So do I.'

He had given her the right answer, for her stiff features softened. 'There was man here, looking for you. A few weeks ago. He said he knew Mister Joseph Klein.'

Davie's grip tightened on the thick wooden banister. 'Did he say his name?'

She shook her head. 'No name. He looked familiar.'

'What did he want?'

'He asked after you, wished to know when you would be home. I did not know and this I told him.'

Davie knew the answer to his next question before he heard it. 'What did he look like?'

She paused, her face crumpled as she thought back. Then she looked up and said, 'He looked like you, David, except older…'

Davie's fingers tensed on the polished wood and he glanced at Bobby, who was listening to the exchange with interest. 'Who is he, Davie?'

Davie licked his lips, which had suddenly turned very dry, and when he spoke his voice was dust-bound. 'My dad.'

* * *

Rab McClymont's eyes clouded as he thought over what Davie told him, the muted sound of Madonna singing 'Vogue' coming from the sitting room. They were in Davie's old bedroom in the Sword Street flat. It had been freshly decorated and the double bed looked very inviting after ten years of stinking Barlinnie cots. All Davie wanted to do was get under the covers, curl up and sleep for a year. However, the fact that his father had been sniffing around would murder sleep.

'You sure it's him, Davie?' Rab asked, his brow furrowed. When Rab's big brow furrowed it looked like a freshly ploughed field.

'Mrs Mitchell said he looked like me, but older. And I'm certain I saw him outside the court that day. And he sent me that photo of my mum. Who else could it have been?'

Rab could not answer that. Bobby said, 'You think it was your dad that set Harris and the other lads on you, Davie?'

Rab frowned at that. Davie replied, 'Could be.'

'Well,' said Rab, forcing a wide smile, 'let's no worry about Danny McCall now, eh? Come on, Davie, got some folk I want you to meet. But first, got something to show you.'

Davie sighed inwardly, but he went along with it. Rab was his mate, and he didn't want to let him down. He knew the guests were crowding into the living room at the end of the hall, but Rab didn't lead them there right off. He stepped across the lobby and threw open the door to what had once been his own room, back when he and Davie shared the flat. He gave Davie a wide grin as he stepped back to let him pass. Davie tightened his eyebrows quizzically and looked in. Rab's big bed was gone of course, but it was what had replaced it that surprised him. One wall was covered in shelving which Davie recognised as having been in Joe's old place up near Barlinnie. And those shelves were filled with the old man's most treasured possessions – his records, line after line of carefully tended vinyl, gathered over years. There was even a substantial selection of 78s, their brittle plastic lovingly protected in padded sheathing.

'Joe left them to us,' said Rab. 'All his Frank Sinatra stuff, his Dean Martin, all they guys. Stuff frae the forties and that, big bands, Glenn Miller, some blokes I've never even heard of.'

Davie stepped into the room reverentially. Joe had loved these recordings and many a night had been spent playing chess while Sinatra, Crosby or Dean Martin crooned in the background. Joe loved Frank Sinatra. 'Others can sing a song,' he used to say, 'but Frankie *delivers* it'. Davie liked the sound, but his real preference was the swing music of Harry James, Tommy Dorsey and other names from that bygone era. He reached out and gently touched one row of album covers, running the edge of his finger along their spine.

'I never much liked that stuff, you know that,' Rab said. 'But I know you did, so…'

Davie slid an album out and stared at the cover. A moody painting of Sinatra in a dark jacket, tie, hat on his head, a cigarette in his hand, leaning against a wall and behind him a lonely street with lamps glowing in a mist. Davie glanced over to the wall and saw that Joe's old photographs had been hung there too. He sought out the one with the old man and Sinatra, taken years before in London. Joe was smiling at the camera, Frank's arm over his shoulder. They both had drinks in their hand, Frank, like the album cover, with a cigarette burning between two fingers. Joe never smoked, never drank much, but he told Davie he did that night. 'When Frankie offers you a drink, even pours it with his own hand,' he once said, 'you do not turn it down.' Davie placed the album back in its place, swallowing hard to combat the growing emotion.

'We kept his record player, too,' said Rab from the doorway. 'We got a bloke to come out and wire it up proper. There's a CD player in the living room but I thought you'd want all this in here. It's all yours, Davie. I think Joe would've liked that.'

Davie made a show of studying the hi-fi equipment set into an alcove of its own on the shelving, unwilling to turn around and show Rab how much the gesture had touched him. It had been top of the range in its day, and Davie knew it would still sound good. 'Thanks, Rab,' he said.

Rab cleared his throat and said, 'Aye, well… I've got no use for it.'

Bobby raised his can of Carlsberg and said, softly, 'To Joe, eh lads?'

Davie and Rab stared at each other for a moment, each thinking of the man who had taught them so much, then raised their own drinks – Rab's can of lager, Davie's can of Coke. 'To Joe,' they said in unison. They each took a slug and stood in silence, each wishing Joe Klein was still around.

Davie gave the albums one last look, then gave Rab a smile. 'This was good of you, Rab. You're a good mate.'

Rab's brows drew together. 'Fuck off. It's just a bunch of noise to me. C'mon, let's mingle…'

The living room was filled with people standing or sitting, talking and drinking, most of whom Davie did not know. One or two faces were familiar and he nodded to them as Rab led him across the room towards a tall, slim woman in her early thirties sitting in an armchair near the window, long dark hair framing a delicate face, her nose peppered with faint freckles. 'Davie, this is Bernadette,' said Rab, a big grin on his face. So this was Mrs McClymont, Davie thought and smiled, holding out his hand. She ignored it, rose to her feet and wrapped him in her arms for a tight hug.

'I'm so glad to meet you, Davie,' she said, her voice soft and warm, as was her embrace, her accent not as broad as he expected. Despite himself, Davie felt something flutter in his groin at the feel of her soft body against his. He felt guilty, this was Rab's wife for God's sake, but ten years without any physical contact was a long time. She stepped away from him and he hoped there was no visible sign of his arousal. 'Rab speaks of you often,' she said.

'Aye,' said Rab, 'and some of it's even true.'

Bernadette looked deeply into Davie's eyes and said, 'It's good to have you home. Rab is so glad to have you back. Don't listen to him, he's missed you, I know he has.'

Rab looked shame-faced. Feelings were for songs, not something men talked about. Davie felt his own cheeks begin to burn and he wondered how a guy like Rab snared such a prize. Bernadette seemed to be a decent person, despite what Bobby had said about her family in Belfast, and in their line of business such people were rare. To cover the awkward moment, Davie turned to face a nervous little man with a shock of thick grey hair who was standing to one side. He looked crumpled, as if he needed a good iron, and was dressed in a shapeless brown suit, the shoulders of the jacket flecked with dandruff.

'This is my solicitor, Gordon Spencer,' Rab said, thankful to divert attention away from what his wife had just said. 'You get in trouble again, Gordon's your man.'

Davie shook the man's proffered hand and looked into a set of watery brown eyes, seeing someone who looked uncomfortable in his own skin. Or maybe he was just unhappy being there. 'Mister McCall,' said the lawyer, nodding to him. His voice was cultured but weedy. Davie wondered how he fared arguing in a court. 'How does it feel to be on the outside?'

Davie shrugged, not really wishing to discuss his feelings with a stranger. 'It'll take a bit of getting used to.'

The man's head bobbed in agreement. 'That it will, that it will, I'm sure. Still, you have one advantage other fellows in your position do not – you are a man of property.'

Davie looked from Spencer to Rab and saw his mate's grin spread even wider. 'Aye, mate,' said Rab. 'This flat's all yours. Joe left it to both of us, but I've got my place out at Bothwell with Bernadette...' he smiled at his wife and Davie saw then and there that Bobby had been correct, the big guy was head over heels about this soft-spoken woman. It made him even guiltier about feeling aroused when she had embraced him. 'Anyway, I've signed the flat over to you. And Joe wanted the proceeds from his house to be split between you, me and Bobby, but when he died relatives came out the woodwork in Ayrshire – did you know he had folk down there?' Davie nodded. Joe had mentioned them once. Polish miners who had been brought over to work down the pits back in the twenties or thirties and settled there. Joe didn't see much of them. Davie knew there had been some dispute over Joe's will, but then he'd gone away and didn't think any more about it. Rab went on,

'Anyway, they got a hefty wedge but there was some left over, so you've got a wee bit of money in the bank, too.'

Davie blinked as he took this in and said to Bobby, 'You never told me.'

Bobby grinned. 'Wouldn't do you much good in the jail, mate. Thought we'd save it as a nice surprise for when you got out.'

The lawyer said, 'It's not a great deal, but it's enough to tide you over until you start earning. And beyond, I'm sure, if you're prudent.'

Rab laughed. 'Aye, he means don't go spending it all on burds and fast cars.'

The solicitor wasn't finished. 'The flat upstairs, too, should also be yours.'

'The one that old dear lives in, the Polish woman,' said Rab. 'But Joe specified that she get to live there rent free till she dies.' Rab pulled a face, showing what he thought of their old boss's softer side. 'Daylight fuckin robbery, so it is, but what we gonnae do? Gordon here thinks there's a way round it, though.'

'That's fine,' said Davie, quietly. 'Mrs Mitchell stays there as long as she wants.'

Rab sighed. 'Davie, son, it's good to have you back, but in the name of God, you'll need to toughen up. You've got a wee bit of cash, sure, but it'll no last forever, the way prices are today. This isn't 1980, son, you'll no believe the cost of living.'

'I think it's right and proper,' said Bernadette, smiling at Davie with her dark brown eyes. 'Good for you, Davie.'

Davie smiled back at her but he was really uncomfortable now. Crowds were never his thing at the best of times, but he was finding it hard to cope with the tingle he still felt at his groin. Rab's wife was attractive, and her physical proximity, the faint aroma of her perfume, her gorgeous brown eyes gazing at him, were all a growing reminder that he had not felt a woman's touch for ten years. There were guys in the jail who could switch their sexual preferences when it suited them, but he was not one of them. He had spotted two girls when he entered the room, one blonde, one brunette, and they were watching him from the settee as they sipped something clear from long glasses. Rab must have followed his gaze, for he smiled again.

'Davie, man, I'm sorry,' he said, 'should've taken care of business first. Sorry, folks, but there's stuff I've got to discuss with my boy here.'

'I thought you'd already discussed business, Rab,' said Bernadette, frowning.

'Aye, love, but there's a few things we never took care of, eh, Bobby?'

Rab jerked his head towards the girls and Bobby craned round to see them. He turned back, grinned, and peeled away from their little group to cross the room and lean over the duo. Whatever he said made them smile as they looked back at Davie.

'C'mon, Davie,' said Rab, gripping him by the arm and leading him away. Davie was grateful, for his face was beginning to flush again. He looked back at Bernadette, who looked puzzled till she saw Bobby chatting to the girls, and a small smile tickled her lips. As Rab led him past the girls, Davie saw them both appraising him, before giving each other a knowing glance. He knew they were deciding which one of them was going to welcome him back into the free world. He also knew that was why they were there, and that Bobby had probably selected them for the freedom they showed with their favours. Not normally Davie's thing, but suddenly he wanted it very badly.

Rab left him in his room – 'Take your time, son. And give her one for me.' – before he closed the door with a wink. Davie sat on the bed, wondering just what the hell he was doing. He wondered which of the girls it would be. A sudden worrying thought struck him – what if, after all this time, he couldn't stand up and be counted? What if he'd forgotten? Then another scary proposition presented itself – what if they both came in? Not being able to perform for one woman was bad enough, but two? He rubbed his face with both hands, wishing now that he had never gone along with this. Maybe he could get out, leave the flat before anything started, just slip away now, go for a walk, get away, be anywhere but here waiting for one girl or the other, or both, to walk through that door.

It was the blonde girl who came in. She stood with her back against the closed door and looked at him. She cast her eye around her.

'Nice room,' she said. She had a smoky voice, low and smooth. Davie wondered where Bobby had found her because she sure as hell wasn't from around here.

'I'm Vari,' she said and smiled. Her teeth were slightly crooked but very white against the pale peach of her lipstick. Her hair was long and straight, her eyes, like Davie's, a bright, piercing blue. When he saw her in the living room he had thought she was in her late teens, but now that he could see her clearly he realised with some relief that she was older, probably early to mid-twenties, which was good. He felt bad enough about the set-up without feeling like a child molester, too.

'Vari,' he said. 'Nice name. Is it Highland?'

She shook her head and moved further into the room. She was slim but rounded in all the right places. 'Different spelling. It's short for something else.'

'What?'

She gave him a coy smile and said, 'You'll laugh.'

Davie shook his head and she looked at him thoughtfully, sizing him up. Then she said, 'You seen a film called *Spartacus*?' Davie nodded. It was a favourite of his and the boys, particularly the scene where Kirk Douglas's men stand up and proclaim 'I am Spartacus' to save their leader, even though they knew it would mean their death. They stood up and were counted. The thought made him nervous once more about what was going to happen. Vari continued, 'So did my dad. He loved it so much he named me after Spartacus's wife.'

'Varinia,' said David, surprised that he had hauled the name up from his memory. He knew he fancied Jean Simmons, though.

She was impressed. 'Right. So, you can see why I shorten it.' Davie nodded, understanding that Varinias were not that thick on the ground in Glasgow. 'And you're Davie, right? Davie McCall?' Davie nodded as she stepped closer to him. 'Davie McCall,' she repeated, as if weighing it up. 'Heard a lot about you.'

'Any of it good?' He asked, his voice betraying his tension. He swallowed to lubricate his throat. He had not been much good at this kind of thing before the jail, now he was even more hopeless.

'Some of it,' she said, very close now, and he could smell her perfume. He had no idea what it was called but its aroma made him feel light-headed. She reached out and touched his face, drawing a finger from his temple to his jaw. Her finger was cool but her touch was electric. 'You're not bad-looking, you know that?'

He shrugged. He knew he looked like his father. He never thought of himself as handsome, simply ordinary looking.

'Nice eyes,' she said, 'like Paul Newman. Anyone ever told you that?' She raised her hand a little to brush his hair with her fingers. 'Nice hair, too, very dark. When you go grey you'll be dead distinguished looking.'

She cupped her hand under his chin, raised his head slightly and leaned in to kiss him. Her lips were cool and soft and he could taste her lipstick. Her tongue snaked between his teeth and probed his mouth. His hands went to her waist and he began to lean back onto the bed, pulling her with him.

And then, as she expertly took off his clothes, he looked down and smiled when he saw that his body had not failed him.

I am Spartacus, he thought.

* * *

Joe the Tailor told Luca Vizzini not to attend the party in Davie's honour. *It would not be fitting*, Joe had said. Now he sat across the table in the café on Duke Street and watched as Luca completed tax forms. The café was empty, so the little Sicilian had taken the opportunity to catch up on paperwork. It was good to divert his thoughts from Bannatyne and Davie McCall. *Tax is important*, Joe always used to say, *pay a little and it keeps the wolf from the door.* Despite the cash rolling in from the drugs, Luca still liked working in his little café. Joe had bought it for him, way back when, and Luca felt at home here.

Joe had not said anything for an hour, he had simply sat there, watching. Finally, Luca tired of working at his figures and moved behind the counter to pour himself a cup of coffee. He carried his cup back to the table and sat down facing his old friend.

'I still think I shoulda been there, Joe,' he said. He knew Joe wasn't really present, but it made him feel good to talk to him.

The old man shook his head. *No, keep your distance.*

'I don't think he suspects nothin,' Luca said.

David, he is not stupid, said Joe. *He knows. On some level, he knows what you did.*

Luca was not a coward, but fear stabbed through him. Luca had been a button man for the Genovese family in New York and he had killed men without turning a hair. But Davie McCall disturbed him and he did not know why. He was just a young punk, after all, and he had dealt with young punks all his life. But there was something about that kid, something he could not put his finger on. Only one other person had unsettled Luca in the same way and that was the boy's father, Danny. They looked so alike, maybe that was it. Or the cold distance in those blue peepers they both shared, a look that made you believe they knew what you were thinking before you even thought it. Rab McClymont Luca understood – he was motivated by profit, therefore he could be manipulated. Bobby Newman was nothing, a hanger-on, a tool to be used when necessary. But Davie? What was it Churchill said about Russia? A riddle wrapped in a mystery inside an enigma. Yeah, that was Davie McCall.

You must stay away from him, Joe said.

'Ain't gonna be easy, Joe,' said Luca. 'He's out now, he's gonna be workin for us.'

He will know.

'He can't know,' protested Luca, his voice taking on a whine he did not like. 'No-one knows.'

Davie will know. And he will come for you.

Luca shook his head. 'Joe, you're all wrong on this, way off base. The kid don't know nothing, I'll stake my life on it.'

Joe gave him that little half smile of his and leaned forward in his seat. *You are staking your life on it, Luca, my friend,* he said.

*   *   *

Alice, the brunette, wouldn't have minded going into the room with that Davie McCall fella. He wasn't bad looking and they all said he was a good guy to have on side if she ever needed him. But she let Vari go because she had another function in the flat that day, a job to do. And the guy who sent her to do it scared the shit out of her. No-one noticed when she slipped away from the flat and skittered down the stairs, but she kept checking over her shoulder just in case. *Don't let anyone see you do it,* the bloke had warned, and there was something in his eyes that told her she would suffer if she let anyone catch her. So she ran down the stairs, listening for footsteps behind her because that Bobby Newman would be the only one likely to notice she was missing. He would find her later, of course, but she'd just tell him she felt ill and had to go. In the end he wouldn't give a damn.

She ran down Sword Street towards Reidvale Street, where he said he would be waiting. She scanned the scrubby trees and spotty grassy area that bordered the railway line, but she couldn't see him. She looked at her watch, wondering if she had got the time wrong, but no, this was when he said to meet him. And she had the impression that being late was not an option.

'You get it?'

His voice came from behind her and she whirled round in surprise, wondering where the hell he had appeared from. 'You gave me a fright there,' she said, her hand clutching her chest as if she was suffering from a heart attack. He smiled, but there was no humour there.

'Did you get it?' He asked again.

'Aye,' she said and handed over the slip of paper on which she had scribbled down the phone number for McCall's flat.

He unfolded the paper and stared at it as if it was the answer to a mystery that had puzzled him for years. 'You have trouble getting it?'

'No, there's one of they old-fashioned phones in there. Got the number written on the wee plate thing in the middle.'

He nodded, folded the paper up again and slid it into the pocket of his coat. 'No-one saw you write it down?' She shook her head and he seemed satisfied. 'You tell anyone what you were going to do?'

Another shake of the head. 'You told me not to.'

'Good girl,' he said and held out a sheaf of five pound notes. But it was the small plastic bag with them she focussed on. As she reached out he pulled them away again. 'Keep your mouth shut, understand? You tell anyone you got me this, it'll go hard on you.'

'Aye, aye,' she said, her eyes on the brown powder in the bag. She'd hit up just before she and Vari had set out for Sword Street, but that had been, like, hours ago, and she was coming down. The bundle of notes would see her nicely for a day or two, she thought, but the smack was just what the doctor ordered. He held it and the money out again and she snatched them greedily. Then she felt his hand clamp on her upper arm and those blue eyes that seemed so cold burned right into her brain. She saw his eyes cloud, as if something was settling in. But then they cleared and he released her, stepping back and abruptly walking away. She watched him go, unconsciously rubbing her arm where his hand had bit into her flesh.

Alone in her flat in Parkhead that evening, she could still feel his fingers biting into her skin as she prepared the hit. She thought about him as she tightened the rubber strap round her arm and inserted the needle into her enlarged vein, thinking about how much he looked like the boy McCall.

It only took a few moments for the almost pure heroin to flood her system. It didn't take her much longer to die.

* * *

The first phone call came in the early hours of the morning.

Davie was alone in the flat. All the guests had left, Bernadette

giving him another long hug, though thankfully this time his baser
urges did not react, thanks to Vari's skilled and enthusiastic minis-
trations. Vari had extracted a promise from him that he would call
her, but he wasn't sure he would. She seemed a nice girl – worldly,
certainly – but nice enough. After Audrey, Davie was certain nice
was not for him. Before Rab left, he told him that if he was up to
it he had a job for him and Bobby the following day, a wee trip
down the coast. *Get you some fresh air, son,* he had said, *do you
good. Nothing special,* he had promised, *just a message to a boy
down Ayrshire way.* Davie had simply nodded. How easily he had
slipped into old ways.

Davie couldn't sleep. The bed was too soft, the room too clean,
the flat too quiet. He'd become used to the coughs and groans of
the old prison, he found, and it would take time to become accus-
tomed to the outside again. So he got up and paced the flat for a
time, feeling restless but too tired to go for a walk. He searched
for some paper on which to draw. He'd discovered an aptitude for
art inside during classes run by a well-meaning lecturer from the
School of Art. His sketches were good, their subjects always recog-
nisable, but he'd never be the toast of the arty-farty crowd. He
found the act of drawing soothing, and thrust away in one of the
plastic bags he'd carried from the jail were sketches of Sammy, other
prisoners and screws as well as landscapes both real and imagined.
He would never show them to anyone. They were a secret part of
him that he would never reveal.

He found some old rolls of wallpaper in a cupboard in the
kitchen so he tore some off and ripped it into manageable sheets.
There were a couple of pencils in a drawer in the living room, which
he sharpened with a small knife from the cutlery tray.

Davie settled in to the old room with Joe's LPs. He found the
one he had held earlier, 'In the Wee Small Hours of the Morning'.
Sinatra's smooth voice filled the room with longing and a sense of
loss, and Davie thought of Joe and he thought of Audrey and it
was her face he drew from memory. There had been a time, and
he had discussed it with Joe on their last night together, that he

believed he could leave The Life behind him, shake it off like a bad cold, and start afresh with Audrey. He had been young then and he thought such things were possible. When he went after Clem Boyle that thundery night and they had fought in the street like two gladiators, he began to realise that even though he might want to leave The Life, The Life might not want to give him up. The incidents with Donald Harris and the others in the jail was merely confirmation. He knew that, so had Audrey. And then there was that dark thing that Sammy had spoken about. Davie knew it lurked within him, waiting for the chance to spring to life. He had felt it before he went into the jail, a force that guided his actions when violence threatened. It had taken over when Harris went for him and dealt with the situation. It was still there, biding its time, waiting for the buttons to be pushed again.

You have a choice when the devil comes knocking, Sammy had said. Rab wanted him to do this message tomorrow. Was Rab the devil at the door? Or was he still to appear?

Davie sighed and tried to focus on Sinatra's voice as he sang of heartbreak and lost love. When he looked at his sketch of Audrey he realised he'd put something else in, a dark shape behind her, little more than a shadow.

And then the phone rang.

At first Davie was going to ignore it but it kept ringing. Must be Rab or Bobby, Davie thought as he walked down the hallway to the living room: they're the only people who have the number. Must be about tomorrow.

He perched on the arm of the settee beside the small table on which the phone sat and lifted the receiver. 'Hello?'

At first there seemed to be nothing on the line, but then he heard the sound of traffic slipping by somewhere.

'Hello,' Davie said again, but still the caller did not reply. He frowned, wondering if someone was playing silly buggers.

'Okay,' he said, 'I'm busy so…'

'You've grown up, son.'

The four words made Davie's blood freeze and something cold

and damp breathed up his spine. He hadn't heard that voice for thirteen years, but he knew who it was. He squeezed the solid plastic receiver, unconsciously pressing the earpiece tight against his head. He felt his breath catch and an old fear steal over him.

There was a slight laugh on the other end of the line. 'What? Not got anything to say to your old man? After all these years?'

'Where are you?' It was not much of a question, but it was the only one in his head.

'All in good time, son. For now, just thought I'd say hello, let you know I was still alive and kicking. How you been?'

'What do you care?'

'I'm your dad, of course I care.'

'You've got funny ways of showing it.'

Another small laugh. 'Ah, still upset, eh?'

Davie stifled the desire to scream at him down the phone. That was what Danny McCall wanted, he sensed. He wanted to hear his son lose it. Davie would not give him the satisfaction. Instead he asked, 'What do you want?'

'Told you, to say hello. Let you know I'm around.'

'If Joe was still alive, you'd not be here.'

'That's true, that old bastard would've had me cut into pieces and fed to the pigs somewhere. I'll tell you, I was never more relieved than I was to hear he'd copped it. Even so, I'd been back to the old town a few times before that. He didn't know that. None of you knew that.'

'Where else you been hiding?'

'Ah, here, there, everywhere. Like the song says. You know that song, son? The Beatles?'

Davie gritted his teeth, rage building inside him and at the same time hearing a roaring in his ears, like waves on a rocky shore. 'I'm not your son. I don't want anything to do with you.'

Another small laugh. 'Ah, that's not true, though. Is it, Davie, son?'

'Don't call me "son".'

'But that's what you are, like it or not, son. My boy. My offspring. The fruit of my loins. Can't change that.'

'Come and see me. We'll see what changes.'

'That's my boy! Heard you were a chip off the old block. To be honest, I did wonder sometimes if you'd let bygones be bygones, but I can tell that's not likely. So we've got unfinished business, you and me.'

'Anytime you want to finish it, I'm here.'

He heard his father chuckle again, as if he was enjoying this. 'Soon, son. When the time's right. Got stuff to do first.'

'What sort of stuff?'

'Never you mind that now. But we'll talk again, you and me. We've got some catching up to do…'

And then he was gone, the connection cut off. Davie stood as if frozen to the spot, the phone still to his ear. He listened to the dial tone as if it would give him a hint to where Danny McCall was, but the monotone buzz had nothing to say. He hung the receiver up almost gently and stared at it, Sinatra's voice still floating through the flat as if the world really hadn't changed at all.

But he knew who had thrown the dark shadow in the drawing.

14

NICE DAY FOR a run down the coast, Rab had said as Davie and Bobby had set off in Bobby's Montego for Ayrshire. He was right. Although there was a bite in the air, the sky was blue and it was the kind of morning that makes you feel good to be alive. Or at least out of jail. Davie, though, had his mind on the phone call. He now knew his gut feeling that Danny McCall had been lurking around the city for ten years was sound. He didn't tell Rab or Bobby about the call. He needed to understand exactly what his father was after. Once he had a clearer picture, he'd tell his mates.

Bobby chatted away as they drove through the south side of the city and down the A77, but Davie didn't take much in, so wrapped up was he in his own thoughts. But one thing Bobby said penetrated, and he turned from the passenger window and stared at him.

Bobby's head swivelled briefly towards Davie then returned to the road ahead. 'I'm giving up The Life, Davie,' he repeated.

Davie watched his pal's face. Bobby knew him well enough not to take his lack of response as disinterest.

'It's no the same anymore,' Bobby went on with a slight sigh. 'Been thinking about it for a while. Just no the same. Not since Joe.'

Bobby trailed off and fell silent. Davie waited, knowing Bobby had more to say.

'It's the drugs, Davie. It's… well, it's just no the same, you know? I mean, this bloke we're going to see today. Glasgow boy, who's moved down to the sticks, right? He's puntin gear to weans, they say. Weans, Davie. And we're helping him.'

Davie knew they were going to deliver some sort of message, but he hadn't asked what it was or why. He was simply along for the ride. Sometimes 'a message' could be a slap or two, other times something worse, but Rab had not suggested that this was anything more than verbal, some business best not trusted to phones. Only Bobby knew what the message was, and until now Davie hadn't been interested.

'So what's the message?' Davie asked.

'The bawbag owes Rab some dough. I've to remind him of his responsibilities. Nothing heavy, just a word or two, a wee nudge, but he'll get the picture right enough. But it's drugs, Davie. Hate them.'

Davie paused for a moment then asked, 'So what'll you do?'

'When I get out?' Davie nodded. 'You mind my Uncle Bobby? The one I'm named after?'

Davie recalled a man who used to give them both comics when they were kids. Bobby may have been named after his uncle, but there the similarities ended. Uncle Bobby was large, round, red-faced and had a bad comb over. But he was kind-hearted and funny and, more importantly, as straight an arrow as you could hope to find.

Bobby said, 'He says there's a place for me in his shop, that wholesale painting and decorating place down the far end of Duke Street, mind it?' Davie nodded, recalling the smell of thinners that

permeated the large storeroom at the back of the store. One summer
Bobby and he were paid a fiver each to redecorate the small toilets
using industrial strength paints and after two hours in the confined
space they had stumbled out into the fresh air, high as kites on the
fumes. It was the first and only time Davie had felt that sense of
euphoria, short-lived though it was. Within an hour they were
both puking their guts out in the alleyway behind the shop, Uncle
Bobby pleading with them not to let their parents know.

'I think I'm going to do it, Davie,' Bobby said. 'And there's something else. I'm getting married...' Davie looked up again, a smile
beginning to grow on his face. Bobby gave him a shy sideways
glance. 'I never said nothing yesterday, it was your day, mate, but
next year, I'm getting hitched. Rab doesn't know yet. You're the
only one I've told.'

'Who is she?'

'You don't know her, she's from over Shawlands way. Connie's
her name. Connie Lorrimer. You'll like her, Davie. She's a wee bit
older than me...'

'How much older?'

'Only five years, I'm no playing grab a granny or nothin, don't
worry. She's been married before, didn't work out. She's a primary
school teacher, can you believe that? I'm going out with Miss.'

Davie smiled, remembering the days in school when they called
the teacher 'Miss', even if she was an old witch who had been
married for forty years.

'Anyway,' Bobby said, 'she wants me out The Life. She knows
all about me... well... most of it. And she doesn't like Rab one bit.
She never gave him a chance, to be honest, just judged him on his
reputation. That's why I never brought her along yesterday to your
party, he's okay with her but I know she cannae stick him. She'll
like you, though.'

Davie wondered about that. If she judged Rab on his reputation,
what would she think of him? But then another thought struck
him. 'There'll be some very disappointed girls down our way.'

Bobby gave a wide, almost shameful smile. 'Aye, well... she

knows I've been a bit of a lad in my day. But, you know something, Davie? See since I've been going out with her, I've no been tempted. I can still pull them if I wanted to, but I don't want to. How was Vari, by the way?'

Davie was thrown by the minor non-sequitor but he soon answered, 'She's a nice girl.'

Bobby's smile grew. 'Thought you'd like her. You going to see her again?'

Davie shrugged. He hadn't really thought about it, there being too many other matters to deal with.

Bobby nodded. 'Aye, same old Davie. Give her a call, man! Have some fun, for God's sake. You come this way but once, know what I'm sayin? Live a little. I'm no sayin marry the girl but, Jesus, it doesn't do any harm to get some now and then.' Then something sounding like awe crept into Bobby's voice. 'Fuck me – would you look at that!'

Davie had been dimly aware during their conversation that they had driven through the small town of Maybole and had passed the ruins of an old abbey on their left. The car crested a rise above Turnberry and ahead of them lay the Firth of Clyde, its waters a deep blue, reflecting the lighter blue of the sky. The dark mound of the Ailsa Craig rose from the water ahead of them and to the right they could see the tail end of the Isle of Arran. It was an incredible vista and neither of them spoke for a few moments, two Glasgow boys more used to the high rise flats and sandstone tenements of the city than the blue-tinged splendour before them.

'Makes you wish you could get out of Glasgow, eh, Davie?'

Davie didn't answer. The sight had brought back memories of the holidays he'd taken with his parents. Ballantrae was only a few miles further down the coast and he was tempted to ask Bobby to take him there once their business was completed in Girvan. But he decided against it. That was the past and it was dead and buried. There was no going back.

Instead he said, 'Congratulations, Bobby. I hope you and Connie are very happy.'

'Thanks, mate. You'll meet her soon, I promise.' Bobby cleared his throat. 'What about you? You going back to work with Rab?'

Davie looked through the passenger window. 'I don't know,' he said, and he was being truthful. That lawyer had told him he had some money in the bank, enough to tide him over. He didn't need to go back to work right away. He didn't *want* to go back to work right away. He was no longer sure there was a place for him in The Life. Drugs had changed everything. Sammy said it, Bobby said it. It had been far from peaceful before but now, with the riches to be found in addicts' veins, The Life was more volatile than ever. And Davie was not sure he wanted any part of it.

* * *

Liam Mulvey was of slight build, his balding head scraped down to the flesh, and was dressed in green and black camouflage trousers and a sleeveless jerkin over a dark t-shirt. He was hefting a rifle case into the back of a four-wheel drive outside his terraced house, once owned by the council but now his thanks to Right to Buy, when Bobby pulled up at his gate.

'Fuck me, Liam,' Bobby shouted through his open window, 'almost never saw you there in your camo gear.'

A frown etched itself into Mulvey's narrow forehead and Davie could tell he was not happy to see them. 'Bobby,' he said, his voice heavy, 'what brings you down here?'

Bobby climbed out of the car and Mulvey moved down the drive to meet him, as if he didn't want the visitor to set foot on his property. 'Well, Liam, it's no a social call, let me put it that way.'

'Rab sent you?'

Davie decided to get out of the car too. He stood on the road beside the passenger door, leaning on the roof, watching the two men talk a few feet away. Mulvey glanced at him and for a second Davie thought there was a flash of recognition in his eyes. Davie searched his memory, but he couldn't dredge up a Liam Mulvey. But then, he had met many people during his time with Joe the Tailor, it was always possible their paths had crossed.

'Just a gentle reminder, Liam,' Bobby said. 'Big man wants his wedge.'

'He'll get his money.'

'Oh, he knows that, Liam,' Bobby said softly. 'One way or the other, he knows that.'

Bobby had learned a great deal over the years, Davie realised. Joe had always taught them that there was seldom any need to go in heavy. A word or two should be enough to bring a man round to your way of thinking.

'So where you off to, Liam?' Bobby jerked his head towards the four-wheel drive.

'Up into the hills there,' Mulvey nodded towards the green hills that loomed above the seaside town. 'Bit of rough shooting. Rabbits, maybe a pheasie if there's a stray one around. Just for sport.'

Davie saw distaste flicker on Bobby's face. He felt a certain revulsion himself.

'Sport, eh?' asked Bobby. 'Don't see how it's sport myself. Now, maybe if the rabbits had guns and could shoot back, might be a different matter, eh, Davie?'

Mulvey looked again at Davie and once more there was that flicker. Davie asked, 'We met before?'

Mulvey hesitated. 'No, don't think so.'

Davie moved around the front of the car. 'You sure?'

'I'm sure. I just know who you are, that's all. But we've never met.'

'Aye, Davie's famous, so he is,' said Bobby, smiling. 'I wouldn't let Rab down, Liam.'

Mulvey's eyes hardened. 'Tell Rab that he needs to come down here, see me himself, no send his errand boys. No matter how famous they are.'

Bobby drew in his breath sharply. 'That would piss him off big time. And you don't want to piss him off, do you?'

'Bobby, I like you...'

'That's nice, Liam.'

'But, see – I really don't give a flying fuck if I piss Rab McClymont off. I've been a good customer to him for a while now and I'm a little late in settling up, so what? I'm good for it and he knows it. He wants to talk to me about it, he can come down see me and we'll talk. Tell him I've got a proposition for him, too.'

'What kind of proposition?'

Mulvey smiled, but there was nothing friendly in it. It gave his thin face a wolfish quality. 'I want the organ grinder, no the monkey. Tell him it'll make him a lot more than what I owe him.'

Bobby shrugged. 'That what you want me to tell him?'

'Aye, that's what I want you to tell him.'

Bobby exhaled deeply. 'Okay, I'll tell him. And you know what? I think he might take you up on your offer. He was just saying the other day he could do with some fresh air and a wee trip doon the watter might be just the job. We'll be in touch.'

Bobby gave Mulvey a little wave and turned back to the car. Mulvey watched as he climbed back in and then his eyes flicked to Davie again. He held Davie's cool gaze for as long as he could then broke eye contact and turned back to his four-wheel drive. Davie climbed back in beside Bobby.

'How much does he owe Rab?' He asked.

Bobby watched Mulvey as he hoisted himself into the front of his four-wheel drive, then flicked the ignition key of the Montego. 'Enough that Rab will want to come and give him a talking to for being so cheeky.' Bobby eased the car away from the kerb. 'Never did like that wee bastard. See the size of that gun? That's him all over. He's a short-arsed wee sod and shooting that cannon, killing animals that can't fight back, that'll make him feel like a big man. Wee man with a big gun, that's him. Penis extension, that what they call it? Maybe I'll hang around long enough to see Rab give him a slap.'

* * *

Mulvey watched in his rear view as the blue Montego pulled away, allowing them enough time to turn out of his street before he steered his four-wheel drive in the opposite direction. He knew they would be heading north, but he was going in the opposite direction. He could've made a call but what he was about to say was not something you trusted to phone lines. You never knew who was listening. So he headed south, following the twisting coastal route to Ballantrae. Fifteen minutes later he stood outside a small terraced cottage. He'd met the man who opened the door many times, of course, but now he looked at him with fresh eyes. Liam paused, as if he expected to be invited in, but he should've known better.

'Rab's boys have just left.' Liam's voice was low. He hated talking on the doorstep but he'd never once been taken inside. He wondered why.

The man nodded. 'Will they deliver the message?'

'Aye. Rab'll want to have a go at me for being so bloody cheeky when I owe him dosh, but he'll also be curious about what I've got to say. Rab McClymont's fond of money, so he is.'

'Good.'

'One other thing…' Liam paused but the man said nothing, just waited. 'It was Bobby Newman that was here.'

'So?'

'He wasn't on his tod. Davie McCall was with him.'

The man did not seem surprised. 'He didn't lose any time getting back in action.'

'Aye. But here's the thing. Me seeing him? Made me think.'

'About what?'

Liam leaned in closer. 'About how much he looks like you.'

Danny McCall didn't even flinch. He turned those cold blue eyes on Liam and said, 'Your point is?'

'Here was me thinking your name was Bill McAllister. But see now that I know who you are? Changes things, doesn't it?'

McCall's voice grew soft. 'How do you work that out, Liam?'

'I know what you done. I know the Law's still looking for you.'

A soft laugh rattled in McCall's throat. 'Liam, son, the Law's forgotten all about me. And I'd suggest you forget what you've just said, too. I'm liable to take it personally.'

'Ah, see, that wouldn't be wise, Danny – can I call you Danny? Suits you better than that other name you gave me. You need me, mate…'

'I could find another partner. Lots of guys out there with ambition, just like you, with connections to Rab.'

'Aye, but I've set the ball in motion now and you need me to see it through. So what I think is, I should get a wee bit extra dosh, just so's I don't drop a word to the boys in blue about who you really are. Cos I don't think they have forgotten.' Liam leaned in closer, dropping his voice even lower. ' I don't think they ever forget about murder.'

McCall considered this. Then he sighed. 'Okay, Liam, fair enough. We'll split everything fifty-fifty. Once we remove Rab and move in on his territory, we're partners. Sound good?'

'Aye, mate, sounds fantastic.'

'Good. Let me know when Rab gets in touch. Make sure everything's ready.'

The door closed, leaving Liam staring at the wood. He didn't care. He was grinning. He turned away, headed back to his motor, thinking *this is a good deal… Seeing that bloke McCall and putting two and two together to make one happy family was a stroke of luck.*

* * *

Davie was quiet most of the way back to Glasgow. Bobby didn't intrude, knowing that when Davie descended into that kind of silence, the best thing to do was leave him to it. Bobby didn't feel like talking much anyway, truth be told. He had admitted to Davie he wanted out and that was the fact of it, but he hadn't told him everything. It was true that things hadn't been the same since Joe died, with Luca and Rab taking them further into the drug trade, but the reality for Bobby was that the world really turned sour the day Mouthy Grant was killed.

Bobby had never spoken to anyone about that day. He doubted if Davie even knew what happened. In all of Bobby's visits to the Bar-L, Davie had never asked about it. Connie certainly didn't know. He'd never be able to tell her about that. Never.

Bobby told himself that he hadn't known what Rab was going to do with Mouthy. He told himself that he really believed Rab was simply going to give the boy a warning and then send him out of the city. As they sat in the car on the journey from Luca's Duke Street café to the waste ground, he told himself that he had no idea this was to be Mouthy's last trip. Deep down, though, he knew what was going to happen. It was inevitable. Mouthy had grassed.

Bobby walked with Mouthy across the waste ground, Rab bringing up the rear. Mouthy was quiet, which was unnatural for him, as he was able to keep up a seemingly non-stop stream of chatter. Hence his nickname. Bobby had wondered over the years if the wee guy knew what was going to happen, and that was what was keeping him silent, but doubted it. Rab had told him they were going to get his stuff and then see him out of Glasgow. Mouthy and Rab were mates. He trusted the big fella. There was no way Rab would do him harm.

The bullet crack was very loud, or maybe that was just the way it sounded to Bobby. Mouthy pitched forward, blood spraying into the dirt. None of it hit Bobby, not in the literal sense. But Bobby knew he had Mouthy Grant's blood on him just the same.

When he saw the message painted on the broken-down wall telling the world MOUTHY GRANT IS A GRASS, Bobby told himself something else – that what had been done was the only thing that *could* be done. Mouthy had broken the code and there was a price to pay. The boy must've known that before he blabbed to the cops, before he helped put Davie away. Bobby continued to tell himself a lot about that day. And he almost believed it, until he met Connie. She was like no-one else he had ever met, and for the first time he felt he could put his old life behind him and start afresh. He wondered if that was how Davie had felt when he'd been going out with that reporter lassie.

There had been a lot of things he'd done of which he wasn't proud. There had been slappings and there had been full-on kickings. But the only thing that shamed him was Mouthy Grant's death.

Bobby Newman wanted no more blood on his hands.

15

DAVIE WATCHED the man complete the paperwork. The guy had obviously done this a million times before and boredom swam around his eyes on the few occasions he looked directly at Davie. Maybe once he had been young and enthusiastic about his job, but not anymore. Maybe once he'd thought he was going to make a difference, that he was going to help people. But that, too, had died. Now he followed the routine and his words were lifeless, his movements listless. He was grey, too, but that fitted his environment because everything about this room was grey – the walls, the furniture, even the air. Bobby had told him to sign on as soon as possible, so he'd made his way to the 'buroo', the unemployment exchange. It was the civil service, so there was a pile of forms to be filled in, questions to be answered. Davie watched the man scribble in various boxes then glanced around the big room, where other guys just like him were sitting at identical desks with other form pushers. Davie knew he'd have to start earning. Or at least draw the dole. He didn't need to worry about rent and Rab had given him a hundred quid to be getting on with, but the big man had been right – the cost of living was scary. When they came back from Girvan, Davie had asked Bobby to drop him off at a supermarket and he'd realised with a shock just how much prices had risen in ten years.

'So what experience do you have?'

Davie returned his attention to the man opposite him, who was now staring at him with those disappointed eyes of his. 'In what way?'

'Well, what have you done in the past?'

He felt the hard cement scraping his flesh, felt the sweat soaking through his clothes, felt the hot breath of Clem Boyle on his face as they each struggled to reach the gun...

'Not much,' he said.

The man frowned. 'You've never had a job?'

Davie jutted his head towards the from he'd filled in earlier. 'Been away for the past ten years.'

The man scanned Davie's handwriting, found the section that explained Davie's absence from the work pool. He nodded and scribbled something down on his own form. 'Do you have any skills?'

The ease with which he'd disarmed Harris. And Harris' face contorted in agony as he twisted his arm from the socket...

'Nothing to speak of,' said Davie.

The man sighed. 'So what kind of job would you be looking for, Mister McCall?'

Davie shrugged. He hadn't thought about it. Get signed on, Bobby had said. Get your Giro every two weeks.

'I mean, you have no experience, you have no skills. The best you're looking at is labouring, or menial work somewhere. And I'll not kid you, your prison record will hold you back. Have you spoken to your probation officer? Maybe he can help.'

'Not on probation.'

The man sighed again and looked around the office. 'I'll be honest, Mister McCall, I don't know what to suggest. I know we have nothing to offer you right now. Look around you – there are lots of young men in the same position, and most of them have worked before.'

Davie knew what the man was telling him. He'd known it himself. Three years of working for Joe the Tailor and ten years banged up was no preparation for life as a straight arrow.

Even if his nature would let him.

* * *

Luca felt his body clench when Davie McCall walked into the café around tea-time. His eyes flitted around the café for a sight of Joe, but the old man wasn't there, which was strange. He really thought he'd see him when Davie showed up for the first time. Luca knew it was bound to happen, knew Davie would come sooner or later. Even so, he was surprised and, if the tingle in his fingertips and the tightness at his throat was anything to go by, scared. He wondered what that was all about. Luca had killed men, he'd beaten them, he'd put the fear of God into them. He'd rubbed shoulders with mobbed-up psychos who'd kill you for just looking at them the wrong way. *But here's Davie McCall, this boy, and all he's done is walk into the café and I'm trembling like a virgin on a first date. Seriously,* he thought, *what's up with that?*

He plastered his biggest shit-eating grin across his face and moved out from behind the counter. 'Davie,' he said, and no-one would've known that this guy was the last person in the world he ever wanted to see. 'What do ya hear, what do ya say?' Jimmy Cagney, *Angels With Dirty Faces.* He'd watched the flick years ago with Joe and Davie and ever since then he'd used the greeting when he saw the kid. He relaxed considerably when Davie smiled at the memory and held out his hand.

'Luca, good to see you,' he said. His voice was different, Luca noted. Deeper. He'd grown up since he was away. Looked even more like his father now. Same blue eyes, same dark hair, same way of holding himself as he took note of his surroundings. Not for the first time, Luca wondered if that was what disturbed him about this kid – no, not a kid anymore, a man. A man like his pop.

Luca shook his hand and said, 'Sorry I didn't make the party, kid. Not got the patience for small talk no more, you know how it is.'

Davie nodded. *Yeah,* thought Luca, *he knows how it is.* Davie was never one for small talk – in that way he differed from his father, who could talk the legs off a donkey. Danny McCall was a charmer, sure, but he was a dangerous man. There was always something working away behind those blue peepers. Luca searched the eyes of the young man before him but saw nothing. He reckoned he was safe. Davie didn't know what he had done.

Luca asked, 'You wanna have something to eat maybe?'

Davie looked around and Luca followed his gaze. The café was quiet, only a mad old bat talking to her shopping bag at one table, and two kids nursing Cokes while they waited for their burger and chips.

Davie shrugged then nodded. He slid into a booth and settled himself into the faux leather bench in Joe's favourite booth. Luca wondered if Davie chose it on purpose. He glanced around again, certain that Joe would appear, but still there was no sign. Davie plucked the plastic-covered menu from its slot in the wall and studied the food on offer. He selected a cheeseburger, chips and a glass of milk. Luca yelled the order to Enrico and took a seat opposite.

'You're lookin good, kid. Could do with some sun, though. You got the Barlinnie Tan, right enough.'

Davie smiled. 'Not much sunshine in the halls, Luca.'

'How's freedom been so far?'

Luca saw Davie's eyes cloud as if something dark had seeped into the irises and he knew something troubled the kid. He wanted to ask what it was, but was afraid what the answer might be. But all Davie said was, 'It's good to be out, that's for sure.'

Luca nodded. Like Rab, he'd never done time, although that bastard cop Jack Bannatyne had sniffed around long enough, trying to root something out. It had taken all of Luca's street smarts to keep himself distanced from the operational end of the business and keep Bannatyne off his trail. Bannatyne had planted the niggling thought that Davie would've worked some things out while he was away. He certainly seemed to have something on his mind. The question was, what did this kid know?

Luca decided to bite the bullet. 'What's up, kid? You look kinda blue.'

Davie's expression didn't change, but his eyes bored deeply into Luca's own. 'I've been thinking about Joe,' he said, and Luca felt icy fingers clench inside his chest.

'What about him?'

Davie sighed and leaned forward. 'You really think Jazz killed him?'

Luca sat back and suddenly Joe was there, sitting beside Davie, smiling at him. 'Why do you ask that?' He struggled to keep his voice even.

'I don't know. Had lots of time to think in the jail. Nothing much else to do. It's just… well, I can't believe Joe would let a scroat like that get the better of him, that's all.'

'Joe got him.'

'Yeah, but only after he'd let Jazz put a bullet in him. I don't think that boy would've been able to get one over Joe.'

Luca swallowed and forced his mind to slow down. He had to be careful here. If Davie suspected his involvement, there was no way he would be here talking about it. Davie McCall had no guile. If he thought he'd killed Joe, he would be fighting for his life right now. No, the kid just had doubts and Luca had to deflect them. For now.

He leaned forward. 'Listen, this ain't gonna be easy to hear. Shit, it ain't easy for me to say. But Joe was getting old, you know?'

'He was fifty-five, Luca. Not that old.'

'Yeah, but his life had taken its toll, y'unnerstand? He was tired, Davie, I know because he told me. And it was a tense time – all that killing, all that blood. Johnny Jones on the rampage. Joe knew he was next on the list.'

'That's my point. Joe was on his guard.'

'Sometimes your guard slips, you know? He was weary, bone weary. He made a mistake.'

Luca watched as Davie processed this. The kid didn't want to believe that Joe was fallible, was all. He didn't want to believe that Joe was human. The fact was, Joe hadn't let Jazz get the drop on him – he'd gutted the scroat before he knew what hit him. It was Luca who pulled the trigger, using Jazz's gun, to put Joe down. His old buddy Luca. Luca saw the betrayal reflected in his old friend's eyes as he died, but it had been necessary.

Davie looked down at the table top and his body slumped as if accepting something he had until now refused to believe. He said nothing more, apart from a 'thank you' when Luca collected his food, laid it down in front of him and wished him *buon appetito*. Luca left him to his meal and took up a position behind the counter. He kept himself busy, washing down the serving area, rearranging the confectionary on display, but all the while he kept a watch on the kid. Luca thought he had convinced him, but he was still troubled. He needed to see Davie's eyes to be sure he was in the clear, but he couldn't get a clear view of them.

It did not help when Joe appeared at his side and whispered, *He knows.*

* * *

He'd only been out a day and everything appeared familiar and yet different. Ten years was a long time and things had changed. Shops had new owners. Buildings were gone. Fashion had changed. He was older.

As Davie walked back to Sword Street, he thought about Luca's words. Joe had been ageing, Davie had noticed it. It was nothing overt. A slowing down, that's all. Maybe he did just make that one mistake and gave Jazz the chance to pull the trigger. It would only take a second. But Joe still had the strength with a bullet in him to stick a knife in Jazz. To Davie, that wasn't what a tired, weak old man would be able to do. And there was only one bullet, he'd heard. If Joe was coming for Jazz with a knife, Jazz could've put another one in him, maybe two, stopped him dead.

On the other hand, maybe Jazz was so shit-scared that he couldn't fire again. Maybe the boy panicked and Joe got to him first. Davie knew the old man was handy with that knife, he'd learned to use it with the Polish partisans in the war. Joe had told him his war stories and Davie knew he was capable of wielding it expertly and swiftly.

And then Joe lay down and died.

He didn't try to call anyone, he didn't try to get help.

He just died.

Davie didn't believe it.

Someone else was there, he knew it.

* * *

She was waiting for him when he reached the closemouth. He'd seen a figure in the car but didn't know it was her until she climbed out. He stared into her green eyes and was instantly transported back to the night in the city's West End when he'd seen her for the first time. He felt the same powerhouse blow to his chest he'd felt then. Some things never change.

'Hello, Davie,' she said, a nervous smile tugging at the corners of her mouth.

'Hello, Audrey,' he said.

'I heard you were out,' she said. He nodded. Of course she would. 'You're looking good,' she said, and he had the impression it was more to say something than anything else.

'So do you,' he said and he wasn't just being polite. Her honey blonde hair was pulled back from her face and tied in a pony tail. She had lines that weren't there the last time he saw her, but then, so did he. Ten years is a long time. She hadn't put on weight, she was still slim yet curvy at the same time. She was wearing a smart dark blue trouser suit and crisp white blouse. She looked gorgeous.

And then he saw the ring on her finger.

'You're married,' he said and she glanced down at her left hand as if she'd forgotten. She reddened slightly.

'Five years,' she said.

Of course she was married, he thought. *Why wouldn't she be? So that was why her by-line vanished – her name changed.*

They stood for a few moments, looking at each other, their awkwardness standing between them like a third person. Her right hand had moved to cover her left, he saw, hiding her ring. He wondered if she knew she'd done that.

'I need to talk to you, Davie,' she said.

He nodded as if a former girlfriend appearing out of the blue after eight years was the most natural thing in the world for him. 'You want to come in?'

She looked up at the red sandstone walls as if the answer was written there. 'Sure,' she said finally. 'Why not?'

The flat seemed even quieter than usual as they sat facing each other in the sitting room. He'd asked her if she wanted tea or coffee but she declined. He didn't offer anything else because he wasn't sure what he had. After that they sat in silence, the only sound the whirring of the electric clock on the mantelpiece above the gas fire.

Davie hated that clock and vowed to get rid of it. If he wanted to hear the passing of time, he wanted a good old-fashioned tick and not an electronic throb. He couldn't think of anything to say, so he left it to Audrey. She was the wordsmith, after all. He was just a ned.

'Davie,' she said, finally, 'I'm sorry about the way things ended. Back then. In the jail.'

He shook his head. 'Not your fault, Aud.'

'No,' she insisted. 'I… well, I ran out on you. I deserted you.'

'Aud,' he said, his voice firm, 'water under the bridge. You did the right thing.'

She gave him a slight smile. He couldn't tell whether she was agreeing with him or if there was something else. 'When you… when you had your sentence extended after…'

'After I beat that guy senseless. You can say it, Aud, I was there, I remember.'

Her eyes dropped. 'Yes… well… I couldn't handle it.'

'I know.'

'I let you down.'

Davie repeated, 'You did the right thing. I wasn't the right one for you.'

She nodded, her right hand absently moving again over her left. 'He's a police officer,' she said, even though Davie hadn't asked. She looked up and saw his raised eyebrow. 'A DC, Stewart Street.'

Davie said nothing. She shrugged, as if she was apologising. He wanted to tell her not to apologise. She never had to apologise to him. She got on with her life and that life was not for him. But he didn't speak, choosing, as usual, to remain silent.

'You're a legend, you know that?' There was that slight smile again. He had missed that little smile, the one she gave him when she was about to make fun of him. He missed the way her eyes sparkled. He missed her. But she was not for him, he had to keep reminding himself of that. 'The way you chased Boyle down Duke Street after he'd shot that policeman…'

'Frank Donovan.'

'Yes. Frank Donovan. He's a Detective Sergeant now, back at

Baird Street. The fight in the street between you and Boyle, it's grown arms and legs over the years,' she continued. 'Last time I heard it mentioned, it lasted half an hour and you were both beaten to a bloody pulp.'

Davie's mind flashed back to that night and he was facing Clem Boyle again – felt the ache in his ribs, in his muscles and where his flesh had been scraped from the bone as they scrambled on the pavement trying to reach a gun. 'Didn't last that long. But we were pretty beat up.'

'Still, it's made you a legend. I was reminded of that yesterday when I met an old friend of yours. Donald Harris.'

Davie frowned. 'Harris?'

'He told me what happened, what really happened. You were telling me the truth back then. I'm sorry, Davie...'

'What did he say?'

'That he went after you, that you got the better of him. That someone paid him to do it.'

Davie was tense, leaning forward in his chair. 'He say who?'

She shook her head. 'He's a junkie now, he'd just shot up and passed out. I wouldn't get much sense out of him even if I woke him. I'm sorry, Davie, I should've believed you.'

Davie dismissed the thought with a flick of his hand, his mind on Harris. He might know who had paid Lomas off. It was a long shot, but he might know something.

He stared deeply into Audrey's eyes, almost losing himself again, but pulling himself back. That was over, he told himself. 'Do you trust me, Aud?'

She thought about his question for a moment then nodded. 'I should've trusted you eight years ago. I trust you now. Why?'

'Because I want you to take me to Harris right now...'

16

THERE WAS NO answer at the door of Jinky's top-floor flat. Davie had knelt down to listen at the letterbox but heard no movement inside, no telly blaring, no radio. That didn't mean anything, of course, because if Audrey was right and it was a shooting gallery, the addicts could all be asleep, like vampires in the daytime. Short of kicking the door in, which Davie might have been tempted to do had she not been there, there was nothing for it but to head out to see if they could find him.

Audrey drove them to the shopping arcade in Cumberland Street. It wasn't a huge mall like the one they had built at St Enoch Square in the city centre. The shops here drew local trade in the main, and the occasional visitor in need of a newspaper, sandwich or a hot pie. But that was not what would attract addicts like Harris. They needed to eat, but they had more pressing reasons to come here. Audrey parked the car opposite the opening to the shopping centre and nodded towards a railing cutting the wide pavement off from the road.

'That's the Beggar's Rail,' she said. 'Watch.'

Davie watched intently. A few people wandered in and out of the shops, women with shopping bags, young mums with children, men heading for the bookies or the pub. But there were others, hanging around with seemingly nothing to do. They appeared restless, nervous even, young women, young men, a few older people, some of them obviously addicts, their thin faces and pale skin as much a giveaway as the continual scratching at their arms or groins.

'When they can no longer find veins in their arms, they start to inject in other parts of their body – their groin, usually,' said Audrey. 'Strip them down and you'll find track marks all over. There'll be ulcers on the arms and legs, scabs, sores, you name it.'

Many of them limped as they paced to and fro, puffing on cigarettes like the nicotine was mother's milk. They paid little attention to their surroundings or the fearful looks from some of the shoppers as they skirted around them. Their complete attention was on the roadway.

'Here we go,' said Audrey, and Davie saw a blue vw Estate park up near the rail. A white-haired man in his fifties and a hard-faced woman who might have been a decade younger climbed out. The addicts didn't move, but they stared at the newcomers expectantly. The white-haired man stood at the rail and nodded to a young man to come forward. A word or two was exchanged and the man held his hand out to the woman, who had stationed herself at the rear of the vw. She opened the door and reached inside, then passed something to the man, who in turn handed it to the younger man. Bank notes were exchanged and the junkie limped off, his purchase clutched in his palm.

'They sell everything,' explained Audrey. 'Smack, jellies, eggs… you name it.'

Davie knew that jellies and eggs were different forms of Temazepam, one a plastic bubble, the other a rock that needed to be melted. He'd been away for ten years, but drugs were far from unknown in Barlinnie. A woman with a baby in a pram was next. The mother was plump and healthy, but Davie guessed she wouldn't stay that way. The drugs would soon eat that fat away. God knew what kind of life lay ahead for the child. She thrust the small package into the pram and hurried away. Davie shook his head at the parade of human misery.

'Not pretty, is it?' said Audrey. 'But that's the business you're in, Davie.'

'I'm not in the business,' he said.

'Not yet maybe. But your pal Rab is, and your other pal, Bobby, is it? This is what they do. They provide the drugs that these people sell.'

Davie didn't reply. There was nothing he could say. Joe had been against this, but the profits it generated were too powerful a draw for some and even he couldn't fight it. He died opposing it.

'Watch this,' said Audrey, and Davie saw a middle-aged woman coming round the railing towards the rear of the vw. She raised the sleeve of her sweatshirt and let the woman inject something into her arm.

'Some people don't like jagging themselves,' Audrey explained, 'so the dealer'll do it for them. All part of the service. Some of these people will be HIV-Positive, thanks to sharing dirty needles. Some of them will be dead this time next week, or next month or even tomorrow, if they don't get help. Some will get help, get clean, and never look back. But they'll always be addicts, always be on guard against slipping back into their old ways. But most will keep going until the drugs or the virus or some other infection kills them. But there're always more poor souls ready to take their place. And plenty of drugs to go round, thanks to Rab McClymont and the rest.'

Davie was sickened by the scene. He wished he could tell Audrey to take him away from there, but they still hadn't found Harris. 'You think this is where Harris buys?'

'It's the most likely place, close to his flat. He could be out thieving to pay for his habit, but sooner or later I think he'll come here. He spoke about it during the interview.'

Davie nodded and sat back in the seat, unable to take his eyes off the free enterprise before his eyes. Joe had been right about the drug trade: it fed on weakness, it thrived on unhappiness, it prospered on despair. And when it had drained every last penny from its customers, it let them wither and die and went in search of fresh blood. Joe was a crook, a thief, even a pimp, but he despised the notion of drugs taking hold in his adopted city. Yet, here it was ten years after his death, and deals were being made in broad daylight. Davie didn't understand addiction, whether it was drink or drugs. He had spent his life controlling his emotions, reining himself in, for fear of what he might unleash should he ever let himself go. Drink and drugs, even tobacco, were taboo for him, a self-imposed restriction certainly, but one to which he adhered rigidly.

The only addiction he had given into was Audrey. Like it or not, she was in his blood. And now she was sitting beside him, close yet unattainable. If this was how junkies felt about their drugs, he pitied them.

'So, how'd you meet your husband?' Davie asked, trying to take his mind off what he was watching. And her proximity.

Audrey shifted uncomfortably in her seat. 'You really want to know?'

Davie nodded, but she still hesitated. 'Don't worry, Aud,' he said. 'It's been a long time. Whatever there was between us... well, it's in the past.' He thought he saw a look of pain in her green eyes but she hid it well. Almost as well as he hid his.

'I was still at the *Times* when I met him,' she said. 'This was a couple of years after I... well, you know...'

He nodded, understanding. She meant a couple of years after he'd had his encounter with Harris and she'd decided she'd had enough.

'Anyway, I'd seen him at jobs, he'd seen me. There was a big murder out on the South Side a few years ago, a wee girl killed near her home. He was on the team, I was covering it. He asked me out one day and I said yes and that was it, really. We were married eighteen months later.'

'Kids?'

'Not yet.'

'You happy?'

She paused. Davie wondered why. 'Yes,' she said, but there was hesitancy to the single word.

'Good,' he said, deciding it wasn't his place to pry. They lapsed into silence again and he was trying to think of another subject to bring up when she leaned forward and said, 'There he is.'

Davie followed her gaze and was shocked. He recalled that the bloke hadn't been especially tall, but he had been thick-set and powerful. He'd felt his strength during their fight, even though Davie had gained the upper hand quickly.

The Bar-L Special sliced through the air in front of his face. He slammed the mop handle hard on Harris' wrist. He wanted to break it, to smash the bone into kindling. He didn't, but when he had Harris on the ground he put a foot to his chest and jerked and twisted at his arm until he felt something give in the shoulder...

Harris wasn't the same man now. The red hair was thinner, not as red, but his body had wasted. *No*, thought Davie, *he'd faded*. It was as if someone had taken an eraser to him and had rubbed away at his bulk, at his vitality, and left this hollow man limping towards the dealer to make his buy. Davie let him complete the transaction and begin to walk away before he opened the car door to follow.

'Davie, don't hurt him,' said Audrey and he poked his head back into the car. Her face was etched with concern – whether for Davie or for what he might do, he couldn't be certain.

He'd hurt him badly back then. Harris had screamed but a scream wouldn't stop him. Nothing would stop him once the dark thing had taken over...

'Not planning to,' he said, and closed the door. He'd only moved a few feet, his eyes on Harris hobbling home, when he heard Audrey's footsteps behind him. She didn't trust him. He couldn't blame her.

Davie caught up with him around the corner. He called out Harris's name and the guy stopped and turned, a look of suspicion in his eyes. At first Harris didn't recognise him but then, slowly, the memories came back and he began to back away. 'I don't want no trouble,' he said, his eyes fluttering like a scared bird.

'Not going to give you any,' said Davie. 'Just want to talk.'

Harris looked from Davie to Audrey, who had just come into his view. He was still walking backwards, his right hand, which held his drugs, cradled against his chest with his left, like a mother protecting a child.

'Don't run,' said Davie. 'I'll catch you.'

Harris looked around him, still searching for a bolt hole.

'Jinky,' said Audrey, her voice soothing. 'He's telling the truth. He just wants to talk.'

He focussed on her then, his eyes calming but losing none of their suspicion. 'What about?'

Davie resisted the impulse to step closer for fear that he would panic him. 'Who got you to come after me in the jail?'

'Promised I wouldn't say, didn't I?'

'It was Lomas, wasn't it?'

A nervy little smile flickered on Harris's lips. 'Might've been. Might no have. I'm no sayin.'

Davie knew it was Lomas. 'Where is he, Harris?'

'How the fuck would I know?' He gave Audrey an apologetic nod. 'Pardon my language, darlin.'

'I'm betting you do know where he is and I'm betting you've been milking him for cash. He's a prison officer who hired a con to go after another con. He'll not want that to get out.'

Harris smiled then and Davie saw the mean bastard of old. 'Shows you what you know, he's no a prison officer anymore...' He stopped abruptly when he realised he'd said too much.

'So you have been in contact,' Davie said and glanced over his shoulder at Audrey. He'd taken a flyer but it had paid off. 'Where is he, Donald?'

A sly glint came into Harris's eye. 'What's it worth?'

Davie sighed, his patience wearing thin. If it were not for Audrey's presence he would've slammed the boy's head against the wall by now.

Thread his fingers through the red hair, bounce his face off it. Just like he'd done back in that prison corridor. Ramming the head against it until the slap of flesh against stone took on a liquid sound and blood burst from Harris's nose and his forehead...

'How much do you want?' Audrey said, stepping forward and touching Davie on the arm, as if she knew what he was thinking.

'Seems pretty important, must be worth... oh... fifty.'

'I'll give you twenty.'

'What? The *Record* on a fuckin wage freeze or something, pardon my language? C'mon, darlin, you can do better than that.'

'Thirty, or I walk away now.'

Harris was strung out, but he caught the finality in her tone. If he continued to haggle she'd walk away and leave him to Davie's tender mercies. Davie fought to conceal a smile. She was something.

'Thirty then, but it's daylight fuckin robbery, pardon my language.'

Audrey dug into her coat pocket and produced a slim wad of folded notes. She slid off three tenners and held them out. Harris reached out with his left hand but Davie got there first, snatching the cash away.

'Information first,' he said.

Harris kept his eyes on the money and sighed. 'Aye, it was Lomas.'

'Where is he?'

'He got retired, given the shove. That Governor, the one we called The Colonel? He poisoned his well for him. He's a security guard now, big booze warehouse up Bishopbriggs way.'

'Where does he live?'

'Sighthill, they high flats next to the cemetery. Can't mind the block or the number.'

Davie glanced at Audrey who nodded. 'I can get it.'

Davie turned back to Harris and held out the money. Harris took a few tentative steps closer then suddenly grabbed the notes from Davie's hand. He counted them, even though he'd watched Audrey peel off the three tenners. Davie shook his head, feeling a mixture of sadness and disgust. 'What happened to you, man?'

Harris thrust the notes into his trousers pocket and looked back at Davie. He pulled himself straight, his chin set in a defiant thrust. For a moment Davie saw the old Donald Harris looking back at him. 'Don't you fuckin judge me, Davie McCall. I'm fucked up right enough but I'm doin it to myself. The only person I'm hurtin now is me. What about you? Can you say the same?'

Then he turned and walked swiftly away without looking back. He knew they had what they wanted and wouldn't follow. Davie was stung by his words but he knew Harris was right. Audrey looked at Davie and raised an eyebrow. 'Pardon his language,' she said.

17

DARKNESS CLOSED in as they left the Gorbals. They headed north across the river to the tower blocks looming over the southern edge of the graveyard that sprawled over the hill to Springburn. Audrey had asked a pal on the *Record* newsdesk to check the voters' roll for George Lomas, living somewhere in the housing scheme. He found one listing and rattled off a block and door number.

'This time, stay here,' said Davie when she'd parked in one of the bays next to the flats. She was about to argue the point but he went on, 'Lomas isn't like Harris. He might get nasty and I'll need to do what I do.' He didn't want to expand any further and she didn't ask him to. She sat back in her seat again as he climbed out.

'Davie,' she said, just as he was about to close the door. 'Be careful.'

He gave her a wave and headed into the flats. The scent of fresh bleach filled his nostrils as he took the lift to the fifth floor. Somebody had certainly kept it clean. He wondered if they had to, lifts often being mistaken for public toilets in this city. It bumped and shuddered as it slowly made its way upwards and Davie began to think he would've been quicker taking the stairs. Finally the doors slid open and Davie stepped out into a long corridor with arrows and house numbers pointing in either direction. He turned right and eventually pushed through a door into a square landing with four flats leading off. He stopped at the one marked 5D, helpfully carrying a tartan nameplate with LOMAS printed in white, and rattled the letterbox. The top half of the door was made of frosted, toughened glass, behind which there was a white curtain. Davie could not see any lights beyond. He waited, feeling tension build in his stomach. He had no idea how he was going to play this. All he knew was that he needed to confirm who was behind the attacks, even though he was certain he already knew. For some reason only clear to his own twisted brain, Danny McCall had not wanted his son to leave Barlinnie.

When there was no answer, Davie gave the letterbox another clatter. Still no movement behind the white curtain. He got down on his knees and held open the letterbox, peering into the dark hallway beyond. No lights, no sound. The flat was empty.

Dammit.

He straightened and considered his next step. Harris had said Lomas was a security guard at a whisky warehouse in Bishopbriggs. Shouldn't be too hard to track down, but Davie wasn't sure if he wanted to approach the man at work. He turned from the door. He knew where he lived. He'd come back again.

And then the heavy door leading to the corridor opened and Davie came face to face with Lomas. He had an anorak over a gray uniform and he looked older and seedier than Davie remembered. He saw recognition flood the man's face immediately and then a sharp sting at his knee as Lomas's boot lashed out. He knew exactly where to kick to cause maximum pain, but the blow had been rushed. If he'd done it properly, with all his strength behind it, he might've shattered Davie kneecap. Even so, it hurt. It hurt a lot. Davie slumped a little, the pain shooting up his thigh as he reached out to grab the sleeve of the anorak, but Lomas jumped away and ran down the corridor.

Davie moved after him, the heavy blow to his knee throbbing. He was limping and Lomas was travelling faster than Davie would've given him credit. The man ignored the lift and headed for the stairwell, the door banging open then swinging shut before Davie could reach it. He shouldered it open and heard Lomas pounding downwards. Davie continued his pursuit, the pain in his leg easing as he moved but still slowing him down.

He reached the exit on the ground floor and stepped out into the cool night air, his breath frosting in the pale street light. He saw Lomas running towards Springburn Road and broke into a lope after the man's receding back.

He didn't see the figure keeping to the shadows, watching him.

* * *

Audrey saw a slightly overweight man burst out of the flats at high speed and sprint across the grass towards the main road. Then Davie followed him, obviously favouring his left leg. *What the hell happened?* Davie said he only wanted to talk but there he was, chasing the guy. And limping.

Then she saw the third man, wearing a dark, thigh length woollen jacket, its thick collar turned up against the chill. She realised that she'd been aware of someone walking past the car, glancing at her, but she had been so focussed on the block of flats she had not noted where he went. The man broke into a jog, following Davie and the first guy, who she assumed was Lomas. Davie was too far away to hear if she called out to him.

She climbed out and went after them.

Lomas swerved onto the pavement of the main road and then headed straight for the graveyard gates, which were still open. Davie assumed he'd know the cemetery well enough to believe that he could give him the slip. There would be no street lights, but there would be places to hide – large bushes, maybe even Victorian lairs. With dark now having fully fallen, he could even conceal himself behind a tombstone and Davie wouldn't see him.

Davie ignored the nagging pain in his leg and picked up his speed. He couldn't let Lomas out of his sight, couldn't let him find a bolthole somewhere. He cursed himself for not being prepared for the kick. He should've seen that coming. It would not happen again.

They were running up a small rise now, the cemetery stretching ahead of them and vanishing into the winter night. The dark shapes of tombstones surrounded them as they ran, tangible reminders of the frailty of man's existence. There was no moon so Davie had to strain to keep Lomas's dim outline in sight. His breathing was relatively even, his muscles not complaining, the dull ache in his leg aside. He had kept himself as fit as he could in the jail, doing exercises in his peter, taking every opportunity to do manual labour. Now he was out he'd get back to Barney Williams' gym over in Bridgeton, where he'd continue to work out. He knew he couldn't sustain this pace indefinitely, however.

Lomas was a different matter. His initial burst of speed must have drained what reserves he had and he was flagging. Davie also slowed, prepared to stop when Lomas did in order appear unthreatening. Davie hoped the man would talk without the need to get physical.

The man halted in front of a stand of trees. He leaned forward, hands on knees, struggling to catch his breath. Davie moved to within five feet, far enough to give the guy his space but not so far that he couldn't launch himself if need be.

'Why'd you run?' Davie asked.

'Why the fuck… you think?' Panted Lomas, manoeuvring round to face him. His face was red and sweaty, Davie saw. He didn't think Lomas had much run left in him, let alone fight.

'I just want a word.'

'Aye,' said Lomas, taking a deep breath and wiping moisture from his upper lip, 'I know your kind of word, Davie McCall.'

'I'm not going to hurt you.'

'Sure – and my heid buttons up the back.'

'I just want to know why.'

Lomas squinted. 'Why what?'

'You know what.'

Lomas nodded, his breathing a bit more regular now but his hands still shaking. 'You've spoken to that shitehawk Harris.'

Davie nodded and waited. Lomas raised a trembling hand to his face again, this time to scrape his knuckles against the sweat on his brow. He stared at the damp smear on his hand as if it was a sign. 'Ach, fuck it – I was paid to set you up.'

'Who by?'

Lomas smiled. It was the same smile he'd seen on Harris earlier, the smile of greedy men thinking they could make a buck. 'What's in it for me?'

Audrey had given Harris money. Davie had no intention of giving Lomas anything. 'Tell me and you stand a good chance of walking out of this cemetery.'

Lomas's smile froze and transformed into a scowl. 'You've no changed, McCall. You're still a fuckin ned.'

'You're the pot, I'm the kettle, Lomas. Who paid you?'

Lomas shook his head. 'You'll get no name from me. There's people out there scarier than you.'

Davie said softly, 'They're not here, Lomas. I am.'

Lomas was fully aware of the threat but shook his head again. 'You'll hurt me, sure. You'll maybe even hurt me bad but see these folk? They'll have me killed. You're no killer, Davie McCall...'

There's a first time for everything, Davie was about to say, but then he saw the figure loom from the trees. A hand wrapped over Lomas's mouth and he was dragged back into the shadows. It was very swift, very fluid and Davie was shocked for a moment but then he ran forward, his eyes searching the darkness for the two men. He became aware of the two shapes ahead of him being enveloped by the gloom, then heard a muffled squeal. He followed the sound, moving slowly, every nerve on alert for an attack.

'Lomas,' he whispered.

A soft groan floated through the darkness followed by the crump of something hitting the ground. There was a rustle as somebody squeezed through bushes, then silence. Davie followed the sounds, ears straining for a footfall, eyes alert for an attack.

He found Lomas on the grass a few feet away, his eyes open and staring at the sky. As Davie knelt beside him he knew the man would never see anything again.

He didn't touch the body for fear of leaving something of himself on it that could lead the police to him. He scanned the area around him, still expecting some kind of attack, but saw nothing, just thick green bushes and the trees behind. Hairs prickling on the back of his neck made him think someone was watching.

Watching, waiting.

'I know you're there,' he said, softly.

A breeze made the bushes tremble, but no-one answered.

'So you've turned chib man now, eh?' He didn't need to turn the body over to find the wound. He could tell by the way that Lomas had been dragged back that a knife was being buried into his back. And even though he hadn't seen the assailant clearly, he knew who it was.

'You always told me weapons were for losers,' Davie went on, trying to goad some kind of response. He stood up, slowly spinning 360 degrees, expecting his father to rush out of the bushes at any moment. But the only thing that disturbed the leaves was the waft of a gentle breeze. Then he heard a flutter of wings, as if something had been disturbed, so he turned in their direction, prepared for an attack. But there was only darkness.

'I know you're still there,' Davie said. 'Why don't you come out? We'll finish it right here.'

Davie waited but saw nothing, heard nothing. He backed out of the circle of bushes, through the trees, body tensed, nerves alert, towards the path. He stood for a few seconds, peering into the deep shadow of the foliage, still expecting to see a face not unlike his own staring back at him. But nothing appeared.

He was beginning to relax when he heard a movement behind him and he whirled, right fist clenched, ready to lash out. Audrey cried out in shock, stumbling backwards and almost losing her footing. Davie grabbed her just in time, pulling her closer to him. Despite what had just happened, she felt good.

'Davie,' she said, breathlessly. 'Where is he?'

He held her by one hand, his other arm around her waist. Her fingers felt cool, her body warm and soft. He didn't want to let go but he did. He tried not to look back at the bushes as he said, 'We have to go.'

Her worry gave way to suspicion. 'Davie, what happened?'

He pulled her away. 'Never mind. It's best you don't know.'

She planted her feet firmly on the cement path and peered over his shoulder to the bushes, trying to see what it was he didn't want her to see. 'Tell me, Davie…'

He knew she would not budge until he told her. 'Lomas is dead.'

Her suspicion gave way to shock. She opened her mouth to speak but no words came. He knew thoughts would be flooding her brain, one uppermost. 'I didn't do it,' he said.

She gazed into his face, searching his eyes for a lie. 'Who then?'

This time he did lie. 'I don't know. I didn't get a clear look.' He didn't need a clear look. He knew.

'There was another man, following you. That's why I came after you.'

'What did he look like?'

'Couldn't really see him well enough. About your height, dark hair, maybe going grey. Dark jacket, thick wool, collar up. That's all I saw.'

He placed a hand on her back and gently propelled her away from the bushes again. He had to get her away from this place. He looked across the graveyard wall towards the city glowing in the dark, at the silhouette of the tower blocks, broken up by squares of light. He didn't think anyone would have seen anything, not in the dark graveyard, but it wasn't a good idea to hang around. As they walked he said softly, 'You were never here, understand? Anyone should ask, you were never here.'

He glanced at her face as they moved and saw her mouth was fixed in a tight line and her eyes were wide and staring. He berated himself for letting her come with him. But addiction was like that.

As they walked away, he heard someone whistling somewhere back in the darkness. He couldn't make out the tune, but it was slow and sad and floated through the tombstones like a ghost.

18

AUDREY DIDN'T ASK Davie any questions as they drove from Sighthill to Sword Street. He knew her mind would be reeling and suspected that she did not fully believe him when he said he'd had nothing to do with Lomas's death. That saddened him, but there was nothing he could do about it. Seeing her today had proved more painful than he could imagine, but there was no future for them. Even if she hadn't been married, there was too big a gulf between them. She now knew he had told the truth about Donald Harris. But tonight's events would mean she could never completely trust him. He couldn't blame her.

She stopped her car at the mouth of Sword Street and he climbed out without a word. But he couldn't leave without saying something. He leaned back into the open door. 'I didn't do it, Audrey.'

'I know,' she said, not looking at him. But she didn't know. She couldn't be sure. He could tell by the way she stared intently through the windscreen, by the way her hands were wrapped tightly on the steering wheel, by the way the muscles on her jaw clenched and unclenched.

'It's best you stay away from me,' he said, his voice sounding very far way. This was the last thing he wanted to say. 'It's not safe. Not around me. Not just now.'

She turned to face him then and he saw her green eyes swimming. 'That's just it, isn't it, Davie? It's never safe around you. You're like some sort of magnet, attracting violence and death. And you stroll through it all unscathed, untouched. How can you live like this?'

He had no answer for her. He stood at the side of the car silently. Then he carefully closed the door and said, 'Goodbye, Aud.'

A tear broke from her eyes and trickled down her cheek. She looked as if she might say more, but thought better. She threw the car into first gear and drove off.

Davie watched the car's rear lights grow smaller as it moved down Duke Street. He felt something hard and painful blocking his throat. She was right, he realised. He was a magnet for violence, for death.

But he didn't come through it untouched.

* * *

Frank Donovan was waiting in his car at the closemouth as Davie approached. Davie recognised him immediately as he climbed out, a welcoming smile on his face, and his first thought was whether Donovan had seen Audrey. He decided that the junction with

Duke Street was too far way to make her out, although he must've seen her car. Then he wondered if Lomas had been found already and they'd somehow linked him to it. But the smile was friendly enough, even if Davie didn't return it. He didn't feel much like smiling and he hadn't forgotten that Donovan was a cop.

'Good to see you, Davie,' said Donovan. 'But I'm getting a hellish feeling of déjà vu.'

Davie knew what he meant. It had been a night like this, although a lot warmer, that Donovan had spoken to him on this very spot about Joe's death. Later that night Clem Boyle shot the detective. Davie was surprised that Donovan was even back here. Showed guts. Even so, he wasn't in the mood for small talk. 'Why you here?' Davie asked.

'To thank you for what you did that night.'

'Didn't do it for you.'

'I know that, but I thought I'd thank you anyway. You helped bring that bastard Boyle down.'

'All I did was fight him. Your boys did the rest.' Armed police had shot Boyle, just before he was about to shoot Davie, but he had never felt the need to thank them for saving his life. Yet here was Donovan, thanking him. He suspected there was something else behind this visit.

'I've been asked to have a word with you, Davie,' said Donovan, his smile vanishing. 'My bosses want to know what you're going to do now you're out.'

'They going to offer me a job?'

Donovan gave a small laugh. 'Not likely. They think you're going to go on some sort of revenge mission. Over Joe.'

Davie nodded in understanding. So the police didn't think Jazz was working alone either. Interesting.

'Do we have something to worry about, Davie?'

'No.'

Donovan stared at him, just as intently as Audrey had earlier, trying to spot a lie. Davie stared back, seeing doubt in Donovan's eyes. Eventually, though, the cop exhaled deeply and nodded. 'Okay,' he said, but in that one word he told Davie that he remained unconvinced. He wasn't stupid, this cop.

'One other thing,' he said and Davie thought, *there always is.* 'Does the name John Keen mean anything to you?'

Davie shook his head. 'Who is he?'

'A ghost,' said Donovan and he looked as if he meant it. 'Maybe a killer. The girl killed the other day up Springburn way, you hear about it?'

Davie nodded. He'd read about it in the paper.

'If you hear anything, I'd appreciate a call. This was a nasty one.'

'What makes you think I'd hear something?'

Donovan hesitated and Davie knew he was battling the impulse to say something he shouldn't. 'You never know. It's a funny old world.' Donovan turned back to his car, then stopped. 'You watch your back, Davie. Things are different now. The world's changed since you've been away.'

'So I keep hearing,' said Davie.

* * *

Davie climbed the stairs to the flat, suddenly weary. It had been a busy couple of days and he wasn't used to this much activity. He'd have to pace himself, ease himself back into old ways. After all, as everyone kept telling him, the world had changed since he'd been away.

The white envelope was stuck to his door with sticky tape. He unpeeled it, careful not to remove any paint, and ripped the envelope open. Inside was a series of five Polaroids, each showing the same room, the same scene from different angles. He felt something inside him lurch when he thought he recognised the room but then realised it was different – wallpaper wasn't the same, furniture wasn't the same, but similar. It was what the pictures depicted that was famil- iar. The overturned chair, the ironing board, the glow of the fire, the standard lamp on its side.

And the woman's body near the wall, behind the old kitchen table. Blood on the wall beside her. There was no shot of her face but Davie knew it would be nothing more than a bloody pulp.

It was a recreation of his mother's murder. Staged, photo-graphed.

But the woman's body wasn't staged. That was real, he knew it in his gut.

He turned the envelope over in his hand but there was only one word hand-printed on the front:

SOON

Donovan had said it was a funny old world. It wasn't funny, Davie decided, thinking about his mother, about Joe, Mouthy and all the other deaths, even Lomas. It was tragic and it was brutal.

And something told Davie it was going to get worse.

19

DONALD HARRIS lay on the battered couch in the Crow's Nest thinking about going out for a hit when he heard the knock at the door. He'd come back to the flat that morning to shoot up and had fallen asleep. When he woke he tidied up a bit, because even he could see the place was turning into a right tip, then he felt the familiar need build again. His body had used up every last drop of the score deal he'd jagged earlier and now it was beginning to crave more. His flesh began to creep on his bones and that familiar itch in his gut, the one he could never properly scratch, started up again. He still had some of the cash he'd got from that reporter burd, so at least he didn't need to go out thieving to raise the necessary.

He decided against answering the door. He wasn't expecting anyone. The people who used the top floor flat all had keys, for the time being at least, until the council came along and boarded the place up. The last tenant had been a mate who'd moved out, headed over Edinburgh way, but she'd left Harris a key. He'd then cut a few more and dished them out to other pals, all for a nominal sum of course, because a bloke's got to live. If the council ever got around to flattening the place he'd have to find somewhere new, but till then it did him just fine.

The bang at the door became more insistent and he tried to ignore it, but the itch under his skin was growing all the time. He'd have to see who it was and get it dealt with, then he could get out. Otherwise he'd be having the screaming hab-dabs soon.

At first he thought it was that bastard Davie McCall standing there but when he looked again he saw that it wasn't. This guy was older, his hair greyer, his face more lined. *But fuck me, it could be his dad,* Harris thought.

'Donald Harris?' The guy said. Glasgow accent, friendly, didn't give any kind of official vibe. Harris saw no harm in nodding.

'Got a present for you,' said the guy, pushing him hard into the hallway and as he staggered back against the wall Harris was dimly aware that the man was wearing rubber surgical gloves. He started to protest, but when the guy turned those cold blue eyes on him he thought better of it. The man locked the door behind him and pointed through to the living room. Harris obeyed, fully aware now of the damage he'd done himself. Time was he could have put up a fight. Time was he could've taken this bloke on, held his ground, did him damage. But no more. Now he was a shadow, a flimsy reflection, of what he used to be.

He was told to sit down in the armchair, while his guest put his gloved hand in the pocket of his black jacket, producing a plastic bag filled with brown powder. Harris knew what it was, of course. He'd stuck enough of it in his veins. And even though he felt his blood quicken at the sight of it, he knew this was not going to be good for him. The man tossed the plastic bag into his lap.

'Enjoy,' he said.

Harris picked the bag up and examined the contents. He licked his lips, the junkie within him crying out for it to be coursing through him. But the sensible part of him, the part he thought had died long ago, screamed at him not to touch it. He wasn't so strung out that he didn't recognise that this was no gift, this was his death warrant. He held the bag out to the man with shaking fingers. 'I'm awright, thanks man.'

The guy smiled. 'No, you're not, son. Look at you. You're desperate for it. Every part of your body is begging for it. So take it. Go on. Fill your boots.'

Harris shook his head, still holding the bag towards the man. 'No, trying to give it up…'

The smile dropped and the man lowered his head, his eyes burning icy holes into Harris's own. 'Take it.' That's all he said, and Harris knew then that he had little choice. Sure, he could make a break for the door, maybe even get out the living room, but he knew the guy would get him, drag him back, beat the shit out of him. Either way he was fucked.

He drew his arm back and looked again at the brown powder. *Maybe it was better this way,* he thought. *Go out on a high, so to speak.* God knows he didn't have much to live for, not since he'd first stuck a needle into his arm and felt the glorious rush. His wee mammy would have nothing to do with him, his brother neither. Walked past him in the streets, just like he'd told that girl reporter. Like he was nothing, which he supposed he was. His mates weren't really mates at all, just junkies. He'd never be able to rely on them the way he used to rely on his gang mates. A junkie's loyalty was always to the next fix. Friendship meant nothing, family meant nothing, honesty meant nothing, although for years before he'd started using, Harris had little more than a passing acquaintance with honesty.

Once again he looked up at the guy, who was watching him with no expression. 'Why you doing this?' Harris asked.

The man thought about the question. 'Why not?'

Harris frowned. 'Who the fuck are you?'

'Does it matter?'

Harris shrugged, because it really didn't matter anymore, and dropped his eyes to the bag. He slowly struggled to his feet and shuffled to the small table beneath the window where he'd left his works. As he heated the heroin in a blackened spoon, he glanced back and saw the blue-eyed man leaning against the wall by the fireplace, arms folded over his chest, watching. He looked bored.

20

FRANK DONOVAN SAT at his desk in Baird Street and stared at the crime scene photographs from the Springburn bedsit. Then he looked at the shots taken in the Oatlands flat thirteen years before. Then he looked at them both together. He'd suspected that the two scenes were almost identical but he couldn't be certain until he received the file. He'd been right. The way Virginia had been murdered mirrored the death of Mary McCall exactly.

He'd asked Davie McCall if the name John Keen had meant anything to him, just on the off chance. He didn't think the guy would know the name. Donovan didn't even think this John Keen existed. There would be men of that name in the city – and they were in the process of tracking them down in order to eliminate them – but Donovan was confident none of them was his guy. He'd told Davie McCall that he was a ghost, and he'd meant it.

Donovan considered what all this meant. Two murders, years apart, with the second being dressed to look like the first. It couldn't be a copycat because the details of the first murder had never been made public. Unless the second killer was a cop, a notion which made Donovan sweat a little, but his gut told him differently. Of course, in the interests of a thorough investigation, any officer on the scene in Oatlands all those years ago would have to be checked out. That'll go down a storm, he thought. Davie McCall would have been able to recreate the scene of his mother's death easily, he would imagine, Donovan being certain it was preserved in his memory like lines in stone. But the younger McCall was no killer, Donovan was certain of that. He could handle himself and maybe someday he'd do someone in during a fight, but not a woman, never a woman. Joe the Tailor had taught him too well. Anyway, he'd been tucked up in Barlinnie the night Virginia died.

So if it wasn't a stranger and it wasn't a cop and it wasn't the son, that left only one possibility.

Danny McCall. The man, the myth. The ghost.

Donovan had only been on the job a year or two when the older McCall murdered his wife, almost killed his son and then vanished into the night. But he knew all about it. The events of 1980 had led him into probing Davie McCall's background and that, inexorably, led to Danny. He'd asked around, done a bit of digging and managed to get a feel for the man.

He'd been an enforcer for Joe the Tailor and was good at his job. What set him apart from others in his trade was his intelligence, the majority of men in his line of business being dumb brutes who broke that bone or sliced that flesh when their bosses told them. When he was sent out to put a scare into someone, he put some thought into it, coming up with novel ways to intimidate. The famous crucified man, hands nailed to the floorboards, had been his work, although no official complaint was made and no-one arrested. Danny McCall had also led a charmed life with regards to the law, for Donovan could only find one conviction, for mobbing and rioting, when he was in his late teens and running with a street gang out of Dennistoun.

He was thirty-six when he disappeared, that would make him forty-nine now. Where the hell had he been all that time? What had he been doing? And what was he doing back in Glasgow? He was calling himself John Keen, but Donovan would bet his pension it wasn't the only alias he'd used over the years as he'd drifted from place to place, dodging the Law and Joe Klein. Couldn't have been easy but a guy with Danny McCall's smarts would have known what he was doing. He'd've made contacts over the years, guys with no liking for the Law, or Joe, who would give him aid. Donovan sat back in his chair and considered what Danny McCall would've done with himself all these years. A bit of work here and there, he supposed, for those same men who sheltered him would have found a use for his particular talents. Donovan gazed again at the photographs spread across his desk. Two murders, over a decade apart. Were there more, he wondered? A request through HOLMES, the computer system beginning to link forces up and down the country, would help there.

His phone rang. 'DS Donovan.'

'Frank, it's Detective Superintendent Bannatyne.'

Donovan closed his eyes. He'd forgotten to let Bannatyne know he'd spoken to McCall. 'Sorry, sir, I've been wrapped up in this murder, forgot to call…'

'Never mind that now, Frank. Events have moved on.'

Donovan was puzzled. Did Bannatyne know about his theory about Virginia's murder? Donovan hadn't mentioned it to anyone yet, not even his DI, but he wouldn't put it past Gentleman Jack to have some way of knowing. 'Sir?'

'You hear about the dead man up Sighthill?'

'Yes, sir,' said Donovan. Another detective from Baird Street was leading that one.

'Dead man is Gerald Lomas.'

'Yes, sir, security guard at a whisky warehouse, I hear.'

'Yes, latterly,' said Bannatyne. 'But before that he was a prison officer.'

Donovan raised his eyebrows. He hadn't heard that.

'Frank, Gerald Lomas was the officer who came upon David McCall battering all kinds of shite out of a boy called Donald Harris.'

Donovan felt something cold steal over him. But there was worse to come.

'And earlier this morning, Donald Harris was found dead in a flat in the Gorbals.'

Donovan's eyes were on the pictures before him but he didn't see them. *Davie*, he thought, *what the hell have you done?*

* * *

'Davie, what the hell have you done?'

Davie had opened the door to his flat to find the Audrey on his doorstep, her face set hard. Wordlessly she pushed past him and then, once he had closed the door, whirled on him in the hall and fired the question at him like a bullet.

'What you talking about?' He asked.

'Jinky… Donald Harris,' she said.

Davie was puzzled. 'What about him?'

'He's dead, that's what about him. So that's the prison officer and now him.'

'How'd he die?'

'Overdose, it seems. But he was an experienced user, Christ he was almost making a career out of it. He was too wise to OD. He knew the score.'

'Aud, it was nothing to do with me…'

'You expect me to believe that?'

Davie took a deep breath and then expelled it slowly. He didn't expect her to believe him but he would have to convince her somehow that he was not responsible. He couldn't bear the thought of her believing him to be a double killer. Not her.

And there was only one way he could think of that might make her understand.

'Come with me…'

She stood her ground in the hallway, eyes burning with anger, arms folded across her body.

'Please,' he said, motioning towards the living room. Audrey relented but her face remained frozen.

Davie picked up the envelope containing the Polaroids from the coffee table and handed it to her. She looked at it and said, 'Soon? What's soon?'

He didn't reply. She sighed and slid the pictures out. She flicked through them, her face turning pale. There was a slight tremor in her hand as she held them out to him. 'What is this?'

'There was a woman murdered the other night, working girl.'

'Virginia McTaggart, I know. How did you get these pictures? Are they police shots?'

Davie shook his head. 'They were taken before the police got there. She wouldn't have been long dead.'

Audrey looked down at the photographs, her brow working as she struggled to understand. 'You going to tell me where you got these, or have I to assume you killed her as well as Lomas and Harris?'

That comment stung Davie like an open razor. 'I didn't kill anyone. I told you, the other man you saw killed Lomas, Harris too, probably. And he killed this girl. These pictures were left here for me.'

'Why?'

'Because what you're seeing there is a replica of the night my mother died. There are slight differences but the table, the overturned chair, the standard lamp – it's all the same. She'd been ironing the night it happened. She hit my dad with an iron when he went after me. He then beat her to death with a poker. He's recreated it, for some reason.'

She stared at him, taking this in. When she spoke her voice was softer. 'Your father did all this?'

'Yes.'

'Danny McCall...' she saw his look of surprise when she said his name. 'I'm a reporter. I find out things, it's what I do. I've known about him since a few days after we met.'

He nodded, understanding. He'd never told her about his father but it stood to reason that she would do some research.

'You have to take these to the police,' she said. 'Frank Donovan's on that case, take them to him.'

Davie knew she was right, but the ingrained mistrust of the law would not leave him. Audrey caught his hesitation and said, 'Davie, you have to do it. And tell them about Lomas, too.'

He shook his head. 'Can't do that, Aud. Can't go to the cops.'

'Davie, if you're right your father is practically a serial killer. He's killed your mother, he's killed these people, who knows how many others he might've done over the years.'

That was just it, Davie thought. It was a truth he was finding difficult to face. His father was a stone cold killer. It was the drink that had led to him murdering his mother, no matter what fanciful theories old Sammy might have had about some dark force inside him. But these killings had been planned, premeditated. Lomas had it coming, maybe even Harris, for he was killing himself by inches anyway. But the girl? Davie couldn't accept that. More than ever Davie feared that whatever lived inside his father also nested within him. There was only one way to purge it, he believed.

He had to get Danny McCall himself.

Audrey knew him well, though. 'Davie, you can't do this alone.'

'Got to, Aud.'

She grew angry again. 'What is this, some kind of macho thing? A man's gotta do what a man's gotta do?'

'Can't go to the police, Aud. This is between me and him…'

'Not anymore, is it? Tell that to this girl,' she held up the photos. 'Tell that to Lomas and Harris and whoever else he kills from now on. Their deaths will be on you, Davie. You could do something now to stop him but you're so fucking pig-headed, so fucking insular, that you can't see sense. Step outside yourself, David McCall, look around. You can't do this your way, Joe's way. You need to talk to the police.'

Finally, Davie snapped. 'He killed my mother!'

She took an involuntary step back at the violence in his tone. She had never seen Davie lose his temper, few people had, and his face had changed with such suddenness that it unnerved her. His eyes seemed to darken and his features harden into a mask. For a moment she thought he had become someone else. Some*thing* else. Then it was gone as quickly as it appeared and he looked ashamed. He turned his face away from her and when he spoke again it was barely a whisper.

'My mother, Aud. And he tried to kill me. Now he's playing some sort of game with me, God knows why. If I go to the police, I lose. He'll vanish again and I'll wonder when he's going to turn up again, always looking over my shoulder. He'll still be there. Still waiting and watching.' He looked up then. 'Him and me, Aud, that's how it has to be. That's the way he wants it. I don't know what his end game is, but I do know that it's going to come down to just him and me.'

And then, as if on cue, the phone rang. Davie's eyes darted

towards it and he felt something like dread. Audrey watched him, warily. 'Are you going to answer it?'

'It's him,' he said.

'How do you know?'

He looked back at her and for the first time ever she thought she saw fear. 'I know.'

They both remained immobile, watching the phone as it rang. Then Davie gave a little sigh and plucked the handpiece from its cradle. He said nothing as he held it to his ear and at first all he heard was the muted sound of traffic on the line. Then he heard his father's voice. 'How's it going, son?'

Davie watched Audrey as she moved to the couch and sat down, perching on the edge as if she was ready to bolt. 'You're one sick bastard, you know that?'

He heard a small laugh. 'Good to hear your voice, too...'

Davie turned away so Audrey could not see him close his eyes tightly. When he spoke again his voice was hoarse. 'Why you doing this?'

'Same reason a dog licks its balls, son. Because I can...'

'You said "Soon" on the note. What does it mean?'

'Just what it says. Soon.'

'You killed that girl just to send me that message?'

'What? You didn't like it? Thought it was a work of art myself.'

'You didn't need to kill her.'

'Now, where's the fun in that? Eh?'

Then Davie asked the question that had puzzled him for years. 'Why didn't you kill me when you had the chance?'

There was a pause on the line and again Davie heard traffic sounds. He was in a call box somewhere, he was sure of it. 'Call me sentimental,' Danny said eventually.

'Yet you murdered your wife.'

That small laugh again. 'What can I say, son? My moods are... changeable.'

Davie felt his rage reach boiling point and his grip tightened on the handset. 'You really are sick.'

'Now, now, sticks and stones. You don't want your girlfriend there thinking you've no respect for your old man...'

Everything froze and Davie shot a glance in Audrey's direction. When she saw his expression, she tensed. Then Danny was gone with a click. Davie dropped the phone and threw himself across the room to the window. He pulled back the curtain, his head darting left and right. There was no call box out there, but he couldn't help himself. He thought about rushing out, finding the nearest box, but his more rational self told him his father would be long gone. But he now knew for certain that Danny McCall was always there, watching, waiting.

Audrey was at his side, her hand gently touching his back. He could feel the slight pressure of her hand and somehow it soothed him. 'You're not like him, you could never be like him. Forget all this lone gunfighter shit. Go to Frank Donovan. Tell him.'

For the first time he could remember, Davie McCall was confused and unsure of what to do next. He wished Joe were there, he would know. Joe would sort it all out. But Joe wasn't there. Maybe Audrey was right, maybe going to the cops was the best thing to do. So what if his father took to the wind again, at least he'd be out of his hair, if only for a while.

In the end, the police came to him.

21

JIMMY KNIGHT sauntered through the Necropolis, a cigarillo clenched between his teeth, casually casting an eye over the gravestones and lairs as he passed them. He wasn't taking in any of the names or dates etched into the various stones. He wasn't interested in the dead of the past. To his right rose the vaulted roof of Glasgow Cathedral, beside it the dark bulk of the Royal Infirmary, both set against a slate grey sky. The low rumble of the traffic on the M8 behind him and the High Street was muted in the damp air. The Victorian city of the dead was peaceful and he met no-one along the way. Very few locals ventured here, at least during the daylight hours. Glasgow people were largely unaware of the history on their doorstep. At night teenagers might climb the fence and trek up the hill to find a place to drink and laugh and explore each other's bodies, while junkies probably sought the seclusion for their pursuits, but only a few city dwellers would visit the place, leaving it to the tourists and the historians. But on a dull November weekday, there were few tourists and Knight wasn't interested in history.

He found his quarry standing alone, looking across the tombstones towards the East End of the city. 'Rab,' said Knight. 'Glad you could make it.'

He spoke as if McClymont had a choice, which he hadn't. Knight had insisted on a meeting and when Knight insisted, Rab had to comply. Knight had built up quite a file on McClymont containing evidence which, if revealed, would put him away for some time. Rab did not want to go away for any length of time. Knight also had Rab McClymont registered as an official informant, codename 'Bluto', which amused the big cop no end. He'd chosen the cartoon name because as Rab grew older he looked more like Popeye's nemesis – dark hair, dark shadow on the chin that no amount of shaving could shift, muscles beginning to run to flab. If it ever got out that McClymont was telling tales, it would be the end of him. The legend RAB McCLYMONT IS A GRASS would be found on a wall and Rab himself face down in a ditch somewhere.

Knight knew Rab also had a file – photographs and tape recordings of Knight making deals that would make his superiors drop their Filofaxes. They had reached a stalemate, the threat of mutually assured destruction binding them even closer together. Neither of them wanted to use their weapon because their partnership had proved to be far too rewarding but it was there, just in case.

'What's up?' Rab asked.

Knight withdrew his cigarillo and blew a cloud of smoke from the corner of his mouth, away from Rab. He knew the big guy hated the stench of his preferred brand and he was nothing if not considerate of other people's feelings. 'Your boy Davie is getting himself in hot water.'

Rab looked surprised. 'What? Already? What's he done?'

'Bloke by the name of Lomas was stabbed over there in Sighthill. He was a screw in Barlinnie while McCall was there. And an ex-con called Harris died of an overdose.'

Rab thought about this, then said carefully, 'So what's that got to do with Davie?'

'Lomas was the screw who caught your boy beating up Harris. His evidence put him away for another eight years. Theory is that Davie boy is settling scores.'

Rab shook his head. 'No, no way. If they'd been damaged a bit, aye maybe, but no killing. No Davie.'

'People change. He's been away a long time. So he's no mentioned any of this to you?'

'Not a word.'

'Think he would? I mean, if he was planning some payback, would he tell you?'

Rab considered his reply, making Knight think he was not so sure about his old pal. 'Maybe, maybe not. Hard to say now. Ten years ago I'd've said, aye, definitely, but now? You said it, people change.'

'So he could've done it?'

'Anybody could've done it. You could've done it, I could've done it, fuckin aliens could've done it. What I'm saying is, I don't believe Davie would've done it.'

Knight puffed thoughtfully on the remnants of his smoke. 'Yeah, me neither. Told my boss that, too. He's asking me to nose around a bit, on the hush-hush. He's had a bee in his bonnet about Davie McCall ever since Joe the Tailor got himself done. Luca, too.'

'Why Luca specifically?'

Knight gave him a sideways glance. 'Have I never told you? Bannatyne thinks Luca pulled the trigger on the old man.'

Rab fell silent, taking this in. 'What makes him think that?'

Knight shrugged. 'Gut feeling. He doesn't think Jazz Sinclair had it in him to do it, or that Joe would let a kid like that get the drop on him. And then there's the GSR, told you about that, didn't I?'

Rab nodded. Gunshot residue, tiny chemical particles that blow back from the gun when fired, adhering to the gunhand. There had been none on Jazz Sinclair, Knight had told him. Rab had never heard of GSR before then. Knight was certain he'd kept it in mind since, though.

Knight said, 'It had to be someone he knew, someone he trusted. Luca fits the bill, so the boss did some digging around.'

'What did he find out?'

'Fuck all. That's what bothers him. What do you know about him?'

Rab shrugged. 'Born in Sicily, went to New York, came here. That's it.' Knight could tell Rab knew more, a lot more, but wasn't going to tell. Rab only passed on information that would do him favours and he wasn't ready to say anything about Luca. Not yet anyway. Never mind, Knight had time. This was one of the reasons behind this meeting, just to plant seeds into McClymont's mind. And from little seeds, big trees grew.

Rab continued, 'Luca's taking less and less to do with business. Getting old.'

'That right?' said Knight, thoughtfully. 'Getting to be a bit of a passenger, is he?'

'Wouldn't say that,' said Rab, but Knight could hear caution in his voice.

Knight dropped what was left of his cigarillo onto the ground and twisted his foot on it. 'Doesn't matter, big guy. Just keep an eye on your boy McCall, eh? Let me know if you hear anything. And watch him around Luca. He might get the same notion as my boss and then there'd be trouble. You know what Davie thought of Joe.'

He patted McClymont on the back and headed back the way he'd come, for he was due to link up with Frank Donovan. He'd taken a few steps when he remembered something else and turned. 'And Rab…'

McClymont looked up and Knight could see by his expression that he was thinking about Davie. And Luca. Specially Luca.

'When you see Liam Mulvey, give him my best.'

The change of expression from thoughtfulness to suspicion was like a cloud passing over the sun. 'How the fuck d'you know I'm going to see him?'

Knight gave him his biggest shit-eating grin. 'He owes you money, I told you I'd heard a whisper he'd come into some. Stands to reason you'd be paying him a visit. Saturday, if I'm not mistaken.'

Rab's eyes narrowed and Knight knew he was trying to suss what game he was playing now. Knight kept his grin wide and open, as ever enjoying keeping Rab guessing. He saw him sigh and there was a weariness in his voice, 'How the fuck you know these things, Knight?'

'Told you before, son – got eyes and ears everywhere. There's no much happens I don't hear some sort of whisper about...'

Knight knew he was going to be late for his meet with Donovan, but there was business to discuss.

* * *

Donovan didn't mind Knight being late because it gave him the opportunity to study the computer printouts in front of him. They gave him chills. He'd put the request through HOLMES, the Home Office Large Major Enquiry System. Seven major enquiries came back from Scotland, England, Wales and Northern Ireland – God bless modern technology. He'd discounted four of them because they didn't quite fit the pattern he was looking for or someone was already doing time. That didn't mean they weren't part of the puzzle, but he had to whittle it down somehow.

So that left three. One from London, one from Liverpool, one from Manchester, all committed since 1985. There might be older cases, but, Jesus – this was enough to get the goosebumps growing.

Three murders.

Three women of varying ages, two of them prostitutes, one a middle-aged mum picked up in a disco. All found in pokey flats, all battered to death with a poker, which was left at the scene. All the rooms similar to the two Glasgow murders, an overturned chair, a standard lamp on its side. All with a fire left burning.

All unsolved.

He knew he should've kicked this upstairs before now, but he still wasn't sure he was on solid ground. After all, it was just his coppers' nose twitching. Even so, he couldn't bring himself to fully believe it. Was Danny McCall really some undetected serial killer, reproducing the murder of his wife up and down the country? And if so, what the hell was going on his twisted mind? And had Detective Sergeant Francis Donovan of Strathclyde's finest simply stumbled on it? Betting man that he was, Donovan would not lay odds on that. And yet his nose was still twitching. He laid his hands on the printouts, as if he could divine some basic truth through his fingertips. More information was needed, but he knew as a lowly DS he was unlikely to get it. This would need someone on a higher pay scale.

He saw Knight enter the CID room, the ubiquitous cigarillo clenched between his teeth, so he pulled together the sheets of paper and thrust them into a drawer. There was no way he was sharing this with him. Knight would either scoff or work out a way to take all the glory for himself.

Knight came to a halt at his desk, plucked the cigarillo from his mouth, smiled, and said, 'So, Frankie boy, you ready to go see your wee pal? You want some time alone with him, to make kissy faces, just you let me know.'

Donovan sighed. He hated working with Jimmy Knight.

* * *

Audrey was still trying to convince Davie to take the photographs and his fears to the police when there was a rapping at the door. Davie knew it was the Law even before he opened it – they had a way of banging like they had the right to do what they wanted.

'Davie,' said Frank Donovan, his face as stiff as Audrey's had been earlier, his voice low, the friendly manner of the previous night now gone. Only the cop was left. 'Need a word.'

Davie flicked his gaze from Donovan to the man at his side. He knew him immediately, even though the last time he'd seen him was only as a face in a courtroom. Jimmy Knight, the one they called the Black Knight, the one who forced witnesses to give perjured evidence. Davie had been involved in the robbery, but the notion that he was convicted on false testimony still rankled. Davie felt his muscles tense. Donovan caught the look and went on, 'You remember Detective Sergeant Knight?'

'He want a word, too?' Davie asked.

Knight said, his voice harsh, 'Let us in, McCall, don't be pissing me about on the doorstep.'

Donovan half-turned his head towards his colleague, irritation flaring then subsiding, trying hard to present a unified front. 'Let us come in, Davie,' he said, his tone conciliatory. 'It's best we discuss it inside, eh?'

Davie sighed and stepped aside. Donovan nodded as he passed, Knight barged on down the hallway. He'd been in the flat before, when he arrested Davie and Rab. He glanced to his right into the kitchen then turned left to the sitting room. Davie followed the cops, knowing this had to be about Lomas and Harris. It was only a matter of time.

Donovan stopped short when he caught sight of Audrey sitting in an armchair, a cold mug of coffee in her hand. 'Audrey?'

Audrey kept her face impassive, but Davie caught the slight flare in her eyes as she saw the two cops. 'Frank,' she said, calmly.

Donovan looked from her to Davie, his confusion evident. Davie guessed she was the last person he'd expected to see. Knight didn't have any time for this, but he knew better than to be as abrupt in front of a witness as he had been at the door. Davie also had the impression he'd recognised Audrey. 'We'd like to speak to Mister McCall alone, miss, if you don't mind.'

'Anything you can say to Davie you can say in front of me, that right, Davie?'

Davie nodded. He was enjoying the way she handled these guys. Being a straight arrow – and a crime reporter on the *Daily Record* – she'd get away with it. To an extent, at least.

Knight's voice became officious. 'This is police business and I'm going to have to ask you to leave.'

'You arresting him?'

'No.'

'You going to caution him?'

A red flush began to stain Knight's cheeks. Davie knew cops didn't like to answer questions. It was a technique Joe had taught them to circumvent police interviews. If you start asking questions, they get flustered.

'Not at this stage,' said Knight.

'You going to haul him downtown?' Audrey's eyes were shining now and Davie could tell she was enjoying herself as well.

Knight glanced at Donovan. Davie followed the look and saw the big cop would get no help there. He'd burned his bridges in the doorway. 'No,' said Knight, the word straining against his temper.

'Then I'm free to remain where I am as long as Mister McCall is happy about it. You happy about it, Davie?'

'Couldn't be happier.'

Knight sighed deeply, his face growing darker by the second. They had first met in a small interview room at Baird Street Police station and Davie had recognised him then as the kind of copper who could turn nasty if his buttons were pushed. He doubted he had mellowed with age. Donovan, though, wasn't going to let it get that far.

'Audrey, do us a favour, come into the kitchen with me, eh?' he said softly. 'Let DS Knight ask his questions. Davie's a big boy, he can handle himself.'

Audrey looked at Davie, who nodded. She obviously knew and trusted Donovan, but Knight she either didn't know or perhaps only by reputation. However, both she and Davie were aware there was no way he could verbal Davie if he was on his own. He needed corroboration. She got up and followed Donovan out of the room. Knight glared at her back, then said when the door closed behind her, 'You two back together?'

Davie was not surprised that Knight knew his history. 'No.'

'Bit of all right. Bet you'd like to, eh?'

'She's married.'

Knight sneered. 'What? You got scruples?'

'Yeah, but I've got ointment for it.'

Knight exhaled through his nose, which might have passed for a laugh. 'You a funny guy?'

'Not especially. What did you want to ask me?'

'You know a guy called Lomas?'

Davie felt a stillness come over him. So it *was* about Lomas. Small world, right enough. 'There was a screw named Lomas in the jail.'

'Oh?' Knight's face tried to look innocently surprised. He didn't quite pull it off. 'How was the Bar-L, son? Holiday camp, I hear.'

Davie grimaced. 'Let's stop the games, eh? So what do you want to know?'

'Where were you last night?'

'Here.'

'All night?'

'Yes.'

'Anyone with you?'

'No.'

'On your own?'

'That's usually what it means when there's no-one with me.'

Knight's jaw tightened. Davie wasn't normally one for snappy comebacks but something about Knight brought it out in him. 'So no-one can verify that you *were* here?'

'Don't know how else to say it. I was here, all alone, on my tod, with no-one with me. Clear now?'

The jaw clenched tighter. 'Crystal. You seen this bloke Lomas since you got out of the jail?'

'No. Why would I?'

Knight ignored the question. 'What about a junkie called Donald Harris?'

'Saw him yesterday,' Davie knew better than to lie. He'd spoken with Harris in broad daylight and anyone could have seen them together, whereas he was certain no-one saw him at Lomas's flat, or at least no-one who could identify him.

'Why?'

'Him and I have a history. I wanted to know why he attacked me in jail, maybe you've heard about that.'

'I've heard it was the other way round.'

Davie shrugged, telling the cop he didn't care what he'd heard. Knight paused. 'You part on amicable terms?'

'Yes. Mrs Fraser was with me, you can check with her.'

'Mrs Fraser? Bit formal, isn't it? If I remember right, you were pretty tight once.'

'We're old friends.'

Knight leered. 'Old friends? That what they call it now?'

Davie didn't answer. He wasn't getting into that. He regretted even mentioning Audrey, but there was no point in lying about her either. If someone had seen him, they'd seen her, too.

'You want to know why I'm asking all these questions?'

Davie shrugged. 'You'll tell me when you're ready.'

'Or won't.'

Davie shrugged again, still trying to convey lack of interest. That was when Audrey burst in and said hurriedly, 'Davie, don't say anything. They're trying to connect you to a murder…'

Davie kept his face impassive. Knight was clearly irritated by the interruption, though. 'Mrs Fraser, I'm not finished here.'

'Yes, you are,' she said. Donovan loomed up behind her, shrugging in apology at his colleague. Audrey went on, 'Davie had nothing to do with that man's death.'

Knight's lips tightened. 'How do you know that?'

'Because he was with me last night.'

Knight raised his eyebrows and glanced at Davie, who felt something sink in his chest. *Audrey, why'd you have to say that?*

'Mister McCall told me he was alone last night.'

Audrey's eyes were defiant. 'He was with me.'

'All night?'

Audrey hesitated then, glancing at Davie. He shook his head a fraction, trying to warn her off. 'No, not all night. But Frank tells me this fellow was killed sometime between 7pm and 8pm. I was with Davie until then.'

Knight threw Donovan a glare then and when he spoke there was a weariness in his voice. 'Anyone else here?'

'No, just us.'

'I see,' said Knight, glancing at Davie. 'And what were you doing together, just the two of you?' That leer was back and Davie could tell it really pissed Audrey off.

'Talking, catching up. We're old friends.'

'Mmm, old friends,' Knight seemed to savour the two words, giving Audrey a slight smile. 'And does your husband know about this, I wonder?'

Davie really thought Audrey was going to launch herself at the smirking cop. Donovan must have too, because he cleared his throat then and stepped between her and Knight. 'I think that's as far as we can go here, eh?'

Knight's eyes slid from Davie back to Audrey and back to Davie again. He obviously did not believe a word of what Audrey had said, but there was no way for him to prove otherwise. He nodded. 'Okay, that'll do. For now. But I'm telling you, McCall, this whole thing stinks. You know something and I'm going to find out what it is, believe me, son.'

He brushed past Donovan and vanished into the hallway. Donovan gave Audrey a stern look then shook his head before following him.

Davie waited until he heard the front door close then slipped into the hallway to ensure they were gone. As soon as he walked back into the sitting room he said, 'Shouldn't've done that, Aud.'

'Frank told me they know all about you and Lomas and Harris. He says they're convinced you had something to do with their deaths.'

Davie thought, *they're not wrong.* He said, 'Why is Frank telling you all this?'

'Because he's a good guy, Davie. He doesn't agree with them – he knows you better than you think. I think since you got Clem Boyle that night he's studied up on you. He told me to get in here and break this up somehow. Telling him I was with you was the only way I could think of on the spur of the moment.'

Davie shook his head. 'That was the Black Knight, you know him?' She nodded and Davie continued, 'If he finds anything to link me to that graveyard last night, you'll be in deep trouble.'

She shrugged. 'I'll cross that bridge when I come to it.'

She looked so calm, so confident and he knew he was falling for her all over again. It scared the hell out of him. 'He'll tell your husband.'

'What makes you so sure?

'You pissed him off, he'll want to get you back.'

She thought about this. Her face clouded for a second then cleared. 'I'll handle it.'

* * *

'What the fuck was that all about, Frank?' Knight was furious. He rounded on Donovan as they descended the stairs. 'What? Could you no keep a wee slip of a lassie away for longer than five minutes?'

'What was I supposed to do, pin her by the arms?'

'You do anything you bloody have to when I'm interviewing a fuckin suspect.'

'You're not even supposed to be interviewing him, you're there unofficially, remember? Anyway, you've got nothing on him and you know it.'

'He could've burst…'

Donovan began to laugh, the idea of Davie McCall being so over-taken with guilt that he spontaneously confesses being worthy of a stand-up comedian. He'd seen it happen, but not to guys like McCall. They never burst. Knight glared at him.

Donovan said, 'He's not the type to use a knife, you know him.'

'First time for everything, Frankie boy.' They were moving together down the stairs towards the street now. 'You think she was with him last night?'

Donovan nodded. 'She'll not lie to you.' However, he knew she had not been with Davie until 8pm, because he'd seen Davie in the street fifteen minutes before that. He was certain McCall had nothing to do with Lomas's death but he had a copper's nose just like Knight. He knew there was a jigsaw here and he didn't have all the pieces.

Knight asked, 'They shagging?' Donovan gave him a reproving look. Knight held his hands up in defence. 'She's tasty. I would.'

Donovan sighed. Knight would hump a hole in a barber shop floor if he had to. 'They were an item, years ago. When Clem Boyle shot me he was aiming at her. But it all ended when McCall was inside.'

'Her man's on the job, I hear?'

'Aye, a DC at Stewart Street.'

'Fraser, Fraser...' Knight tried to place the name. Donovan knew he had the kind of mind that retained names and faces and he was accessing it now. 'No, Les Fraser, is it?'

'Aye,' said Donovan.

'He's okay, that guy.'

'Yes, he is. Don't tell him about this.'

'Won't breathe a word, unless I have to.'

They were in the street now and Donovan gave Knight a look that told him he didn't believe it. 'Jimmy, there's nothing going on between them, I guarantee it. Don't cause trouble unnecessarily.'

Knight's eyes were dancing with amusement as he regarded Donovan. 'Frankie boy, I'll decide what's necessary...'

Donovan nodded. 'Why don't we take it to Gentleman Jack, then? See what he thinks.'

Knight paused to smile, but there was a chill in his eye. He knew his boss had asked Donovan to speak to McCall. It had annoyed him but events had moved on. 'I wouldn't, Frankie boy. Bannatyne's asked me to look into this under the radar. He's obsessed with McCall because of his connection with Joe Klein. You know why he's asked me? Cos he knows I'll get the fuckin job done. You know why he didn't ask you? Cos he knows you won't. You go tellin him tales, he'll no be best pleased, know what I'm sayin?'

Donovan knew Jack Bannatyne used Knight like a Rottweiler, setting him loose on jobs that needed his special talents. Bannatyne thought Davie could be mopping things up and feared where that would end. But Donovan didn't believe McCall was a killer. Maybe, one day, if he was attacked, but he wouldn't set out deliberately to kill. Donovan looked into Knight's smiling face and not for the first time wished he could pound it into mush.

'I'll make my own way back to Baird Street,' he said.

Knight shrugged and walked towards his car. Donovan turned towards Duke Street without another word. He really hated working with Jimmy Knight.

22

VARI HAD THOUGHT about turning up unannounced at Davie McCall's door a few times, but each time had decided against it. She'd been invited to the party for one thing and one thing only and she had performed as expected. But something about him had stayed with her. Sex for her was something she enjoyed, when it was done right, which was seldom if truth be told, but in the end it was still only a shag. There was no mystery to it, no shame in doing it if she felt like it, not now at least. She was glad Alice hadn't really seemed interested, God rest her soul. If Davie McCall had been ugly enough to turn milk she'd not have gone near him, no matter what Bobby Newman wanted, but he wasn't bad looking. It was those blue eyes of his that got her going, so sad, so distant. They hadn't been cold when they were together but she'd bet her life they could turn frosty when he wanted. And he seemed a nice guy, too. She'd heard the stories, how he was a ned, a hard man, a bad guy, but she hadn't sensed that in him. When they'd been together he was gentle and considerate. He seemed almost caring. She'd been with guys for whom a shag was more like a wrestling match; pinning her down, almost forcing themselves into her. But Davie had been tentative, as if he was afraid he'd hurt her. For the first time in a long time she wanted to see a guy again.

That was why she'd thought about going round, but something told her he wouldn't welcome that kind of approach.

Vari knew men. She'd had enough of them, starting when she was twelve years old with her uncle – pillar of the church, local councillor. He'd felt her up two or three times over the months and then finally, one night when they were alone, he'd climbed into her bed and done the deed. She'd never told anyone about it, not at first, they'd never believe her anyway, he was such a *decent* man. He told her that, all the time. They'd never believe her. She'd be seen as a liar, a dirty wee lassie with sick thoughts. Her family was deeply religious, she'd heard her mum and dad discuss the distressing nature of society with its lack of morals, its over-emphasis on filth and permissiveness. She knew they wouldn't understand. She knew what her uncle said was true.

He came back for more whenever he could over the next year or two, leaving her presents each time, money sometimes, more often clothes, perfume, records. She began to think it was the way life was, that it was normal. He told her that, too. He said she'd've been surprised how many girls did their uncles wee favours.

Finally, though, it came out. She was fourteen by then and her mum found a pair of crotchless panties her uncle had given her. He'd wanted her to wear them for him, under her jeans. The idea that only he would know about them seemed to excite him. She'd never actually worn them, but she told him she had. She could remember that Sunday dinner when he'd breathed in her ear, asking her if she had them on, and she'd simply nodded, just to get him away from her. He sat across the table from her and every time he looked at her she knew he was thinking about those panties. She'd felt sick then and had to be excused. She hid the underwear right at the back of the wardrobe but her mum found them and everything came out.

He was right, they didn't believe her. At least, they said they didn't. Her uncle denied it all, saying he'd seen Vari out at night with boys. He'd tried to help her, he claimed, but she enjoyed being with them, enjoyed touching them and letting them touch her. He said he'd never told her parents because he hoped it was just a phase. He'd never, ever, touch a young girl like that, not like that. But she saw the look in her dad's eye as he listened to his brother's protestations and Vari knew he had his doubts. In the end, though, they sided with her uncle and she was branded a wee whore by her own family. A dirty slut who wore disgusting underwear.

She left two years later. Just ran away one night, unable to take the cold looks anymore, the continual suspicion, the checking up on her every move. They didn't come looking for her. Something told her they were relieved she was gone. Four years ago, when she was eighteen, she'd written them a letter letting them know she was okay. They didn't reply.

Her uncle, though, was still a pillar of the church, still a local councillor, still a decent man.

She fantasised that one day she would tell Davie McCall about it and he would find her uncle and beat him bloody. She'd heard Davie McCall did things like that. He'd do it for her, she knew he would. He'd liked her, she could tell, not just because of the way he responded to her physically (that was to be expected because he was a guy after all), but because of the way he'd spoken to her, the way he'd looked at her. With tenderness. And he'd said he'd call her, he'd promised. He hadn't yet, but it had only been a few days.

So when she got back to her Dennistoun flat that evening after work, she was not surprised to find an envelope pinned to her door. She opened it on the doorstep and smiled when she read the words.

Meet me at Alexandra Park gates, 8pm.
Davie

A ripple of excitement washed through her as she looked at her watch. 6.30pm. Time enough to have a shower, make herself respectable. As Vari unlocked the front door to her one-bedroomed flat, she couldn't believe how excited she was.

* * *

Liam Mulvey steered his truck along the narrow country road above Girvan, his mind on Danny McCall and their conversation just before he left the house. McCall had phoned him at home, given him another number and hung up. Liam knew he had ten minutes to get a call box and dial that number. It was the first time they'd spoken since the day Newman and Davie McCall had paid him a visit.

'Where the fuck are you?' Liam had asked.

'Glasgow,' said Danny McCall.

'I need you down here.'

'I'm busy.'

'It's all set up, with McClymont. Tomorrow night.'

'You know what to do.'

Liam frowned. 'You not going to be here?'

'You don't need me. You made sure you've got enough muscle?'

'Stringer's bringing a coupla boys down from Kilmarnock.' Liam was very much a one-man operation, although he had ambition, but if he had such a thing as a right-hand man, it was Stringer. That's all anyone knew him as. If he had a first name, Liam believed even Stringer had forgotten it.

'That going to be enough?' There was doubt in McCall's voice.

'Believe me, it's enough. Big Rab and whoever he brings with him will be crow bait by the time I'm finished.'

Liam could tell McCall remained unconvinced, but he didn't give a damn. The guy didn't press it. 'You made sure all the weapons are clean?'

'Aye,' said Liam, a hint of irritation in his voice. It had cost him a fortune to get the weapons, not that he was paying for anything. McCall was bankrolling this whole thing. He'd tried cutting a deal with the armourer, hoping to skim a bit off for himself, but the bastard had stuck to his price. Liam hated parting with money, even when it wasn't his. That much he shared with Big Rab.

'Then get it done,' McCall said. 'Don't mess about tomorrow night, when they show up, put bullets in their heads, the lot of them.'

'What if your boy's there? You want him done too?'

'He won't be there. He'll have other things on his mind.'

'You sure?'

'I'm sure. Don't let me down, Liam. And don't mess about either. Get in there, get it done and get out, understand?'

'Don't worry, for fuck's sake. I told you, Rab McClymont's a dead man...'

But Danny McCall was already gone. Now, as he replayed the conversation in his head, Liam wondered just what McCall's game was. He knew the sleekit bastard wasn't telling him everything. He didn't know what the fuck his whole plan was, only that it would get Liam back to the city and into the big money, but whatever it was it had better work. McCall wanted to control everything and Liam didn't like being controlled.

His headlights picked out a hedgehog skittering across the road up ahead. It didn't look squashed, so he veered and did the job. He hated fucking hedgehogs.

* * *

When Vari saw the figure at the gates of the Park where Alexandra Parade meets the Edinburgh Road, she thought it was Davie. It was dry, but dark clouds threatened rain. He smiled as she came closer and she realised this guy was older. 'Vari,' he said, 'Davie sent me.'

She studied his face under the street lights. He could be Davie's older brother. Or his dad. But she'd been told Davie's dad was dead. 'Where is Davie?' She asked.

'He's waiting, close by. There's been some trouble the past couple of days, he doesn't want to be seen in public. You know how it is, eh? But he really wants to see you. You okay coming with me?'

She hesitated and his smile broadened. 'Don't worry, hen. I'm an old friend of Davie's, from way back when. I knew his maw.'

She cocked her head, studying his face. 'You look like him, you know that?'

He laughed. 'Aye, it's been said before. Come on, I'm parked just a wee bit down the road.'

He took a couple of steps away but she hung back, still not sure. He moved closer to her. 'I understand your caution,' he said, reasonably. 'You've never met me. I get that, I really do. And if you don't want to come with me, that's okay. I'll just tell Davie you didn't want to come, eh? He'll be okay with it, I'm sure.'

She thought about it. He seemed okay, at least on the surface, but Vari was wise enough not to believe everything a man said. She had no way of being certain Davie had left that note or if he sent this guy. And there was something about him, something hiding underneath the pleasant exterior and the friendly smile. Vari had been with enough bastards to recognise one when she saw him.

'Tell Davie I'm sorry,' she said. 'Tell him to gimme a shout when all this is over. But I'm not going away with you, mister. I don't know who you are.'

He stepped back, spreading his hands in front of him. 'Fair enough, hen,' he said. 'I understand. And can I say, you're a smart girl? I hope my lassie is as smart as you when she grows up. No hard feelings.'

He held out his hand. She looked at it then back to his face. He was still smiling, but something else lurked in those blue eyes. Nevertheless, she reached out, shook the hand, but let it go almost immediately. He smiled and without another word turned in the direction of Cumbernauld Road. Vari watched him walk confidently down the street, his hands in the pockets of his black woollen mid-length jacket, collar turned up. He didn't look back.

As Vari made her way back along Alexandra Parade to her flat, she felt certain she had done the right thing. Davie was a pal of Rab McClymont's, she knew that, so it was reasonable to assume he would be involved in things that might mean he had to lay low, but that guy just didn't seem right. If Davie had wanted to see her he would not have sent a complete stranger, he'd've asked Bobby Newman to come get her. She considered walking down the hill to Sword Street but decided against it. She still didn't want to just turn up at Davie's door. No, she'd get home and give Bobby a phone, let him know. That would be the best thing to do.

It only took her five minutes to walk from the park to her street, but as she arrived she felt the first gentle drops of rain caress her cheeks. Then suddenly it came lancing down as if someone had flicked an ON switch. She ran the final few feet to her close but was soaked through before she reached shelter. She suddenly felt quite tired, so maybe it was best she hadn't seen Davie that night. It had been a tough day in the supermarket, she felt as if she'd not sat down all through her shift. Her shower had revived her slightly, but now she felt washed out again. She just wanted to get in the flat, get out of her wet clothes, make a cup of tea and sit down in front of the telly. Didn't matter what was on, she'd just watch it. She rooted around in her little handbag for her keys as she climbed the stairs. They were in her hand as she reached the door.

She didn't hear him behind her.

Not until it was too late.

She turned just as he reached her, one hand fastened over her mouth, the other wrapped round her throat, his face pressed into her ear.

'You should've come with me, hen,' he whispered. 'Now it'll be even worse...'

23

DAVIE HAD NEVER envisaged Rab as a husband and father, let alone a suburbanite, but nevertheless, there he was, standing in his spacious kitchen in Bothwell, a large striped apron strapped to his expanding belly as he dropped some sliced potatoes into a pot on the stove. The only concession to the young man Davie once knew was the can of Tennents Lager in his hand and the scowl on his face as he heard about the pictures taped to Davie's door. Davie didn't mention Lomas's death or the visit by the Black Knight. There was a time he would've told Rab everything, but not now. Too much had happened and though Davie still trusted the big fellow, it was only to an extent. With Joe's passing, Davie found himself trusting people less and less. He couldn't put his finger on exactly why he trusted Rab less these days, he just knew he had to keep his own counsel about certain matters. Maybe it was because Rab was involved in the drug trade, with which Davie was uncomfortable, or maybe it was the sight of him in the apron that was just so damned off-putting.

When they had shared the Sword Street flat Rab had prepared every meal, Davie's idea of providing food being limited to unwrapping a fish supper. Bobby had told him that Rab's culinary skills now stretched further than a fry up, although he was no great chef. The food he made was fairly simple – roast chicken on this occasion – and Davie could smell the bird cooking in the oven.

He could hear music from the living room. Rab told him it was Gary Moore, his album 'Still Got the Blues' being Bernadette's current favourite, and she was in charge of the CD player in the living room, where she was chatting with Bobby's fiancée, Connie. She was a tall woman, a good foot taller than Bobby, but that didn't bother him one bit. She had thick dark hair, an open, pleasant face and a laugh so dirty it needed an x Certificate. She was a primary school teacher, but Davie couldn't tell from her language, which was salty enough to preserve beef. He wondered how she controlled her tongue in front of the kids. If Davie had to use one word to describe her, it would be 'earthy'. And although she tried to disguise it, she could not completely conceal her dislike for Rab. Even if Bobby hadn't told him, Davie would have spotted it right away. It was the way she avoided the big man's eyes, kept away from him, turned her body away. If Rab noticed he didn't say anything, being the perfect host. Connie, though, loved Bernadette. The two women were obviously the best of friends, but then Davie had begun to realise that Bernadette was one of those people everybody liked.

Davie had also met Rab's son, Joseph. Davie felt something tug at his chest as he realised that Rab had named the lad after Joe. Davie didn't think he would ever have kids, so he was glad and grateful that Rab had somehow memorialised the old man. He was a quiet boy, slim and sallow, and he seemed happy in his own company. He was in his room, watching a video, while the adults had their get together downstairs. Davie was glad for that because he had little experience with children and felt uncomfortable around them.

Davie wasn't the only uncomfortable one. Bobby was squirming in an ornate wooden chair at the small table in the large kitchen – the actual meal would be eaten in the dining room Davie could see through a set of French doors. Bobby was finding it impossible to find the right way to sit. 'What's the deal with this chair, Rab? Was this thing designed by Torque-fuckin-mada? Would Bernadette think less of me if I asked for a cushion?'

Rab turned from the stone and gave Bobby a narrow-eyed stare. 'Fuckin chair cost me seventy quid.'

'You'd think for that money you'd be able to sit in it then. I've tried one cheek, then the other, then both cheeks at once, but it's like sitting on a board here.'

Davie smiled as he sipped at an ice cold can of Coke Bernadette had brought to him. He still felt the touch of her fingertips on his own as she passed it over with a sunny smile. He had always thought Rab would end up with some hard-faced hairy from the schemes, not this soft-spoken, freckle-faced beauty with the soft Irish accent. Her eyes had lingered on his face just a touch longer than it should have and he was certain the brush of her fingers had been deliberate. He wasn't too experienced in these matters, but he felt sure she was showing him more interest than he felt comfortable with.

Rab decided to ignore Bobby's protestations. He stooped to stare at the chicken through the glass door of the oven, then sat in his chair at the table. Bobby watched how Rab positioned himself, trying to spot some sort of knack. He wriggled again.

Rab asked, 'So what's your da playing at, I wonder?'

'Dunno, Rab,' Davie replied. 'He's trying to goad me, I think, draw me out.'

Rab nodded thoughtfully as Bobby shifted his weight from one buttock to the other and asked, 'What do you think will happen when you finally meet?'

Davie didn't answer. The music in the living room changed to the Steve Miller Band and 'The Joker', which was right on the nose, for that was what his father was, some kind of joker, playing tricks. They would go up against each other someday, he knew that with a certainty he found disturbing. Him and me, he'd said to Audrey, but he was wrong. *It'll be him, or me*, he thought.

He looked through the wide picture window to Rab's spacious garden. It was a nice bit of ground, broad expanse of grass bordered by mature trees, illuminated by a series of lights set into the earth. It was warm indoors, but Davie felt something cold and dank wrap itself around him, as if there was some kind of threat out there in the gloom.

He became aware of Rab watching him intently. 'What's up, Davie? You're sitting there like you're ready to make a run for it.'

Davie realised he was perched on the edge of the chair, his hands gripping the Coke can tightly, denting the flimsy container's sides. He forced himself to sit back, smile, shrug. He willed himself to relax.

'Nothing,' he said, 'still not used to being out, that's all.'

Rab glanced through the window, scanned the garden himself, saw nothing, then nodded. 'It'll take a while. It's no easy.'

'It's these bloody chairs, Rab,' said Bobby, still fidgeting. 'They're like something Vincent Price would invent.'

'Quit your moaning, ya bastard,' said Rab, smiling.

Bernadette appeared in the doorway and said. 'Who's moaning, and why?'

'Bobby here cannae get comfy,' said Rab as Bernadette moved behind him to lay both hands on his shoulders and stroke them. 'Seventy quid a whack and his skinny arse cannae get comfy.'

Bernadette laughed, her eyes looking at Bobby then lighting on Davie, giving him another long look. Davie was certain some kind of signal was being given. Or maybe she was being friendly. Or maybe he was imagining it. He really wasn't very good at this.

'When's this going to be ready?' She asked. 'I'm starving.'

'Just about, doll,' Rab replied. 'Can't rush it – it's a skill.'

She laughed and kissed the top of his head, arms round his neck, flattening her breasts against his hair. Her laugh was almost musical, Davie noted. He watched the couple for a second, feeling like a peeping tom, then the chill returned to his flesh and he looked towards the garden once more, half expecting to see his father's grinning face in the shadow of a tree.

'Do us a favour, doll,' Rab went on, jerking his head towards Bobby, 'and get this eejit here a cushion to sit on. He's giving me a pain in my arse...'

'That's nothing to the pain in the arse this chair's giving me.'

Connie said from the doorway. 'I'm going to have to fatten you up, snake hips, get some flesh about you. Gimme something to hang on to.'

Bobby laughed. 'Cannae fatten a thoroughbred, darlin.'

Connie laughed too. 'Aye, son, you keep telling yourself that. Thoroughbred, my fanny.'

Bernadette smiled. 'I'll get you something soft to sit on.'

'Ach, if it's something soft he needs, he can sit on my knee like one of those ventriloquist's dummies. I'll stick my hand up his arse and make him talk. Maybe we'll get more sense out of him that way.'

'Do that, hen, you'll never get a word out him, cos he talks out his backside,' said Rab with a smile and Connie smiled back, briefly bonding with him in a mutual need to have fun at Bobby's expense.

Bobby gave her a smile. 'I love you too, honey...'

Connie smirked. 'Can't blame you.' Then she gave Davie a wink. That's the kind of woman she was. Davie liked her.

Bernadette laughed as she and Connie left the kitchen again, just as the song switched to Sinead O'Connor telling the world 'Nothing Compares To You'. Rab waited until he knew they were safely back in the living room before he said, 'Going to Girvan to see that bastard Liam Mulvey tomorrow night. Want to come?'

It was Davie's turn to shift in his chair. 'I dunno, Rab...'

Rab gave him a sharp look. 'What don't you know?'

Davie inhaled then exhaled deeply before he answered. He knew this conversation would come sometime, but he'd hoped it wouldn't be this soon. 'Drugs, Rab. Don't think it's for me.'

Rab blinked at him, then sat back in the chair. He gave Bobby a brief glance as he took a sip of lager. 'What do you mean, you don't think it's for you?'

Davie paused to consider his words. 'Joe never wanted involved.'

Something flashed on Rab's face then, irritation perhaps, maybe shame, Davie couldn't tell which. 'Joe's no here, Davie.'

'Okay. I don't want involved.'

This time it was genuine irritation. 'Fuck's sake, Davie, it's just business! Supply and demand, that's all.'

'Rab, look…'

'We don't force people to buy our stuff. We don't sell to kids or nothing like that. Tell him, Bobby.'

Bobby raised a hand. 'Leave me out of this, big man. I'm finished after tomorrow, remember?'

'You don't know where the stuff's going, Rab,' Davie said. 'You punt to dealers, they sell to whoever they want.'

Rab's jaw set hard. 'Who you been talking to? That reporter bint?' Davie felt something bristle inside him at Rab's tone but he didn't say anything. Rab went on, 'Here's the simple truth, Davie – if it wasn't us, it'd be somebody else. Drugs are a fact of life now, no getting away from it. Joe would've woken up to it eventually, he'd've seen the money getting made, just as Luca and me have. You were there that night when Luca said it was going to happen no matter what, so we might as well be in control. Anyway, I'm no asking you to punt nothing. I'm asking you to come with me tomorrow night, to have my back. Like the old days.'

Davie stared back at his friend, unable to put into words why he did not like Rab's business. As Bobby had said the day he got out, it's not like the old days. It's dirtier. Davie had witnessed that for himself in the Gorbals.

'We're no delivering nothing,' Rab pressed. 'We're just collecting some dough and hearing what this boy's got to say, that's all. No drugs, nothing like that. I need you there, Davie. I mean, what you gonnae do, son? Get a job stacking shelves?'

Davie thought about it. Rab was a friend, even now. Davie had changed, but had he changed so much that he would desert a friend when he needed it? He also felt guilty about Bernadette and he didn't know why. Then he thought about his visit to the labour exchange and the guy's expression as he noted his details. Stacking shelves was probably the best he could hope for, right enough. Nothing wrong with it, but it wasn't for him. Davie knew the past was always with him. He could no more shake it off as he could his own shadow. The Life was his life. He knew it. He sighed and nodded. Rab's face loosened into a smile. 'That's my boy. Knew you wouldn't let me down.'

24

THE HAUNTING ECHO of Gary Moore's blues guitar and the ache of his voice were in Davie's head as he walked home. It seemed a fitting soundtrack to the night-time city, with the rain drilling the asphalt. Connie had moved in with Bobby in his semi-detached house on the Edinburgh Road, so that was where Davie got him to drop him off after the dinner. He was happy to make his own way back to Sword Street. Before he'd been jailed it had been his habit to take late night walks, latterly with Abe. He loved the city at night, loved the feeling of solitude. There was still noise – traffic, the occasional shout, people singing, for this was Glasgow and alcohol brought out the performer in many a drunk – but it was generally muted, as if the darkness had brought a thick blanket with it. There was little noise on this night, though, the icy rain slicing from the pitch black sky enough to keep people indoors.

Even though he had been away for ten years, Davie knew the streets and lanes between Edinburgh Road, Alexandra Parade and Duke Street intimately. He had never lost the map in his head and the street layout had not changed. It was pretty much a grid, still dominated by red and blonde sandstone buildings. Many of them had been cleaned up, he noticed, thanks to a programme of building refurbishment begun in the late seventies which had progressed into the eighties. New windows, stone sandblasted, doors replaced, mostly paid for out of the public purse. Rab told him he'd bought into a couple of companies who siphoned off some of the cash for themselves, selling the idea to tenement owners that they could have their building cleaned up at no cost by over-estimating the price. That way the council grants available paid for everything. He said they'd made a nice little profit out of it.

Davie was on Craigpark Street, its junction with Duke Street in sight, when he felt the chill again.

It started at the nape of his neck, as if something was breathing icy vapour towards him that had little to do with the weather. He felt eyes upon him. He stopped, looked behind him. The street was empty. He listened but heard nothing untoward. He remained still for a few seconds, every sense stretched, but saw, heard, felt nothing more. He shook his head, telling himself he was imagining things, that this thing with his father had him jumping at shadows.

And then he heard the whistling.

He couldn't pinpoint where it was coming from but he knew it was the same tune he'd heard at Sighthill. He recognised it now – 'Streets of Laredo', an old cowboy ballad his father used to sing to him. The song was about a young cowboy dying after being shot, calling on his friends to bury him. It was the only song to which Davie knew the words and one verse in particular jumped into his mind as the melody drifted through the rain,

Oh, beat the drum slowly and play the fife lowly,
And play the dead march as you carry me along;
Take me to the valley, and lay the sod o'er me,
For I'm a young cowboy and I know I've done wrong.

Davie always loved the song, always wanted to be a cowboy, but now, hearing the sad tune being whistled somewhere in the dark, it became threatening. He whirled around in the street, trying to locate the source, but the sound echoed from the tenement walls. He felt cold sweat trickle down his back and his fingers tightened into fists as he waited for an attack. But still he saw no-one, just heard the melancholy melody floating in the damp air.

Davie wanted to shout out Danny McCall's name, tell him to show himself, but he resisted the impulse. He knew that was what his father wanted, a visible sign of fear. Cat and mouse, that's what it was. Danny was playing with Davie, but Davie would not play by his rules. So he kept his mouth shut and waited it out. Let his father make the move.

Then the whistling stopped.

Somehow the silence was worse.

Davie started to walk again, slowly, muscles still tense, eyes probing shadows, searching for movement, every nerve on the alert for any sign of attack.

Then Davie saw him.

He stepped out of a lane about fifty feet away. He stood under a street light which cast a shadow on his face, but Davie knew it was him. He wore a dark, mid-length jacket, the collar turned up, and his hands were thrust into his pockets. He remained stock still, his breath clouding around him the only sign of life.

Watching.

Waiting.

Davie slowed to a halt and the father and son surveyed one another at a distance. Davie thought about closing the gap at speed then launching himself, bringing all this to an end. He knew Danny McCall was leading them towards something. Was this the time? Was this the place? Would he let his son dash across that fifty feet and let it happen?

Then, as if he knew what Davie was thinking, Danny McCall raised his right hand and waved. It was just a single pass of the hand, just as he had done outside the courtroom ten years before, and then it was back in his pocket. Davie began to move, just a few slow steps at first, then began to pick up the speed.

Danny remained where he was.

Davie was walking fast now, ready to break into a run.

Danny McCall waited.

It was when Davie finally hit a run that the older man finally moved, whirling and darting back into the lane. Davie's feet splashed on the concrete as he pushed himself forward, desperate to reach him before he vanished. But by the time he got to the mouth of the lane, Danny McCall was nowhere to be seen. Davie listened again, trying to track any footfalls, but there was nothing. Just the sound of a taxi whirring by on Duke Street, its tyres hissing on the wet surface.

Davie took a few steps into the dimly-lit lane, eyes roving from dirty red brick wall to dirty red brick wall, placing his feet carefully on the uneven, weed-covered ground. Wooden doorways set into the bare brick dotted the length of the alley, leading to the back courts of properties on either side, and as he reached each one he studied the shadows, always on guard for a dark-jacketed figure leaping towards him. But the lane was empty. Davie stood in the darkness for a few more moments, hoping his father would show himself, hoping he would not. He didn't think he could have made it to the far end of the lane in time, so he must have either gone through one of the doorways into the rear of the buildings, or had shot over the wall. Either way, Davie knew he was gone. There was no whistling, no chill in his bones. Davie was alone in the lane – he knew it.

He retraced his steps towards the street, his body still on edge despite his certainty that any danger had passed. At the very end of the lane his eye was drawn to something fluttering in the breeze on the wall. He moved closer, saw it was an envelope taped to the brick. He peeled it off slowly, noting his hands were trembling. He closed his eyes, momentarily wondering what this one would contain. There had been two envelopes before – one with his mother's picture, the other with shots of the dead girl in that room in Springburn. When he opened his eyes again he focussed on the two words, the ink smudged by raindrops but still legible on the front:

Be fast

Davie frowned – *be fast for what?* – and pulled the flap of the envelope open. He tipped the contents out, another Polaroid, this time showing the face of a badly beaten girl. A face he knew.

Vari.

He couldn't tell whether she was alive or dead, not from the photograph. But the message seemed to suggest she was still alive. The problem was, he didn't have her address. She could be anywhere. He looked towards Duke Street and saw a telephone box on the corner. He ran towards it, hauling the door open to be met by the stench of new booze and old urine. He dialled Bobby's number and was greeted by a guarded, 'Hello?'

'Bobby, it's me…'

Bobby must have caught the urgency in Davie's voice for any leeriness over his phone ringing after midnight morphed into concern. 'Davie, what?'

'Vari's address, I need it.'

Davie heard a smile in Bobby's voice then. 'Fancy a wee bit, eh?'

Irritation flashed in Davie's voice. 'Bobby, just gimme the address.'

'What's up?'

'She's in trouble. Don't have time to explain.'

'Okay, okay, okay…' Davie heard a drawer being opened and he visualised Bobby taking out an address book, rifling through pages. He rattled off an address on Alexandra Parade, but before he could ask another question, Davie hung up and darted out of the phone box.

Be fast, that was what his father written on the envelope.

Be fast…

* * *

The taxi dropped him off at the closemouth and he threw banknotes at the driver, knowing he had paid far too much but not caring, before shooting out. He took the stairs two at a time, only slowing as he approached the front door. It was lying open. He hesitated before pushing it open, listening for any sounds from above or below, but the close was quiet. He nudged the door with the back of his hand, pushing it fully back to reveal the hallway beyond. He heard the sound of the TV playing loudly. Vari's flat was similar to his own, but only had one bedroom, through a door to his left. He glanced in, saw a neat little room, obviously a female's, cosmetics on the dresser, soft toys on a chair in the corner. Another door to the right led to a bathroom, a second one further down to the kitchen. Both empty. He moved down the hallway and turned left into the living room.

There were no lights on but the room was illuminated by the flickering shadows of the TV screen on which he saw Vincent Price facing off against Boris Karloff. A coffee table lay on its side, magazines and a bowl of pot pourri strewn across the floor. Vari lay on her back just beyond the table on an old fireside rug, her matted hair plastered to her face, which was bloody and bruised. Her clothes were torn open to reveal her flesh, her skirt ripped and raised, her underwear torn off. There was blood streaming down her thighs.

Dave knelt beside her and eased her head onto his lap, saying her name softly. He tugged the remnants of her blouse across her body, smoothed her skirt down. She groaned. Not dead, he realised, relief diluting his anger. He edged a strand of blood-soaked hair from her cheek. She opened one eye, the other being swollen shut. She saw his face and fear stabbed at her single eye. She jerked, trying to get away from him but he held her down as gently as he could, not knowing how badly she had been injured, feeling it best she didn't move.

'Easy,' he said. 'It's me. It's Davie.'

She searched his features, still seeing the man who had hurt her, then realising that she was wrong. 'Davie...' Her voice was a parched whisper with barely the strength to leave her cracked lips.

'You're okay,' he said. 'You'll be okay.'

'Davie...' she said again, then her tongue came out in an attempt to wet her lips.

'Don't talk, just lie still. I'll get help, get you some water.'

'Davie...' she said again, her voice slightly stronger now, a hand coming up to clasp his. He looked down and saw there was an urgent appeal in that single eye. She wanted to tell him something.

He asked, 'What is it?'

She swallowed and he saw it caused her pain. She raised a finger and beckoned for him to lean closer. He lowered his head, putting his ear closer to her mouth.

'He said...' she began and he waited. She tried again. 'He said... that I was to give you a message.'

He felt something stab at him then. His father did this just so she could give him a message. Cat and mouse. Playing a game. Pain and fear. Davie closed his eyes and sucked in a halting breath, trying to block out the rising sound in his ears and the growing pressure on his chest. Danny McCall had hurt this young woman simply because she had been with Davie once. And he did it because he could.

'Davie!'

He lowered his head once more, straining to catch her words for she was fighting to remain conscious. Her voice was hoarse, the words slurred but he managed to make them out. 'He said this is only the start...'

Her eyelids fluttered and her head slumped as she sank into a dark pit Davie knew from his own childhood. There was no pain there, he knew, but there were memories which would never die. The sound of rushing feet in the hallway made him look up as two uniformed police officers filled the doorway. They looked at the girl on the floor, saw Davie cradling her head and then one of them said, 'Right, you bastard, what the fuck have you done?'

25

DAVIE HAD BEEN in rooms like this before. It was small, poorly lit and smelled of despair and fear and rage. A uniformed cop leaned against the wall, absently picking at a hangnail on his right thumb. He looked bored and Davie could understand why. Other suspects might have engaged him in conversation, talked about the football, the telly, the weather even, but Davie was not like other suspects. Such conversations were not for him even when he did not have other things on his mind.

An anonymous call had sent the two uniforms to Vari's flat. The male caller had mentioned something about a girl crying out but that could have simply been something on the telly. As their report would later state in the formal manner of police officers everywhere, on arrival at the locus they discovered the main door to the flat lying open. Upon entering they found in the living room a white male with the badly beaten body of a white female. The male was identified as David McCall and was duly cautioned. He made no reply and was conveyed to London Road Police Station for further inquiry. Medical assistance was summoned for the injured female, subsequently identified as the tenant of the flat, Varinia Simmonds, known as Vari, who was conveyed to Glasgow Royal Infirmary. She had suffered severe contusions to the face, head and body and early indications were that she had also been sexually assaulted.

At London Road Davie was charged and held for questioning. They asked him if he had a solicitor and he dredged up Gordon Spencer's name. A look of distaste creased the face of the sergeant at the uniformed bar, but he said nothing as he wrote the lawyer's name down. Davie knew the cop had dismissed Spencer as a 'ned lawyer', but it was the only name he could come up with. A tall, thin Detective Constable with the look of a man who found the whole thing utterly dreary made a half-hearted stab at questioning Davie in the interview room but received nothing in return. Davie had the impression that the DC was merely going through the motions, waiting for someone else to arrive. That mystery was solved half an hour later when Frank Donovan came into the interview room, jerked his head to the uniform to leave them alone, then sat down opposite Davie at the table. Even though this was London Road and Donovan was a Baird Street cop, Davie assumed there was some kind of flag against his name that Donovan was to be alerted if he was ever lifted. He was alone, he didn't start the tape recorder that was bolted to the wall beside them and he wasn't taking notes, so Davie guessed this was an informal chat.

'So what happened?' Donovan asked, his brown eyes boring into Davie's face. Davie said nothing. He was good at that. 'Davie, I can't help you if you don't help me. Now, what happened?'

Davie stared back. 'You think I did that to her?'

Donovan held Davie's gaze, then shook his head. 'No. But you know who did. And you need to tell me.'

Davie held his silence again, his mind working. Audrey trusted this guy, which meant something, but he was still a cop.

Donovan sighed. 'Davie, look… this is a mess. We've got three bodies and they all lead back to you somehow. Now there's this lassie…'

'How is she?'

'She's in a bad way, but she'll pull through.'

Davie nodded, relief allowing him to relax slightly. But only slightly. Then he realised what Donovan had said. 'Three bodies?'

Donovan sat back in the plastic seat and drummed his fingers on the tabletop, clearly trying to decide how much to say. Still watching Davie carefully, he said, 'That girl beaten to death in a flat over in Springburn? The scene was identical to the night your mother was murdered.'

So Donovan had pieced that together, well done. Davie tried not to give anything away but something must have guttered in his eyes for the detective leaned forward again. 'Davie, what do you know? For Christ's sake, man, people are dying out there and you know something about it. You want to get out of here? Then tell me.'

Davie kept his eyes on Donovan's face as he struggled with himself. He knew he should tell him everything but that ingrained suspicion of the law proved too strong. He held his silence. He saw anger rise in Donovan's eyes.

'Okay,' said the detective, 'that's the way you want to play it, fine. Here's what we've got. We've got a young girl almost battered to death, we've got her blood on your clothes, we've got a neighbour who saw a man answering your description entering the close earlier, we've got your history of violence. It's looking very tight, son. We'll hold you over for court on Monday – don't even think about Spencer getting you out on bail, cos that just isn't going to happen. And in the meantime, the guy who actually did this, and the one who I think killed that girl in Springburn and killed Lomas and Harris and maybe others, will still be out there and God knows who's going to be next.'

Davie tensed. 'Others?'

'Maybe, down south. Three other women, all the same as your mother and Virginia McTaggart.'

Donovan glared across the table at him. Davie knew he was waiting for him to speak but he was too shocked to say anything. Another three women. And his father responsible. The cop sighed, mistaking Davie's silence for lack of co-operation, and stood up. 'You people,' he said, shaking his head, then stepped towards the door.

He had his hand on the door handle when Davie said softly, 'It's my father...'

* * *

Davie retrieved the envelope with the photographs of the murder scene from where they were wedged between two of Joe's old record albums. Donovan flicked through them, his face clouding. 'Why didn't you tell me about this before?' Davie didn't answer and Donovan nodded, knowing the answer. 'And what was it that Vari said?'

'That it was just the beginning.'

Donovan frowned. 'The beginning of what?' Davie shook his head. Donovan stared at the photographs thoughtfully. 'What's he trying to do? He kills poor Virginia here, he kills Lomas, he kills Harris, all presumably to get at you, or implicate you, or whatever the hell is going through his head. If I'm right, he killed those other women too. But why?'

Davie had been thinking a lot about that but had no answers. His father was not sane, he knew that for certain now, but if Sammy was right, he had some aim in mind. However, at this stage, Davie was as much in the dark as Donovan.

'So what now?' Donovan wondered. 'Where does he go from here?'

Davie had been wondering that, too.

26

'DON'T LIKE THE fuckin countryside.'

Rab stared through the window of the Range Rover, Bobby in the driving seat. They had driven through Girvan and then taken the hill road inland, following Liam's directions. They had found a turn-off from the single track country road onto a bumpy track which led to a conifer plantation operated by the Forestry Commission. As promised, the gate into the forest was unlocked and they had bounced along for about ten minutes before they reached a clearing, where they parked up. It was late afternoon and already growing dark. Above them they could hear crows calling. Rab was looking at the spiky evergreens crowded around them in the gloom with mistrust.

'Something about it just gives me the heeby-jeebies,' he said. 'Too many trees.'

Bobby looked surprised. 'You've got trees in your garden at home, for Christ's sake.'

Rab stared through the window at the darkness crowding around them. 'These are different. These are wild...'

'And what are yours? Housetrained? A tree's a tree, big man.'

Rab grunted and Bobby grinned at the back of his head. 'Dendrophobia,' said Bobby, and Rab twisted his head away from the view outside to look at him. 'Fear of trees,' Bobby explained. 'Read it in an article.'

'Didn't know the fuckin *Beano* had articles like that,' said Rab.

'It was a magazine that Connie gave me. *Cosmo*, I think.'

'Oh, aye? And did you take the quiz on how big your man's willie was, too?'

Bobby ignored him. 'She thought it was interesting, all these phobias, and there's names for them. Dendrophobia is the fear of trees, Geniophobia is a fear of forests. You've got both of them, Rab.'

'Never said I was feart of them, just said I didn't trust the countryside. There's something unsavoury about it.'

'I think it's because you're scared of the trees, that's my opinion.'

'Don't want your fuckin opinion.'

'Allodoxophobia – that's a fear of opinions.'

'Is there a word for the fear of me smashin my fist into your teeth?'

'Just trying to educate you, big man, no need to get shirty.' Bobby smiled broadly. They had been friends for a long time and only he could get away with talking to him like that. Davie, too, if he was the type who said much. Not that Bobby would have done it if any of the guys were around, but Rab had vetoed the idea of bringing extra muscle. Liam Mulvey was a cheeky wee scroat, he'd said, and the day he couldn't handle the likes of him was the day he'd hang his coat up for good. They fell silent again for a moment. Rab was back to looking out the window again when Bobby said, 'Arachibutyrophobia.'

Rab turned back again and said, 'Bet you can't say that again.'

Bobby inclined his head, conceding that point. 'No even going to try. Proud as punch I managed to say it once.'

'So what's it a fear of?'

'Peanut butter sticking to the top of your mouth.'

Rab began to laugh. 'Who the fuck would be scared of peanut butter sticking to your mouth?'

Bobby laughed too. 'Beats me, but somebody must be, otherwise why have a word for it?'

Rab was intrigued now so he and Bobby discussed other phobias while they waited. They both fell silent when they saw headlights bouncing along the track towards them.

'Showtime,' said Bobby.

As they climbed out of the Range Rover, the crows above them spun around the air like hungry buzzards. Rab looked up at them and said, 'You know what they call a lot of crows? A murder of crows. Or a slaughter.' He caught Bobby's look and said, 'What? I can read, too, you know.'

'Wasn't thinking that, big man,' said Bobby.

'What were you thinking then?'

'That it was a fucking cheerful thought…'

* * *

Luca was used to seeing visions of Joe in the café, but when a real-life ghost stepped through the door from Duke Street, he felt what he could only describe as cold-blooded dread. Luca had come to terms with his fear of Davie McCall and what he might do, but the man before him had truly unsettled him.

'Hello, Luca,' said Danny McCall. 'Long time, no see, eh?'

Luca had his hand on the pick axe handle he kept under the counter. It was highly unlikely anyone would try anything, not with him, but you never knew. So he kept the heavy club nearby just in case. He didn't keep anything more lethal, for Jack Bannatyne's visits had made him ultra cautious. All the same, the sight of Danny McCall after all these years made him wish he had an automatic down there.

Danny McCall's instincts remained as keen as ever, for he held his hands up in a placating manner and said, 'Down, boy – no need for unpleasantness here.'

Old nerves tensed in a way Luca had not felt for a long time. He cast his eyes at the customers packed into the booths then at Enrico in the kitchen and said quietly, 'What are you, nuts? Coming back here?'

Danny smiled. 'No place like home, Luca. Be it ever so humble.'

Luca lowered his voice even further. 'You're still hot, Danny, you must know that.'

Danny made a dismissive motion with his hands. 'What's life

without risk? Joe used to say that, remember? Anything worth doing was worth taking a chance.'

Luca's hand was still wrapped round the pick axe handle. If McCall took as much as one more step towards him, he would come out swinging like Ty Cobb. 'Why'd you come back, Danny?'

'Been back for a while, off and on.'

'Where'd you go? Back then, after...' Luca's voice trailed away, for some reason not wishing to put into words what Danny McCall had done.

McCall smiled and leaned closer conspiratorially, keeping his voice low. 'You mean after I murdered my wife? It's okay, Luca, you can say it. I know what I did.'

Luca hushed him with one hand and then gestured for him to come around the counter. Danny smiled and followed Luca into the small kitchen. Luca told Enrico to step outside for a cigarette then leaned against the sink and said, 'So where'd you hide out?'

'Oh, here and there, hither and yon,' Danny said, casting his eyes around the cramped room. 'Joe wasn't the only one with friends, but then you know that, eh Luca? You used some of them to set up your supply routes. Joe didn't know that, did he? What you were up to?'

Luca ignored the question. He did not wish to discuss Joe with this man. 'What do you want, Danny?'

'I want in, Luca. What is it you guys say? I want a piece of the action. I want to wet my beak.'

'I'm just a café owner...'

Irritation warmed up those cold blue eyes then. 'Don't play games, Luca.'

'I don't play games, Danny. That's your thing.'

McCall leaned forward. 'I know all about the drugs, about the wee cartel you set up back in 1980. I know Joe wanted nothing to do with it. And I know you killed him.'

Luca was about to deny the charge but thought better of it. He sighed. 'What do you bring to the table, Danny? Apart from being a wanted man who could bring unnecessary heat, of course.'

Danny smiled again, the ice melting the earlier fire. 'You're going to need me, Luca, old buddy.'

'Danny, I need you like I need a kidney stone.'

'You're afraid of what my boy might do when he works out who actually did for the old man. He's having a wee chat to the police right now, did you know that?'

Luca felt the air around him cool and he swallowed hard. 'I don't believe you. Davie's no fink.'

'Maybe not. But you'll never be certain, will you? You'll never know what he'll do when it comes to getting Joe's killer. And you know that, sooner or later, he's coming for you. Even if he's not singing his wee heart out now, he'll put all the pieces together sometime and then he'll come looking for you. I can stop that.'

'How?'

'That's my business. Just believe that I can do it. I've changed since I've been away, Luca. Cleaned up my act, so to speak. Haven't had a drink in eleven years. If I went to any of those meetings I'd be getting a fucking medal. Used to be I was a head-on kinda guy, remember? Joe would point me like a gun and I'd fire away. Different now. Nobody points me. Now I do it all for myself. And they don't see it coming.'

Luca shook his head. 'You're still the same guy, Danny. Deep down, you're still the same. Why should I trust you?'

Danny smiled. 'Because after tonight I'll be all you've got...'

* * *

Rab and Bobby waited while the four wheel drive came to a halt a few feet away from them and Liam climbed out, followed by a squat man with a circle of dark hair on his head and two others who wouldn't look out of place on a wanted poster. The four of them strung out in a line, staring straight at him and Rab. Bobby began to feel even more uneasy about this meeting and wished he had been able to convince Rab to bring some boys along. If Davie had been here he'd've felt a bit better. He didn't like this one bit.

Rab said quietly, 'I don't see any kind of bag. You see any kind of bag?' Bobby shook his head, he didn't see any kind of bag. Rab's anger was beginning to rise. 'Then where the fuck's my money?'

'Maybe he's gonnae pay you by cheque,' Bobby said and received a quick glare from Rab in return.

Rab didn't bother with any pleasantries as Liam and his crew drew close. He seldom did. 'Hope you've got my fuckin wedge, Mulvey. If you've brought me all the way down here to sheep shaggin country for nothing I'll be hyper unchuffed.'

Mulvey simply sneered then waved a hand at the balding guy on his left and said, 'Show him, Stringer.'

Stringer nodded and reached behind him to produce an automatic pistol from his waistband. The two other guys to the right of Mulvey brandished similar weapons. And they were all pointed at Rab and Bobby. Bobby felt his mouth run dry and his brain told him to run, to run fast and to run far, but his frozen legs weren't listening. All he could see were those three big black holes pointed straight at him.

'See, here's my notion,' said Mulvey, as if he was talking about what he was planning to have for supper. 'You've got the market pretty much tied up, between you and that wee Tally. No much room for a bright young entrepreneur like me to make my way. Now, old Luca, he's still got control of the sources and the routes and all that, but you? You're only the muscle. So, the way I see it, if we get rid of you, Luca'll need knew muscle, know what I'm saying?'

Rab said, 'Luca won't go for it. He'll never trust you, son.' Bobby was amazed at how calm Rab was. How the fuck could he be so calm in the face of three bloody great cannons?

'Got a guy talking to him right now,' said Mulvey, then he treated himself to a small smile. 'Making him an offer he can't refuse.'

Rab nodded. 'And who would that be?'

Mulvey's smile became sly. 'You'll never guess.'

Bobby glanced at Rab and saw he was smiling. Smiling now? Fuck's sake...

'Okay, so the plan is you do us in, right?'

'Right.'

'And then Luca takes you on instead of me? And you use these guys?'

'Something like that.'

'And you can trust these boys?'

Mulvey's smile broadened. 'They're my boys.'

Rab's own grin widened. 'You sure about that, son?'

Something in Rab's voice made Mulvey's smile falter and he glanced first to his right, to the two men he did not really know, and saw they had lowered their weapons. He then turned to his left to find Stringer was now facing him, the gun aimed straight at his head.

'Stringer, what the fuck?!' He said.

Rab said, 'See, Liam old son, I've been one step ahead of you all the time. I mean, I didn't get to where I am by being a stupid fuckwit of a prick, did I?'

Bobby felt his stomach muscles loosen. Rab had told him this bloke Stringer was on side but when he saw those shooters he still felt as if he'd crap it solid in his pants.

'Stringer?' Mulvey said. He sounded hurt. He sounded betrayed. Bobby understood how he felt, but didn't give a damn.

'You've got ambition, so does he,' said Rab. 'I got word about your plans for this meeting. I just rearranged some of the pieces.' He looked at the two men to Mulvey's left. 'Take this bastard away and put one in his eye.'

Mulvey looked scared then, and with good reason. As the man closest to him grabbed his arm and began to pull him away, he shouted, 'You can't do this, Rab!'

'Fuck I can't. You were gonnae do it to us.'

'You don't know who it is you're dealing with here. It's no just me…'

'I don't care who this mystery man is, I'll put one in his eye, too, when I get round to it.' Rab grew impatient. 'Get him out of my sight, make sure he's no found. Must be places up here that people don't go.'

The man nodded and pushed Mulvey away. Liam appeared to stumble and in the gathering darkness no-one saw his hand sneak under his jacket. The first Bobby knew that he was armed was when he heard the report of the gun and the man nearest Mulvey pitched to the side, blood erupting from his shoulder.

'Fuck!' Rab yelled as he threw himself behind the Range Rover. 'Did no-one check he wasn't tooled up?'

Bobby had thrown himself to the ground as Mulvey rounded on Stringer, loosing off a shot, but Stringer had already jerked to the side and was rolling across the grass towards the trees. The third guy was so stunned by the sudden violence that he couldn't move and Mulvey put two rounds into him before he knew it.

Bobby knew he was a sitting duck out here in the open so he began to rise, planning to make a break for the comparative safety of the Range Rover. He heard Mulvey scream – 'Fuck you, McClymont!' – and heard another shot. At first he thought someone had punched him from behind, that's what it felt like, but then something seared its way though his body. He wanted to keep moving but his legs wouldn't respond, they just wouldn't play ball tonight, and he tumbled forward, his face hitting the dirt.

Rab saw Bobby go down and he wanted to get to him but another shot banged into the Range Rover near his head and he was forced to duck back down again. Then he heard another two shots, a different gun, and he peered out again to see Stringer up on one knee, his automatic held in both hands, blasting away at Mulvey as he legged it into the woods. Rab looked again at his old friend, knowing he should stop and tend to him, but was determined that Mulvey would not get away. He moved quickly across the clearing to one of the guns dropped by Stringer's mate.

'Look after Bobby,' Rab shouted to Stringer as he scooped up the gun without stopping.

27

RAB FOLLOWED A fire break into the depths of the pine plantation, stepping carefully on the lumpy ground. The conifers crowded on either side, their intertwined branches preventing any kind of access, even for a short-arse like Mulvey, so Rab knew he must have gone down this way. The earth was springy and wet and his boots squelched as he walked. He stopped and listened for the sound of his quarry thrashing about, but all he heard was the breeze singing softly through the pine needles. He tightened his grip on the butt of the automatic and moved slowly forward again, ignoring the damp sensation seeping though his shoe leather, his senses on the alert for any break in the natural rhythm of the woods. Not that he knew much about the woods. Who was he, Davy Crockett? He was a Glasgow boy and he hated being out of his comfort zone. But that bastard Mulvey was somewhere up ahead and he'd planned to put Rab down. He'd actually managed to put one in Bobby and for that alone he'd pay.

Rab stopped again, feeling at a disadvantage. The chances were Mulvey knew these bloody woods intimately – Bobby had said he was a shooter – so he was probably up here every chance he got, blasting away at whatever moved. Rab began to regret taking off alone after him, but seeing Bobby lying there with the blood gushing from his back had pissed him off. He paused again and listened but heard nothing. Fuck it, he thought, best go back, get the bastard later. What the fuck was he doing out here like Hawkeye, tracking a man down? He didn't know how to spot a broken blade of grass or tell if a fuckin stone had been turned over. He sighed, not liking the idea of letting Mulvey away, but turned back.

The crack of the gun to his left was like a thunderclap and Rab swore he heard the bullet rustle through the branches above his head. He threw himself face down and rolled, his gun hand coming up and blasting off three shots in quick succession in the direction of the sound and the blink of muzzle flashes. It was more instinctive than calculated but he got lucky, for he heard a grunt and the rustle of a body crashing through pine needles. He waited for a few seconds, gun still levelled, but he heard nothing more. Cautiously he rose to his feet and edged forward.

Liam Mulvey was on his side, reaching with a trembling hand towards his gun, which lay a few feet away. Rab kicked at the hand and retrieved the weapon himself, the automatic in his hand aimed right at Mulvey's face. Mulvey groaned as he rolled over on his back and Rab saw a hole seeping red on his shoulder. 'You are one stupid bastard, you know that, Mulvey?'

Mulvey was obviously in agony, but he managed to give Rab a sneer. 'Never mind the talk, Rab – just get on with it.'

Rab was impressed and nodded in agreement as he raised the gun to draw a bead on Mulvey's face.

'But see if you do, you'll never know what I know,' said Mulvey, his teeth gritted against the pain. 'You're gonnae want to know who's really behind all this.'

Rab lowered the gun. 'Okay, who?'

Mulvey shook his head, the movement making him wince. 'Need your word you'll no do me.'

'What makes you think I'll keep my word?'

'You always do what you say, Rab. It's one of your strengths, isn't it? And one of your weaknesses. I mean, you didnae need to come down here tonight, did you? Obviously I was set up – fuck knows how you got to Stringer – but still, coulda gone pear-shaped dead easy. But you came...' Mulvey broke off as a paroxysm of pain punched through him. When it passed he visibly relaxed, but there was still a tension around his eyes as he looked again at Rab. 'So promise me you'll no put a bullet in me and I'll tell you everything you need to know. You're gonnae want to hear this, believe me. You and your mate Davie.'

Rab's curiosity was piqued with the mention of Davie. 'Out with it, then.'

'Have I got your word?'

'Aye!' Rab snapped. 'Now spit it out before I change my mind.'
And so, Mulvey began to talk.

* * *

Danny McCall was sitting with Luca in the café when the phone
call came. Luca was still uncomfortable, but he sensed no personal
threat from the man and so they chatted amiably enough. What
the hell, they'd been friends once. The Saturday night rush had
cleared considerably and there was only one young couple in another
booth, sharing a plate of chips between them, so Luca had told
Enrico to go home early.

Luca excused himself when the phone behind the counter rang.
He was relieved when he heard Rab's voice and his eyes darted
towards Danny McCall, who was watching him carefully. Luca
kept a smile on his face and his voice low. 'Rab, Jesus! I've been
shittin bricks here! You know who's sittin right here in the café?'

Rab's voice was careful. 'I'll take a flyer and say an old friend
we thought we'd never see again.'

Luca knew his smile dropped and he couldn't prevent the frown
from slicing his brow. He turned away so Danny could not see. 'How
the hell did you know?'

'Met a chum of his tonight. We had words. You heard from Davie?'

'He's with the cops, I hear.'

'Need to talk to him, he's gonnae want to hear this. Can you
keep our old pal there? I'd really like to see him again.'

'Sure, I...' said Luca, turning back to face into the café again.
His voice caught in his throat when he saw that Danny McCall was
gone. 'Goddamn ghost,' he said, softly.

* * *

Rab hung up the phone and stared at it for a moment. So Danny
McCall was with Luca. Interesting. He hadn't forgotten what Knight
had told him about Luca being in the frame for Joe's death. Now
he was getting cosy over coffee and crumpet with Davie's dad.
Something would need to be done about the wee Tally. And soon.

The Kilmarnock street was deserted as he stepped from the call box. He could've called from Girvan, but he was always cautious. He was certain Luca's line was clean, but it didn't do any harm to be careful. He didn't want any record of a call being placed from Girvan. Kilmarnock was still too close for comfort, but he didn't want to delay contacting Luca any longer. Whatever alibi he arranged for tonight would have to factor in the town. Shouldn't be a problem. His Range Rover was parked on the opposite side of the street, Stringer drove Mulvey's vehicle with Mulvey bleeding in the back seat. Stringer's wounded mate was in the passenger seat, the dead one folded up into the rear.

Rab leaned into the open passenger window and said to Stringer, 'You know how to get me when you get back to Glasgow?' Stringer nodded. He was as taciturn as Davie McCall. Rab liked that. Knight had said he was a good man to have around and so far he was right. Rab turned his attention to Mulvey, whose flesh was bleached white through blood loss. 'Make sure he's no found.'

Mulvey perked up then, his eyes widening. 'You gave me your word. You said you wouldnae do me in!'

Rab smiled. 'I'm no doin you in, mate,' he said, then jerked his head towards Stringer. 'He is.'

Mulvey's mouth opened to say more, but Rab gave him a cold, dead look that told him the die was cast. Rab felt nothing as he saw Mulvey's face ripple with conflicting emotions: first anger, then outrage, then fear and finally submission as he came to the realisation that protesting wouldn't do him any good at all and his wound prevented any kind of physical action. At the end, Rab was telling him that he had gambled and lost. Rab stepped away from the vehicle as Stringer fired up the engine and pulled away. Through the rear window Rab saw Mulvey's white face still watching him. He felt no guilt, he felt nothing as he crossed the street to his own vehicle. He'd need to arrange a cast-iron alibi but also find a way to implicate Stringer in the killings should the need arise. He might be a good man to have around but Rab believed in insurance.

He climbed into the driver's seat and looked into the rear,

where Bobby was lying face down across the back seats, his back soaked with blood. 'You okay there?' Rab asked.

'Considering I've been shot in the arse, I'm fine,' Bobby said, his voice weak.

'Hang in there, we'll get you fixed up, mate,' said Rab, turning the key. He'd been relieved when he returned to the clearing with Mulvey in tow and saw Bobby wave to him. There had been a lot of blood and Bobby had passed out from the shock, but as far as Rab could see, the bullet hadn't hit anything vital. Even so, Mulvey had to pay. Big boy's rules. Just as he pulled away from the kerb, Rab began to laugh.

Bobby asked, 'What's so funny?' Rab was still laughing. 'Glad this strikes you as funny, ya bastard,' said Bobby, although a tremble cracked his words. They both knew that the situation was not humorous, but they had come through it. One man had died, another would be dead shortly, but they had survived. Rab felt no pangs of conscience over what had occurred that night but he knew Bobby would, once the pain of his wound eased. Rab understood his old friend and knew why he wanted out of The Life. Bobby had never told him, but Rab knew Mouthy's death weighed heavily upon his shoulders. For Rab, though, it had simply been something that had to be done to protect himself.

He was still chuckling when he said, 'Fucker coulda blown your brains out.'

'Aye, aye, glad I could brighten your day, big guy,' but Bobby was beginning to laugh quietly too. But then he cried out in pain. 'Ah, fuck!'

'What?' Rab said, concerned now, his eyes shooting to the rear view.

'It hurts when I laugh...'

28

DANNY MCCALL HAD known by the way Luca turned away from him that things hadn't gone to plan. He didn't need to hear Rab McClymont's voice tell him that Liam Mulvey had screwed up. He walked swiftly along Duke Street to where he'd parked his car, silently cursing the shaven-headed little shit. He had no idea how it had played out, but he was certain the bastard had put a foot wrong somewhere. It had all been so simple – get McClymont out there with the promise of money and a way of making more, then just put him down. McCall had waited for years before he found Mulvey, thinking he was a perfect fit. He wanted back to the city, he was greedy and he wasn't stupid. It should have worked.

He unlocked the car and sat in the driver's seat for a few moments. He had to get away from the city again, for a while at least. He'd been too quick in revealing himself to Luca, he knew that now. He'd grown over confident. What was it Joe used to say? *Never show your hand until it's time to take the pot.* He should've waited until he'd heard the outcome of the Girvan situation. He should've been patient, for God's sake.

He was driving now, the unconscious part of his mind paying attention to the road. He'd leave the city right away, he decided. Head down to the cottage he'd been using as a base for the past year or two, pick up his things and clear out. Regroup, reassess. Sometime down the line he could come back, have another go. As he thought about it, he realised he wasn't angry or even disappointed. It had been fun while it lasted and he could have more fun in the future.

He realised that he had turned into Sword Street, some secret part of him guiding him to his son's close. He stopped the car and stared up at the window. There was no light, but he sensed the boy was in there.

McCall took a deep breath. He couldn't leave, not yet. His plan to push his way into Luca's operation had failed but he still had other work to do. He had tipped his hand to young Davie and he knew the lad wouldn't stop until he found him. The Law he could handle, even Joe Klein's attempts to track him down he could predict and avoid. But young Davie was different. He was a part of him and he did not relish spending the next few years looking over his shoulder, expecting to see him at every turn.

He had to finish this game with his son before he went travelling again. He thought about going up to the flat now, ending it right away, but he rejected that immediately. That was Davie's territory and Danny McCall knew better than to tackle someone on their own turf. No, he had to draw the boy out somehow, face him on his own terms, do something to keep him on edge, give him an advantage. That was what all this had been about, after all – that tart in Springburn, the phone calls, the photographs, that slut in Alexandra Parade, even that junkie and the screw. All moves designed to keep young Davie off kilter until he swooped in to finish it. It had worked, too – Danny had seen the look on his son's face the other night as he walked home. He looked haunted and he had put that look there.

No, he couldn't leave just yet. But he had to get Davie out of the flat, preferably away from the city, away from what he knew.

And he'd just thought of one final piece to move.

* * *

Davie flicked at the curtain and stared down into the street below. He was in his bedroom, in the dark, because he needed a few minutes to himself. Donovan was in the living room, talking on the phone to his old boss. He needed his help in keeping the brass off his neck while he tried to make sense of what Danny McCall was up to. Davie understood now that Donovan's heart was in the right place, even if he was a cop. Davie was in the frame for the assault on Vari, but Donovan knew he had nothing to do with it. Even so, he needed some heavyweight backing to explain why he had taken a suspect out of another station without a single charge being lodged.

Davie did not recognise the car pulling away from the close-mouth, nor could he see who was at the wheel. He watched it move down Sword Street and then turn out of sight. For a few seconds after it vanished he still watched, something fluttering at the edge of his consciousness.

A knock at his bedroom door made him turn. Donovan pushed the door open and nodded at him. 'It's all sorted, Jack Bannatyne will clear everything. But he says we'd better bring something concrete pretty quick, Davie. This is all highly irregular, you being involved. As far as anyone at London Road or Pitt Street are concerned, you're assisting me with my inquiries and I've got you in protective custody.'

Davie understood. He didn't want to be working with a cop either, the fear of being labelled a grass deeply ingrained. Davie knew he would have to speak to Rab as soon as possible, make sure he knew the score. He didn't need to be watching his back for that as well as remaining alert for his father's next move.

* * *

Les Fraser was known as a bright lad, ambitious but scrupulously honest, which did not endear him to the Black Knight, who viewed the scrupulously honest with deep suspicion. Life was what you took from it and any cop who didn't take a little here and there was not to be trusted. Knight felt more comfortable in the company of men like Rab McClymont, who tended to take with both hands and when that wasn't enough brought in a bloody huge digger. Nevertheless, he had nothing in particular against the young cop, now a DC at Stewart Street. He was just going to ruin his night.

Knight walked into the sixties-style station and flashed his warrant card, saying he was popping through to CID to see a mate. The officer at the uniformed bar barely lifted his face from the paperwork in front of him and let him through. Knight saw Les Fraser leaning back in his chair, sharing a joke with an older colleague, and realised it must be a slow night. The young cop saw him moving purposefully towards him and frowned. 'DS Knight, isn't it?'

'Good memory, son,' said Knight, giving the older colleague a look that told him to back off. The detective turned to his desk and made himself busy. 'Need a word.'

Les's brow crinkled further but he led Knight to a deserted corner of the room. 'What's up?'

Knight made a show of hesitating before he spoke. 'This isn't easy for me, son, but I feel you should know…' He stopped again, all part of the act. The truth was, he was relishing what he was about to do.

'Know what?' The younger man's voice grew slightly strained as his concern heightened.

'Don't know how to put this, so I'll just come right out and say it, one cop to the other – one man to the other.' He paused again for dramatic effect. 'Did you know your wife was seeing an old boyfriend?'

Les Fraser's face remained blank as he soaked in the meaning of the words. 'What do you mean, seeing an old boyfriend?'

'Fella by the name of Davie McCall. Heard of him?' Fraser shook his head. 'Wee scroat, hard man, likes to be anyway. Him and Audrey were quite a hot number a few years back. She never tell you?' Fraser didn't reply, but Knight saw his jaw beginning to work. 'He's out the jail now and she's been seen with him more'n once.'

'Bollocks,' said Fraser, his voice ragged.

'Sorry, son, but I saw them myself, in his flat over in Sword Street. Now, I don't want to see a promising young cop like you having his future in doubt cos his wife's shagging an evil wee scroat.'

Fraser spun abruptly and took a few steps away. Then he halted and Knight saw his shoulder slump. *Christ, I hope he's not going to lose it,* he thought. *Can't handle a man crying.* But when the young man turned back his face was set in hard lines. 'You done, Detective Sergeant?'

'Listen, mate, I'm sorry to be the one that –'

'Cos I've got work to do, you know?' He sounded tough, but Knight heard a catch in his voice. He nodded and Fraser walked back to his desk, his shoulders sagging. Knight struggled with the small smile that was determined to tickle his lips. He wanted to pay back that reporter bitch for pissing him off the other day – and McCall, for that matter. He walked out of the CID room, confident his work here was done.

29

RAB'S FACE STUNG from the slap Connie delivered when he took Bobby home. He'd been patched up by their pet GP. The doctor had been unwilling to treat the wound, but Rab had been insistent, a trip to the hospital not being on the cards. A gunshot wound raised a number of questions that Rab was unwilling to answer. After all, there were two bodies somewhere between Glasgow and Girvan that may surface at some point in the future. It had cost a little extra, but the doctor finally agreed. Luckily, the wound was a through and through, into the fleshy part of one butt cheek and out the other, leaving no serious damage. A lot of blood and a heap of pain, but no permanent harm.

Once they had settled Bobby into bed, face down, his backside a mound of bandages and his body filled with painkillers, Rab and Connie returned downstairs where she whirled and lashed out with the slap that rent the air like a gunshot. 'You bastard,' she said. Rab rubbed his face and was about to argue back but she went on, 'Don't say a fucking word, Rab McClymont, not one single, solitary syllable. You could have got my Bobby killed...'

'Was never gonnae happen,' ventured Rab, still massaging his stinging cheek. Forewarned was forearmed, thanks to Knight.

She hit him again, this time with her left. It was just as painful as her right. 'Get out,' she said. 'Get out now and don't ever come back.'

Rab, both sides of his face burning with the force of the blows and his rising anger, stared back at her. He wanted to wrap his fist round her throat and pummel her for treating him like that. He'd never let a man demean him in that way, he sure as hell wouldn't stand for a bint doing it. But he didn't move, Joe's old teachings holding him back.

Connie's anger was subsiding now and she began to tremble slightly as the tears welled up. 'Just go,' she said, then added, 'please.'

Rab stared at her but decided against saying anything in his defence. The truth was he had been confident that neither of them had been in any danger from Mulvey and that the bullet Bobby took was just a wee stroke of bad luck. The doc had said he'd be fine in a few weeks, hadn't he? And it could've been a lot worse. She should be happy he's not dead. But Rab said nothing as he brushed past her and walked into the new day.

* * *

Les Fraser didn't know how he got through the rest of his shift. He swore to himself that he didn't believe what Knight had said. Yet it kept eating at him. Why would he tell him something like that if there wasn't something in it? What did he have to gain? And if Audrey was seeing this McCall character, and there was nothing in it, why hadn't she ever told him about it?

Somehow he reached finishing time and drove to their flat in Langside. The sky bore various gradations of grey and things were only to grow worse, the weather girl on the radio said, with high winds expected later in the day. They'd hit the west coast hard, she said, and ferries were already being cancelled. That was nothing to what was going to hit Langside if Jimmy Knight's story was true, Les thought.

The flat was silent when he let himself in. She was usually up and waiting for him when he came off night shift, a pot of coffee already made, Terry Wogan rabbiting cheerily on the radio. But this time there was nothing. He pushed the bedroom door open and glanced in, expecting to see her still asleep, but the room was empty, the bed made up, not slept in. He checked the living room and the kitchen but the flat had an empty feeling, as if no-one had been there for hours.

He stood in the hallway, his mind filled with Knight's words.
Saw them myself...
Sword Street...
Saw them myself...
He picked up the phone and dialled the number of a mate in London Road.

* * *

Davie blinked when Rab told him what Liam Mulvey had said about the man with the plan. Donovan had left just after midnight, telling Davie not to go anywhere or do anything without letting him know. 'My neck's on the line here,' he said. 'Don't let me down.' Davie promised him he would not.

'So where did Mulvey say my father was staying?' He asked after Rab had finished his story and he was certain Bobby was going to recover.

'Ballantrae,' said Rab. 'A rented cottage.'

Davie closed his eyes. *The bastard,* he thought, *he'd gone back to the same place he used to take them on holiday. The same town, the same cottage. The bastard.*

When he opened his eyes he saw Rab watching him closely. 'What do you want to do, Davie?'

Davie's voice was flat when he spoke. 'Finish it,' he said.

* * *

Donovan had been asleep for only five hours when Jack Bannatyne called him. His wife, Marie, grumbled at being disturbed but left him to answer it, knowing that it would be for him at that time of the morning. He snatched the receiver from the bedside table before the ringing could disturb their daughter Jessica in the next room.

'We've got trouble, Frank,' said Bannatyne, and Donovan felt his heart sink. 'Just had a call from DCI John Flynn at London Road – you know him?'

'We met once: a send-off in the police club.'

'He's a good mate of mine, knows of my interest in Vizzini and McCall and the others. He says a DC on his team just had a call from a DC Les Fraser at Stewart Street. He wanted McCall's address.'

'Oh, shit,' said Donovan while thinking, *Knight, you bastard.* He knew Knight would do something.

'What's his interest, Frank?'

'He's married to Audrey Fraser, Audrey Burke that was. She used to be Davie McCall's girl.'

'So?'

'So we saw her with McCall the other day. She gave Knight a hard time.'

Donovan heard the DCI breathing heavily down the phone. 'Get back to McCall, Frank, and I mean right now. If you're right and Jimmy's done something stupid, then we need to defuse the situation.'

Donovan had no doubt the use of the word 'we' actually meant only him. 'Right away, sir,' he said and hung up, already climbing out of bed.

'Frank?' Marie's sleepy voice from the bed behind him.

'Got to work, darling,' he said. He heard her tut, but she merely rolled over and went back to sleep. Her father had been a cop. She knew the score.

* * *

Davie opened his front door to be met with a good-looking guy in his early thirties and a fist heading in his direction. He ducked under the blow and pushed the man away with both hands. The guy stumbled back a couple of paces before he righted himself and surged forward again, both hands outstretched and fingers tensed like claws, aiming at Davie's head. Davie didn't know who the hell he was, but he wasn't about to waste a lot of time. So he jabbed with his right fist and connected with the guy's nose. The man stopped as if he'd hit a wall and staggered back once more. But his anger was too great and he wasn't about to let the punch stop him so on he came, his own right swinging towards Davie's jaw. Davie could tell the guy was fit, but this was his world, and he easily dodged the blow to step in close, sinking a punch deep into the guy's midriff. The man's breath burst from his mouth with a groan and his back folded, but Davie wanted to end it there and so he turned his fist into a club and battered it down heavily to the side of the man's head three times. Pain shot along his own arm, but the man went down to his knees then onto all fours, where he swayed unsteadily. Davie stepped back, prepared for another lunge but it looked like the guy had had enough. For the moment.

Rab pounded up the hallway behind Davie. He stared down at the bloke retching on the landing and said, 'What the fuck?'

Davie shook his head, telling his pal he'd never seen the man before. 'I think you picked the wrong guy, mate,' said Rab.

Les Fraser didn't look up. He spat some blood that had seeped from his nose into his mouth and said, 'Davie McCall.'

Davie frowned and searched his memory for some clue as to who this bloke was but came up with nothing. 'That's me, but who are you?'

'Fraser... Les Fraser,' said the man and Davie understood.

'Audrey's man?'

Les nodded and tried to draw himself to his feet, but he was still groggy. He sat back, falling squarely on his backside on the hard stone floor of the landing. 'Where is she?'

'Not here.'

Fraser gave his head another shake, as if trying to clear it, then wiped blood from his upper lip with the back of his hand. 'Fuckin liar,' he said with all the vehemence he could muster.

'It's gen up, pal,' said Rab. 'She's no here.'

Les Fraser looked up at the two of them, focussing on Davie. 'Then where is she? Cos she's not at home. And I know she's been seeing you, so don't deny it, ya bastard.'

Davie felt something electric pulse through him. He glanced at Rab and said, 'Help me get him inside.'

* * *

When Donovan arrived the three of them were sitting in Davie's living room, Les Fraser with a wet tea cloth held to his nose. Rab McClymont looked distinctly uncomfortable in the company of two cops, but there was no way he was leaving Davie alone with them. Leave a boy alone with two of Strathclyde's finest and who knew what they would claim? When Davie led him into the room, Donovan gave the other cop a serious glower. 'What you doing here, DC Fraser?'

The man didn't respond, so Davie answered for him. 'Audrey's missing.'

'What do you mean, missing?'

Rab piped up, 'She's not at home, she's not at work. Your man here thought she was with Davie.'

'What happened to his nose?' Donovan looked from one to the other but no-one had anything to say. He decided to let that lie. 'Okay. She with friends, maybe?' Fraser shook his head. 'Parents? Relatives?' Fraser looked pointedly at Donovan. Donovan sighed and turned to Davie. 'So where is she?'

Davie kept his face impassive and jerked his head towards the door. Donovan, his irritation very evident, tightened his lips then turned and walked quickly out, Davie at his back. In the hallway Donovan suddenly whirled as if he couldn't help himself and snapped, 'What the hell's going on, McCall?' Davie shook his head to convey *not here* before moving past the detective and leading him into the room lined with Joe Klein's albums. Once the door was firmly closed, Donovan said, impatiently, 'Well?'

Davie turned to face him and said, softly, 'He's taken her.'

Donovan didn't need to ask who, he merely caught a breath and then said, 'You can't be certain of that.'

'Yes,' said Davie, 'I can.'

Donovan looked around the room for a phone. 'Then we need to get help. I can't deal with this on my own, not now. You got a phone in here?'

'No phone calls,' Davie said with such finality that Donovan brought the cop's gaze back to him.

'Davie, if you're right, if he's got Audrey...' Donovan couldn't bring himself to say anything further. He knew Audrey, he liked her. He also knew Danny McCall was a maniac.

'He sees one uniform, Audrey's dead. I'll get her back.'

Donovan pulled himself erect. 'This is a police matter, Davie, you can't go careering off –'

'It has to be me.'

'I can't let you.'

'You can't stop me.'

They were facing each full on now, Donovan trying to use his slight height advantage to its fullest extent, but Davie didn't notice. His face remained blank as he stared back at the cop. If the police were involved he would kill her, Davie was certain. If Davie turned up team-handed, he'd kill her.

They heard the handle turn behind them and Les Fraser stood in the doorway, the tea cloth hanging in his hand at his side, blood crusting round his nostrils, bruising spreading under both eyes. Donovan looked past Davie at the younger cop and said, 'Les...'

Fraser ignored him and looked straight at Davie. 'I'm coming with you.'

Donovan stepped between them and said, 'Look, Les, this is...'

'He knows where she is, Frank. I'm going with him.'

Donovan saw the cold, determined look in Fraser's eyes and knew it was useless to stand in his way. He shrugged at Davie as if to say, *he's all yours*, and stepped to one side. Davie gave the young detective a careful look. 'It's not a good idea,' he said.

'I'm going, simple as that.'

'What I'm going to do... what I'm going to have to do... you can't be involved. You're a cop.'

'I'm her husband,' Fraser said. His words were soft but delivered with such force that they left a deafening silence in their wake. Davie studied the other man carefully. He could handle himself, he'd felt that during their brief encounter on the landing. Davie might've got the better of him, but Fraser had been fuelled by anger and that was never a good thing. But they were going up against Danny McCall and even Davie was unsure of the outcome. He shook his head.

Fraser's face was rock solid as he said, 'Then you'd better knock me cold, Davie McCall, because if you don't, the minute you're gone, I'm following you. She's mine, understand? My wife. Mine. She married me, not you. So get it done and truss me up but tie the knots tight because I'm coming after you.'

Davie remained still during the speech and for a few moments afterwards. He could lay the guy out flat, he knew that, but the quiet strength of his words had touched him. He gave Donovan a single glance, received a shrug in return, and then nodded. 'Okay, but there are rules. Just you, no-one else. We get Audrey back and then you leave this guy to me. You walk away, you don't look back.'

Donovan was uncomfortable with this. 'Davie, you can't…'

'This is the way it's got to be, Frank. Him and me, we get Audrey back and then I finish this. My way. His way.'

Donovan knew there was no point in arguing. He looked from Davie to Fraser and back again, seeing two men in love with the same woman determined to do whatever it took. 'Les,' he said, 'you know what you're getting into here?'

Fraser was staring at Davie. 'I know.'

'It could be the end of your career.' Fraser's eyes slid towards him then and Donovan knew his future was not a consideration. He nodded back at the young cop and said, 'Fine.'

Fraser faced Davie again and said, 'We going then?'

Davie nodded and stepped past him into the hallway. 'You're driving,' he said. A grim little smile stretched Fraser's lips as he dropped the tea cloth onto the floor and followed Davie out of the flat. Donovan listened to their footfalls descending the stone stairs as he absently stooped to retrieve the wet cloth then walked into the living room where Rab sat alone.

'Davie gone?'

Donovan nodded. 'Fraser too.'

Rab's eyebrows jerked at that but he said nothing. Donovan raised his head and stared straight at him. 'Where they going,

McClymont?' He saw a lie forming in the big guy's eyes so he cut it off. 'Don't tell me you don't know because I know you do. You also know who they're going up against. Now, you're Davie's mate – you want him out there on his own? That what you want?'

Donovan saw McClymont's brow crease as he considered this. He knew he and Davie were tight, but he also knew there was little honour amongst thieves. He was far from certain that Rab would do the right thing, so he was slightly surprised when Rab finally said, 'Ballantrae.'

31

AUDREY COULD HEAR the twin sounds of wind through tall grass and the scrape of water on shingle. The damp air around her was filled with the tang of salt and rotting seaweed. She knew she was on the coast somewhere. *Clever girl*, she thought, *now let me see you undo these bloody ropes and the blindfold. That would be a neat trick.*

She was scared but she was also angry, at herself more than anything. How the hell could she have been so gullible? How many stories had she done over the years about opening the door to strangers? And yet when she was presented with such a situation she practically threw the door open and invited the bastard in. So, clearly, that sort of thing only happened to other people, not her.

And yet it had happened to her.

As she lay on her back, her arms tightly bound behind her, her legs roped together, a cloth tied around her eyes, listening to the sound of the sea rolling onto the pebbles nearby and feeling God knew what crawling over her skin, she thought about the night before. At least she assumed it was the night before, she had no idea how long she'd been unconscious. She'd been alone in the flat, watching the telly, Les on nightshift, when the doorbell rang. She looked at the clock, saw it was after eleven, but thought nothing of it. They had a spare key for the young couple two floors up because one or other of them had a habit of locking themselves out. It wasn't the first time that they had been bevvying and had come home having left their bag/jacket/whatever somewhere and weren't able to get in. All the same, she peered through the spyhole first, just to be sure. It wasn't either of her neighbours but she wasn't sure who it was. The bulb on the close wall outside had obviously gone so all she saw was the dark shape of a man, slightly distorted by the fisheye lens, his face in shadow.

'Who is it?' She asked, one eye still pressed to the spyhole. The figure stepped a little closer, the head turning to the side to speak quietly.

'Davie sent me,' the person said. 'He's in trouble. He needs you…'

She shouldn't have believed him, but she did. She shouldn't have opened the door, but she did. She shouldn't have been so stupid, but she panicked at the thought of Davie in trouble. She believed him, she opened the door, she was stupid. She knew it as soon as the fist slammed into her face.

And then she woke up here, wherever here was, listening to the waves nearby, feeling insects crawling over her, still dressed in her dressing gown and pyjamas, her feet bare. She was cold, she was angry at herself, but she wasn't scared. If Danny McCall – for she knew who it was who had snatched her – had wanted her dead, she would be lying beaten and bloody in some room somewhere. No, he was using her as bait, to draw Davie out. And she had no doubt about it, Davie would come for her. If there was one thing that was certain on this earth, it was that Davie McCall was on his way right now.

Davie was coming. He would save her.

* * *

They drove fast and mostly in silence. There wasn't much to be said. As they had left the city, Les Fraser asked who it was that had taken his wife, so Davie told him. The young cop didn't respond, he merely stared straight ahead, but Davie saw his fingers tighten on the steering wheel. He knew what Fraser was thinking, that Davie was the cause of all this, and Davie agreed. He had known years ago that he should have distanced himself from Audrey, that there was too much baggage in his life, too much danger. But when he saw her outside his flat that day, something had rekindled inside him. He had known then that, despite his better judgement, part of her had taken root under his skin. He was still unsure what love was, and if he was capable of it, but whatever it was he felt for her would never die, he knew that.

When Fraser had turned up at his door and said Audrey was missing he'd felt fear flap in his gut, but he didn't let the cop or Rab see it. Davie McCall had never felt anything like that before. He knew he feared his father, he always had, but the thought of Audrey being with him generated a terror he did not know existed. There was anger, too, although not Fraser's white hot fury. Davie's anger was more of a slow burn, but it was a cold flame which failed to consume the dread he felt over the prospect of facing up to the bogeyman of his nightmares.

* * *

Audrey heard the rasp of wood on rock and a blast of cool air heavy with the stench of rotting seaweed swept over her body. The sound made her wonder if she was being kept in a shed of some sort. The door was pushed shut again and she felt movement beside her, then hands under her arms dragging her upright to prop her against something harsh but softer than the stone floor. First the gag, then the blindfold, was untied and she could see again. Daylight struggled against the grime on a single window but it was enough to reveal her surroundings for the first time. It was a shed, a fairly large one, filled with the detritus of professional fishing – lobster pots, discarded netting, an old row boat upside down with a gaping hole in its hull. She looked behind her and saw she had been placed against an old sack filled with sand, presumably used to help protect the shed against flooding. Through gaps in the old wooden slats around her she could see sand, boulders and pebbles leading towards a grey sea.

Then she looked to the man standing over her and felt the shock of how much he resembled Davie. His face was impassive as he regarded her, his eyes roaming up and down as if appraising her. She tried not to let her fear or anger show. That was what men like him wanted – fear or anger. They got off on the power.

'Danny McCall, I presume,' she said, her tongue sluggish from having the gag in place for so long. He didn't seem surprised that she knew him.

'Spotted the family resemblance, have you? Me and Davie, two peas in a pod.'

'You only look like him. He's nothing like you.'

He smiled but it did nothing to warm his eyes. 'Sure about that, are you?'

She gave him a slight laugh, still keeping up the pretence that she was unafraid, but the truth was that, with him looking at her the way he did, she was utterly terrified. He dropped the cloths he'd used to gag and blindfold her onto a chair with one broken leg that sat in the corner of the shed. She squinted slightly as she gave him a sad shake of the head. 'You're off your head, you know that?'

He laughed. It might have been a nice laugh from anyone else, but from him it just sounded hollow. 'I knew you'd have spirit. I knew my boy wouldn't fall for some little princess.'

'Undo me and we'll see how much spirit I've got.' She was proud of herself but she knew it was mere bravado. McCall recognised it for what it was, too, for he laughed again but did not respond. Instead he picked up a plastic bag with the Safeway logo on the side and said, 'You hungry?'

She didn't answer, but the truth was she was famished. Being punched unconscious, kidnapped, tied up and left in a rotting old shed near the sea really gave her an appetite.

'If I untie you, don't try to be Wonder Woman, okay?' He said. 'You know you'll come off worse.'

She neither agreed not disagreed and he didn't wait for an answer. He dropped the carrier bag beside her, jerked her upper body forward and picked at the knot on the rope binding her wrists. She felt them give, generating a feeling of intense pleasure and relief, and she pulled her arms to the front, one hand rubbing the other wrist, then vice versa. The rope had been tight, it would leave a mark. He moved away from her and she opened the bag at her side. She found store-bought sandwiches wrapped in plastic and a can of Fanta. She ripped open the plastic around an egg mayonnaise sandwich and bit into it hungrily. Danny McCall watched her eat, an amused look on his face.

'What's so funny?' She asked, her mouth full of food.

'Was just thinking about life, love, the whole damn thing. It's a funny old world.'

'Philosopher as well as a psycho, are you?'

'I'm a man of many parts,' he said, obviously not taking offence to being called a psycho. 'You'll be surprised, once you get to know me. I can even be charming.'

'I don't think we'll get too chummy, do you?'

He smiled again. 'You think he's gonnae come for you, don't you?'

She swallowed some bread and washed it down with a mouthful of the fizzy orange before shaking her head. 'No,' she said, 'he'll come for you.'

32

THE SMALL TERRACED cottage was just as Davie remembered it. It sat in a narrow street, jutting off the A77 through Ballantrae towards the sea. If the sun had been shining this little street would have trapped the rays, the stone cottages soaking up the heat and basking in the light. But there was no sun this day. Dark grey clouds whipped across the off-white sky and a sharp wind sliced in from the water. The occasional strong gust buffeted the car, making it rock a little.

Davie told Fraser to park the car a little way down the road and they sat silently once more, each man staring at the door of the cottage as if they could force it open with their minds. Finally, Fraser said, 'So what's the plan?'

Davie had been thinking about this on the journey down. 'He knows me, he knows I'd want to come alone. We use that to our advantage.'

'How?'

'I'll go to the door, get in. You head round the back – there must be a back way in – and, well, burst in. You think you'll manage that?'

Fraser's eyes were cold. 'I'll be there.'

'That should distract him, give me the edge I need. I'll take him down then.'

For the first time, now they were saying it out loud, the coldness Fraser had shown all day began to thaw and the police officer that had lain dormant began to show himself again. 'You're not going to kill him?'

Davie shook his head. 'I'll just bring him down, that's all.' That was something else he had been thinking about. His initial thought had been that he had to remove Danny McCall from the world, like a cancer. But he knew that would make him little better than his father. No, Davie was going to hurt him, he was going to hurt him a lot, but after that it was jail for Danny McCall. He'd despise the regimented life, the rules, the routine. That would be worse than death for him. His words were confident but they belied the apprehension that had grown on the way down. 'Just make sure you get through that door, that's all,' he said to Fraser.

'I'll be there, don't worry.'

Davie knew the young cop was waiting for him to make the first move, but he found he could not get out of the car. He felt something knot inside him and moisture dot his palms. He threaded his fingers together on his lap to prevent his hands from trembling. He was finally going to face his father, who had haunted him throughout his adult life. He thought about the wrongs Danny McCall had perpetrated – beating him as a teenager, murdering his mother, sending men after him in prison, battering Vari and now taking

Audrey. And that was just the personal acts – he had also murdered that girl in Springburn just to taunt him and he had killed Harris and Lomas. God knew what else the man had done over the years.

A wind blew, distinct from the one surging around the car, carrying the sound of waves crashing onto rocks. But only he could hear it. He ignored the deep-seated fear and forced himself to throw open the door and climb out. Fraser followed. They stared at each other over the roof of the car for a beat, their agreement unspoken, and then they parted, Davie walking up the street towards the cottage, Fraser sprinting in the opposite direction to find a way to the rear of the terraces.

Davie kept his focus on the blue-painted door as he drew close. It hadn't been blue when he'd been here before. He couldn't remember what colour it had been, but definitely not blue. His vision narrowed in on the door as he approached, on the heavy metal knocker in the centre, while still fully aware of his surroundings. That was his gift, and it had been honed over the long years inside. As a teenager he would have concentrated solely on what was before him, on the person in front of him, while everything else faded or vanished.

He grasped the knocker and gave it a series of heavy bangs. He waited on the doorstep, not sure what he would do when the door opened but trusting in his instincts, in his gift. The dark thing, Sammy had called it, something sinister and insidious inside him that would consume him if he let it. He needed it now. For now, it was his friend.

There was no sound from beyond the blue door and Davie touched the wood as if he could see through it with his fingertips. The paint was not new and some of it flaked off under his touch. He laid his hand flat against it, pushing against it, but there was no give. He stepped back and stooped against the window to the left, both hands up beside his face to shield the daylight and try to see into the gloom beyond but a heavy lace curtain concealed the interior. He was straightening up again when a woman's voice said, 'You looking for Mister McAllister?'

She was coming out of the cottage next door, a tartan shopping trolley in her hand. She was in her mid-fifties, small and squat, her face friendly and open. She locked her door and looked to him for a response as she unfolded the trolley handle.

'Yes,' he answered, the name McAllister throwing him only momentarily. 'I thought he'd be in. He's expecting me.'

'Aye, well, he's no in, saw him go out a wee while ago.' She dropped her keys into her open handbag and turned away. Davie felt first relief then, instantly, guilt. Danny had Audrey, he reminded himself.

Davie asked, 'You know him well?'

She stopped again. 'No, no really. He's no here all the time. Travels a lot. He's nice enough, though. Quiet. Doesn't bother anyone.'

He didn't know why he'd asked her about him. A need to know what others thought of his father, perhaps, someone who didn't know the history. His next words really surprised him. 'He's my father.'

She leaned in and studied his face. 'Aye, I see that now. You've got his look about you, so you have. He said he'd been married but he never mentioned he had a boy. No seen him for a while, have you?'

Davie shook his head, still wondering why he felt it necessary to tell this woman what he had. 'Any idea where he could be?'

Her eyes narrowed and a guarded look crossed her face, but she said, 'He's got a shed down on the beach, just beyond the harbour there. It's an old fishing hut type of thing. He sometimes sits down there, sunny days. Can spend hours there by himself, reading, watching the sea. Although,' she looked up at the grey sky, at the gathering clouds, and tightened her coat around her neck with one hand, 'cannae see him down there in this weather. Still, it's worth a try.'

Davie thanked her and she nodded once before she wheeled her trolley up the street. As Davie watched her go he heard the door open and Fraser peered out. 'She gone?' Davie nodded and Fraser widened the door and stepped back. 'You need to come in and see this.'

Davie gave the woman's back another look but she didn't turn round, so he ducked inside and closed the door behind him. Fraser had left the small entranceway and was standing in the cottage's living room to the left, studying something out of Davie's eyeline. Davie followed him and stopped when he saw what Fraser was looking it.

The blackboard was sitting in the middle of the room, its surface covered in photographs and bits of paper. There were shots of Rab, Luca and Bobby, all taken without their knowledge. There was another couple of Vari and a slip of paper pinned nearby with her address. Even the dark-haired girl who had been at the party who'd left without so much as exchanging a 'hello'. But mostly there were pictures of Davie. Most had been taken since he'd got out of Barlinnie – one was even of him shaking hands with Bobby at the gates. There were snaps of him in the street, leaving Luca's café, talking with Rab. But others were older, their colours fading. Him and Joe, separately and together, Rab and Bobby again. Even Mouthy Grant. And Audrey. There was a handful of Audrey, including one of them together in Glasgow's city centre, outside the Dial Inn. Their first date. Danny McCall had been watching him for years, even before Joe died. He'd been following his friends while he was inside, recording their lives, looking for ways in. The blackboard was like a giant chess game and the people on it were the pieces. The realisation hit him like a punch to the gut and it sent something shimmering up his spine.

'There's more,' said Fraser, his voice shaking and he pointed to a photo album on a table in the corner. Davie moved past the blackboard, grateful for the opportunity to take his eyes off the pictures, and flicked the book open. The first few pages were filled with newspaper cuttings, some about him, others with a single by-line.

'Audrey's stories,' said Fraser. 'He's been stalking her, too. He's got more pictures of her at the back. Her and me. One outside the church we got married in.'

Davie felt chill fingers caress the nape of his neck as he flicked the pages and found the photographs Fraser mentioned. His mouth was suddenly very dry and he licked his lips.

Davie stared at the picture of a smiling Audrey, in a cream dress, hanging on a kilted Les Fraser's arm outside a church. The sun was shining and they were smiling, laughing, happy. And Danny McCall had been there. Davie had not. Davie had been banged up in Barlinnie and Danny McCall was out, taking pictures of Audrey. He could have snatched her anytime he'd wanted.

Fraser said, his voice hoarse, 'What the hell kind of creep is your dad?'

'A dangerous one,' he said.

* * *

Les Fraser watched Davie as he studied the pictures, knowing that the guy was as horrified with the idea of the bastard following Audrey around as he was. He'd got through the back door easily, a couple of kicks under the lock had splintered the frame no problem. Fraser didn't really care if anyone heard, that was the idea. If Danny McCall was inside they'd bring him down in no time, he was confident of that, if he wasn't and a neighbour heard then so what? But the house was empty. He heard Davie talking to the neighbour outside so he'd taken the opportunity for a quiet poke around. He found a very interesting item in the bedroom, which he slipped in his pocket, before he'd entered the living room and came upon the picture gallery. He felt something sour churn in his belly as he gazed at the images of his wife, snapped without her knowing.

And now, as he stared at the younger McCall, watching him turn pale as he understood just how sick a puppy his father was, his hand snaked into his jacket pocket, where he felt the comforting weight of the automatic he'd found in the bedroom. His training as a copper told him he should have left it where it was, but he wasn't a copper today. Davie McCall had talked about having an edge earlier on. This was his edge. And something told him he'd need it.

* * *

Audrey winced as the rusty metal sliced the flesh on her wrist, but she didn't stop sawing at it with the bonds. She'd spotted the old hoe propped against one cobweb covered corner while she'd eaten the sandwich Danny McCall had brought her. She purposely did not look in its direction again throughout the period he was with her, for fear he might see it too. So she dutifully munched the food and drained the orange can then let him bind her wrists once more and thrust the gag back into her mouth but not the blindfold, which was something at least. He hadn't said anything more throughout his visit. He'd gone into a kind of funk, as if he was about to do something he really didn't want to but some force was dictating his actions. And then he'd left her. She waited for a few minutes listening to the sound of his receding footsteps crunch on the pebble beach outside, then began to writhe across the floor towards the old garden tool, her bound feet pushing her along. It was difficult but she made it in a few minutes and sat with her back to it, the ropes around her wrist resting on the blade. Then she began a sawing motion, hoping the rusting metal was sharp enough to cut the fronds. Every now and then her wrists slipped and the metal nipped at her flesh but she ignored it, although she did make a mental note to have a tetanus shot as soon as she could. It was slow going and she had no way of knowing if it was working but she knew she had to try. So she kept rubbing at the ropes, occasionally tugging her wrists apart to see if there was any give. She had no idea how long he would be gone but she had one chance at freedom, she knew that.

But the damn bonds would not loosen...

* * *

Davie led Fraser from the street to the grassy area that separated the shorefront houses of Ballantrae from the beach, which was no wide expanse of sand but a pebble and rock-strewn area that stretched southwards to more desolate shoreline and north to the harbour peppered with branches, barrels and wood thrown up by the tide He knew there was a similar beach beyond the harbour, running towards the hills and cliffs of Bennane Head. The wind was strengthening now, coming straight off the water, and he could taste salt in the air. He paused for a moment, trying to dredge a memory of a fisherman's hut up that way but he had no recollection of it. He remembered many things about his holidays here, back when things had been good. He had played on the putting green, he had explored the shoreline in each direction, he had visited the ruins of the castle at the edge of the village, he had listened to his dad's stories. He spoke of smugglers and cannibals, for a cave at Bennane Head was said to be the home of Sawney Beane, a robber turned eater of human flesh. His dad was a great reader and he had regaled the young Davie with all these legends and he had lapped them up. He also told Davie of the Kennedy family, who had owned much of the land around here in bygone days. His dad was filled with tales of the internecine struggle within that family for dominance and had taken him to the vault of Gilbert Kennedy in the village kirkyard and told him how he had been murdered by his own kinfolk. Brother had turned against brother and father against son.

And now here he was, seeking out his own father.

Beyond the harbour, the woman had said, and he could see the red-tinged stonework of the sea wall at the end of the grassy area. Waves crashed up against the sturdy buttress, sending salt water spray over the top like a plague of insects, while the grey sea beyond rose and fell as if something huge was swirling beneath the surface. The wind snatched at their clothes and picked at their hair as they set off at a lope towards the harbour.

* * *

She didn't know how long she'd been sawing at the ropes, didn't know how many times she'd nicked her wrists, but she did know she was bleeding because she could feel the blood sliding under the bonds, making them slippy. She worried about slicing open a vein and her skin stung where she'd been cut but she didn't stop, didn't give up. If anything she became even more frenzied in her efforts. And she was crying, not because of the pain, but simply because she couldn't help it.

And then, suddenly, her arms sprang loose.

One minute she was scraping away, the next she felt the bonds give and she was free. Gingerly, she raised her wrists to inspect the myriad of slashes she'd inflicted on herself, each one streaming blood. None of them were particularly deep, thankfully, but they nipped like buggery. She wiped the blood onto her dressing gown and wiggled her frozen fingers before she pulled the gag from her mouth and then got to work on the knots at her ankles. It took a minute or two, because her fingers really were not in the mood, but she finally managed to free her feet. She rubbed the skin where the ropes had left red welts, and then tried to stand. She'd been immobile for too long and she was numb with cold so it took a few moments for the strength and circulation to get back into her legs. She was unsteady as she moved to the door, using the long handle of the hoe as a makeshift walking stick to help her along. She hadn't heard a chain clanking or a lock turning when he had left earlier so she was confident it would open. She leaned against it, noting with satisfaction it moved fairly freely, then opened it enough to peek out.

A strong wind bit at her face as she pressed it to the gap. A deserted shoreline stretched off to hills one way, houses and the harbour in the other. The grey sea drove relentlessly onto the rocky sand before her, the white-tipped waves rising then dying against the land. She could hear nothing but the roar of the wind and the crash of the water. She knew she was on the Ayrshire coast as she could just make out the dark outline of the Ailsa Craig, although the Isle of Arran which should have been visible beyond it and to the right was lost in the gloom and the mist. The salty tang of the air was mixed with the sickly stench of the decaying seaweed that carpeted parts of the shoreline. Taking a deep breath, as if this was the first gulp of air she'd had in a long time, she put her shoulder to the door, eased it wider and stepped out. She turned to her left, knowing it was wiser to make for civilisation.

He was waiting for her just out of sight around the corner of the wooden boathouse. She didn't see him at first but her heart hammered when she heard him say, 'Took your time, darling. Thought you were never going to work it out.'

She whirled to see him leaning against the wall of the shed, smiling at her. And in that instant she realised he'd been playing with her. He did that, she knew. He played with Davie, he played with her, maybe he even played with his victims. He enjoyed tormenting people. And she knew that she hated him. She hated his smile. She hated the way he thought. She hated the fact that he looked so much like Davie.

She'd swung the hoe before she even knew she was moving. He hadn't been expecting it, either, for she saw his smile falter just before the wooden handle cracked against his temple. His head snapped to the right and he staggered back a couple of paces but she didn't wait to see if he lost his footing completely because she was moving herself, running across the beach towards the harbour walls. They were only a couple of hundred yards away but it felt longer as shattered shells and sharp stones pierced her bare feet and she slid on slimy seaweed. She didn't want to look behind her but she did it instinctively and saw him pushing himself off the wooden slats of the boathouse wall and coming after her. There was a trace of red at his forehead and she felt some satisfaction at having hurt the bastard. Then she concentrated on reaching that harbour and the houses whose roofs she could see to the left. There had to be someone there, someone who could help her, anyone.

But she could hear him now, his booted feet not being sliced and torn on the uneven ground. She could hear him pounding closer and she shot another glance back. He was there but he was still unsteady, so she'd hurt him worse than she thought. Good, she thought. But he was still gaining so she ignored the pain, ignored the blood oozing from the many tiny cuts and gouges on her soles and ankles and forced her legs to move faster because she could see a partially tarred rise ahead, leading to the harbour, more sheds like the one she'd escaped from and the safety she felt certain that lay beyond. The wind swept across the sand, whipping loose grains up and creating a fine mist at ground level. Seabirds and black crows were sheltering from the gale here but she ran through them, putting them up in a scramble of wings and screeches. They flapped around her body and head, unable to get much higher because of the weather. Waving her arms around her to keep them at bay, she powered through the flurry of black and white before stumbling onto the pathway and limping towards the crest, the wind easing as the huge red wall across the small harbour stood guard against the elements.

Audrey forced herself up the slight incline, her strength all but spent but she really thought she'd make it, really thought she'd get there, really thought she'd pulled it off.

But she hadn't.

He grabbed her just as she reached the sheds at the top, just as she could see the line of neat bungalows and the stretch of grass before them and the beach continuing southwards beyond the harbour.

And she could see the two figures racing towards her and her heart leaped as she recognised Davie and Les. She was about to cry out to them, to wave her arms, to tell them she was here when she felt her head being jerked back as Danny McCall grabbed her by the hair and dragged her closer to him. He buried his face into her ear and breathed, 'Nice try, darling.' He reached down with his other hand and snatched the hoe from her grasp, tossing it aside. Then he pulled both her wrists together and clamped them in an iron grip.

She struggled but it didn't do any good, he had too firm a hold. He pressed something cold and hard against her throat and whispered, 'Don't make me do it, hen.' She didn't know what was biting into the soft flesh of her neck but she knew it was sharp. So she forced herself to remain immobile, her eyes fixed on Davie and on Les, who was holding onto the pocket of his jacket as he ran, clearly something heavy in there. But then she was looking only at Davie, who was the faster of the two and he slowed down a few feet away, his face immobile as he came to a halt.

Then she heard Danny McCall breathe the word 'Shit', and she knew this was not part of his plan at all.

33

DAVIE COULD SENSE that Les Fraser wanted to lunge at his father but the time was not right. He held out his right hand to slow the detective down and, thankfully, the guy did as he was told. Davie saw the terror in Audrey's green eyes and wanted to reach out to her. He glanced at her feet, at the blood streaming from tiny cuts, and his anger began to swell. But he kept it in, kept his expression blank, kept his eyes on his father from then on. An uneasy feeling had crept through him as he saw the carpet knife dimple the skin at Audrey's throat, but he took some comfort from the cautious look on Danny McCall's face. He had not expected to see him. Not yet.

Danny McCall looked over Audrey's shoulder straight at his son, his eyes beginning to dance with something close to amusement. 'So you found me, eh, son?'

Davie contemplated not responding but felt it was better to start some kind of dialogue. 'It was easy.'

Danny raised an eyebrow then flicked his gaze to Les. 'You're the husband, right?'

Fraser wasn't in the mood for chatting. His voice was low, his lips stretched tight as he spoke. 'Let her go, fucker.'

Danny gave him a disdainful sneer but Fraser was not going to be ignored. The next thing Davie knew, there was a gun in the cop's hand. 'I said, let her go.'

Davie had no idea where the weapon had come from, but he knew it would do no good. His father stepped even closer to Audrey, his body concealed by hers, only part of his face visible behind her head. She struggled but stiffened as he tightened his grip. 'Crack shot, are you, son?'

Les's hand wavered slightly, even though he had steadied it with his left.

'You've not thought this through, have you?' Danny said, smiling, but keeping Davie in his sights. 'You sure you'd get me?'

'Let her go,' said Les, but his voice trembled.

Danny gave him a dismissive shake of the head, while still watching Davie. 'Chuck it away before you hurt someone.' It was only when Les failed to move that Danny glared at him, while simultaneously pressing the blade harder against Audrey's throat. 'Do it.'

Les shot a glance at Davie, who gave him a brief nod. The gun was no good here. Les looked back to Danny and Audrey, exhaled with a ragged sigh, then threw the gun to his right, where it landed among some tall grass.

Danny McCall smiled as he stepped out from behind Audrey and looked back at Davie. 'Needed a hand, eh, son? Disappointing, that.'

Davie remained silent, refusing to be goaded. He was convinced his father was on the back foot. Not only had he not expected to see Davie in Ballantrae, he was unhappy with the idea that he was not alone. He knew that Mulvey was gone but he didn't know that he had talked. For the first time Davie felt he had something like an upper hand. Now, if he could just get Audrey away from him...

'So what now, son?' Danny said. 'We stand like this for the rest of the day?' He looked around the sky. 'It'll be really dark soon.'

Davie wanted to finish it, there and then, but it was too risky, not with that carpet knife at Audrey's throat. He needed to get closer. And there were things he needed to know first. 'Why'd you do it?'

'Do what?'

'Everything.'

Danny McCall's face creased as he thought about this. 'Why not?'

'Why now? You've been watching me for years.'

Danny's eyes widened. 'You've been in the house?'

Davie nodded. 'You were back in the city before Joe was killed.'

'Only a few times, didn't want to risk that old bastard catching me. Just wanted to keep up to date on my boy, you know? I saw you fight Boyle that night, you didn't see me. I saw you with him and another lad, wee while before that, in Duke Street. Thought he was going to do for you then...'

Davie thought back. He hadn't seen anyone when he and Clem Boyle tangled for the last time but then he had other things on his mind that night. The other encounter, along with Jazz Sinclair, had taken place a few nights before. Davie ran it over in his mind and recalled a drunk man, weaving along the road. He wondered if that had been his father. He really didn't care, though. He flicked a glance at Audrey, who was watching him carefully. He hoped she knew what he was trying to do, edging forward slightly, keeping his father distracted with his questions. 'Did you kill Joe?'

Danny shook his head. 'Believe me, I wanted to. But no, it wasn't me. And it wasn't that young guy, either. Joe was too canny a player to be caught unawares by the likes of him. Someone else did for him, someone he trusted.' He squinted at his son, seeing this did not surprise him. 'But you know all this, don't you?'

Davie nodded. 'So why all this? Why kill that girl? Beat up Vari? Lomas. Harris. The pictures. What was it all about?'

'Simple. I want back in. Couldn't do that with you around.'

And then Davie understood. It was all a strategy to keep him on edge, to keep him guessing, to create fear. His father would have known that he was the bogey man in Davie's mind and he played on it, ramping up the pressure, tightening the screws on Davie's nerves until he made a mistake. He knew that sooner or later they would clash and he wanted to have the edge when it came. And with Davie stressed out, spooked, that might be enough.

But there was more to it. He enjoyed playing these games.

With Rab supposedly being taken out by Mulvey and Davie gone, Danny could have sidled up to Luca easily, made himself useful. Then, sooner or later, Luca would have been in the way, too. But Rab getting the better of Mulvey threw a spanner into the works completely. Audrey's abduction was a hasty affair, risky, and Davie was not meant to simply arrive in Ballantrae, not yet anyway. For the first time in years, Danny McCall was making it up as he went along, and he didn't like it.

But as he looked at his father's face, at the flesh of Audrey's throat where it was puckered by the blade, Davie still felt as if there was a cloud of angry insects fluttering in his gut. He was close now, close enough to get to his father if he wanted, but something held him back. 'Let her go,' he said, then added, 'dad.'

Danny McCall was taken aback by his use of the word. He turned his head towards Audrey, looking at her as if seeing her for the first time, then frowned and stepped an arm's length to his right, his left hand still welding her wrists behind her. 'Her?' Davie held his father's eyes but saw nothing there that suggested he was going to let her go. 'You want her?'

Davie didn't move. He calculated the distance between them and he knew he could reach his father before he knew what was happening.

But still he hesitated. He didn't know why. He wanted to spring forward, wanted to get his hands round the older man's throat, but his mind was in conflict with his body.

'You know something?' Danny McCall said, as if they were all having a chat in the pub. 'You really can't look after your women, can you? I mean, there was your mum. You were next to useless there, weren't you, son?'

Davie felt a chill seep into his bones, making his hands tremble. It was just two or three feet, four at the most. He could be there before the old man knew it. But still he could not move.

'Then there was that tart the other day – what's her name? Vari?'

Davie tensed, willing himself to move, yet he was frozen. With a feeling of shame he realised it was terror. Earlier he thought he was ready. Now he knew he wasn't.

'Now there's her.' Danny McCall jerked his head towards Audrey and Davie looked at her, saw her eyes focussed on him, saw the plea for him to do something. But he couldn't move. He had been waiting for this moment for thirteen years, looking forward to it, dreading it, relishing it. Fearing it.

Danny shrugged. 'Fuckin pitiful, so it is…'

With a cry, Les Fraser threw himself forward. It was a strangled sound, part scream, part roar, all rage. He simply moved on instinct, both hands reaching out. Danny had forgotten about him, so intent was he in needling his son. Davie saw the surprise on his father's face but he recovered quickly and stepped back, the blade swinging from Audrey towards Les, missing him, allowing the detective to bulldoze into him, knocking him backwards, Audrey breaking free from his grasp. Danny put a step or two between them and lunged with the blade again. Les seemed to run right onto it, the sharp edge plunging into side. He stopped, looked down as Danny slid the blade from his flesh and moved out of reach. Audrey screamed. Les began to crumple. Audrey moved to catch him.

Davie was already on his father.

He made no sound as he shot across the few feet between them, surprising even Danny McCall with the speed of the attack. He tried to bring the knife up but Davie swatted it away with his left hand as he balled the fist of his right and swung it at his father's neck. It was a heavy blow and it hurt the older man. He fell back, his left hand reflexively rising to the source of the pain but Davie wasn't about to let him get away. He moved in again, both fists slamming home, pummelling at his father's face, his body, anything. Danny McCall lashed out blindly with the blade, slicing across Davie's chest, cutting through his jacket, his shirt, leaving a deep gash on his flesh. Pain jolted through Davie's body, making him miss a step and the older man leaped closer, the blade arcing up and away, carving a thin line on his face. The sting was sharp and intense and Davie staggered back again, feeling the warm blood coating his cheek chill in the bitter wind.

Danny circled, his body crouched, prepared for another attack. Davie took a moment, wiped the blood away, knowing more would ooze from the sliced flesh. He had lost the element of surprise now and Danny knew it.

'Come on, son,' he said, his voice guttural as he jerked his head backwards to where Les lay, Audrey pressing her hand against his wound. 'You let this one do your work for you. You not think I saw you getting closer? You think I missed it? But you bottled it, didn't you? You hesitated. Big mistake, son, big fuckin mistake...'

Davie sprang again, colliding with his father just as Les had done. Danny stumbled backwards, lost his footing, went down on one knee but was still slashing with the knife, aiming for Davie's thigh, gouging another deep wound.

The pain was excruciating. Davie felt his leg give way and he tumbled down the tarmac incline. When he righted himself he saw Audrey scrambling towards the grass where her husband had thrown the gun.

Danny saw her too.

He moved so quickly that Davie was barely aware of it, whirling, grabbing Audrey by the hair, jerking her head back. She struggled, lashed out with her fists but she couldn't connect. She froze when she felt the blade against her throat once more. Davie rose but his father glared back at him and snarled. There were no words, just something basic and primal rumbling from his throat. He pulled Audrey's head further back for emphasis, stretching the skin at her throat tighter, the knife already pricking the surface, drawing a trickle of blood.

Davie halted. He saw Les trying to rise. He stared into Audrey's eyes and saw the plea there, and the terror. And then he looked at his father and saw the dark thing staring back and Davie knew he had to act fast. He hurtled forward, determined to reach them before Danny moved again. He ignored the pain in his leg and his chest, the sharp nip at his cheek, was almost there before his father knew he had even moved…

But he was still too late.

Everything slowed down to half speed, his forward trajectory, the hand sawing across the throat, Davie closing the gap, the blood erupting from the artery, Davie's bellow of shock and anger and grief, the brief pain in Audrey's face, Danny McCall straightening to meet his son's attack, Davie's right fist slamming into his eye, Danny stumbling backwards, Audrey pitching forward, tendrils of blood streaming in the wind, Davie catching her.

And he held her in his arms, his eyes finding hers and he watched the pain leave her and the life bleed from the green pigment leaving only unspoken words.

You could have saved me, they said.

You could have got him, they said.

You could have saved me, they said.

Then the light died and Audrey with it, the life leaving her in a single tear that trickled down her cheek. And Davie knew that what he had seen in her eyes would haunt him for the rest of his life.

He forced his attention back to his father, who was standing a few feet from them, the blade at his side, blood dripping to the ground. He seemed frozen, perhaps shocked by what he had done. A thought flashed through Davie's mind: *was this how he felt after he killed my mum? Was this why I was allowed to live?* But then he dismissed it. It didn't matter. It wouldn't save him. Not now.

Strength had returned to Les Fraser's body and he pulled himself towards Audrey. Davie took one last look at her face, the eyes still open, still accusing, and he laid her carefully down to allow the injured man to touch her. He heard the sobs burst from the detective as he rested his head on her chest, saying her name over and over.

When Davie rose, his own eyes were dry. He started towards Danny McCall but a screech of tyres made them both turn. Donovan and Rab dashed out of a car that had halted at an angle nearby and were running towards them. Davie faced his father again just as the man began to run. He could not reach the beach because Davie blocked the way. He could not head to the town because Donovan and Rab were there. He ran in the only direction left to him, towards the harbour wall. Davie ignored the scream of his wounds and stalked after him. He didn't run. He didn't need to. He knew his father was not trying to escape, merely giving them space to finish things. For beyond the harbour wall there was only the swirling water.

* * *

The wind howled across the water, ripping the waves up, whipping spray over the top of the high wall and sending it in a freezing cascade onto the stonework. The marina to the right was filled with little boats, safe from the storm in the lee of the harbour wall but still bobbing on the choppy surface. A few birds tried to brave the elements, but they were beaten back down by the shrieking wind. On the wall's parapet, reached by stone steps, Davie saw two black crows as he limped past, their dead black eyes watching him. He barely glanced at them as he kept his eyes on his father up ahead. He was no longer afraid. He had seen Danny McCall for what he really was, a coward. An abuser of women and children. A monster. Davie no longer feared the bogeyman, for he never existed.

Danny McCall came to a halt on the edge of harbour. Davie saw him looking down into the inlet beyond before he turned and faced his son. He wasn't smiling now. Davie walked slowly to within a few feet, hearing the waves buffeting the sturdy stone to his left. Occasionally sea water exploded over the top of the wall, drenching them both in spray.

Davie studied his father as if seeing him for the first time. So this was what had haunted him all these years: this strutting, grinning piece of woman-killing shit. He looked older now, as if murdering Audrey had aged him. Davie saw the lines, the pale skin, the grey hair and how the blue eyes he had inherited had lost their sheen. Danny McCall looked older than he really was. Davie's disdain must have shown on his face, because his father saw it and the smile returned. It was little more than a ghost of the cock-sure grin from before, as if killing Audrey had somehow sapped some of the madness. But Davie knew it was still there. It would be back.

Danny's voice was subdued. 'You think you can take me, eh, boy?'

I know I can, Davie thought, *now*. 'So do you, otherwise why send those guys after me in jail?'

Danny frowned. 'What guys? I never sent anyone after you. I always wanted it to be this way, just you and me. That's why I did that lassie Vari, to keep you away from Mulvey. I needed you out of the picture, but I wanted to do it myself.'

Davie examined his father's face for some shadow of a lie but saw nothing. He knew deep down that the man was telling the truth – he hadn't paid off Lomas, he didn't send those other boys. Someone else wanted him dead or damaged. His mind churned like the raging sea water around them. Who? Who didn't want him to come out of that prison?

Davie tensed as Danny raised the carpet knife up to his face. He stared at it for a second before tossing it into the foam below him. Then he looked past Davie and shrugged. 'Well, son, doesn't look as if we'll ever know which of us would've come out on top…'

Davie half-turned to see Les Fraser on one knee a few feet behind, a large red stain spreading from his side as he held the 9mm automatic in the shooter's pose, elbow slightly bent, left hand wrapped round right wrist to steady the aim. Davie called out 'No!' but Fraser ignored him.

The wind snatched the sound of the gunshots away but the bullets found their mark. Danny McCall's body jerked twice, three times, tiny geysers of blood erupting from his chest. He teetered on the edge, his body useless now, but he still managed to raise his head to stare at his son. He smiled, blood bubbling from between his lips. He tried to raise his hand as if to wave, just as he had outside the court room, just as he had that night in the street, just as he had in Davie's nightmares, but before he could complete the gesture he tumbled backwards and vanished. Davie looked back again towards Fraser, who was rising unsteadily to his feet, the gun still aimed at where Danny McCall had been standing, his wife's blood matted on his clothes and hands, his own blood still seeping from the wound in his side. His waxen face glistened although Davie could not tell whether it was the sea spray or tears.

Davie moved to the edge of the harbour wall and looked down to his father's body drifting on the swell. He was lying on his back, arms outstretched, eyes staring sightlessly upwards. The smile was gone, everything was gone. Only the flesh remained, floating on the bloated current. And then, as Davie watched, a larger ripple surged through the inlet and caught the corpse, pushing it further towards the marina, before drawing it back out again.

And is it did so, it caused one arm to move, just slightly, as if he was waving.

Davie turned and walked back alongside the wall. He stopped beside Fraser, his gaze finding Audrey's body, seeing Donovan and Rab standing over it but watching them. He twisted his head to study the detective's pale features, the eyes still fixed on the point where Danny McCall had vanished, as if he expected him to rise up once more. He saw the agony cutting deep lines on Fraser's face and was impressed at the strength of will he had shown to walk to the harbour. Davie's gaze travelled down to the gun now hanging loosely in the man's hand. He looked back once more to Audrey's body. She looked as if someone had simply thrown her there, used up.

Fraser's gaze did not waver from the harbour edge. His body twitched in a slight shrug and his hand covered his wound, as if to hide it from the world. 'She's dead,' he said, his voice flat, lifeless. 'But he didn't kill her. He cut her but he didn't kill her.' Then his eyes, flooded with tears, swam towards Davie. 'You did that. You killed her, the minute you met her…'

34

DAVIE SAT IN the armchair in Vari's flat and watched her sleep. She lay on her back on the settee, her face swathed in bandages, a quilt pulled to her chin. She breathed softly and despite the bruises, she looked so young. She said she'd been happy to see him but he could see fear shadow her eyes when she looked at him. He knew she saw Danny McCall in his face. They had talked for a while, but he could see she was tired. She needed to sleep a lot, she'd explained, it was part of the healing process, the body going into some kind of stasis in order to fix itself. He didn't know who had told her that and he didn't ask. She asked him if he'd stay while she had a nap and he agreed, knowing that she was afraid to be on her own. So he carried the quilt from her bedroom and he laid it across her as she stretched out on the couch and he gently kissed her on the forehead, feeling her flinch slightly as he leaned closer. Then he sat in the armchair and watched as she closed her eyes, listening to her breath deepen as she descended into sleep. Occasionally, she shuddered and moaned softly, as her mind replayed something, but mostly she slept soundly.

Davie knew about bad dreams. He no longer dreamed of the field. Now his nights were filled with Audrey's face, scarlet tails whipping from her neck in the high wind. He saw her eyes as she died, accusing him, reminding him he had failed her, just as he had failed his mother, failed Vari. Danny McCall had been right. He could not protect any of them.

He and Les Fraser had limped back to where Donovan and Rab stood over Audrey without anything further being said. Fraser had said it all. Davie knew he was to blame for everything. He should never have allowed her back into his life, but he couldn't help himself because he had loved her, it was as simple as that. He had loved her. And now she was gone, just like every other person he had ever loved – his mother, Joe, even Abe was out of his life.

By the time he and Les Fraser reached them, Donovan was shivering in the chill air, his jacket draped over Audrey's upper half. And for that Davie was grateful. Donovan silently eased the pistol from Fraser's hand and removed the clip containing the remainder of the bullets. He jerked the slide to clear the chamber, retrieving the ejected round from the grass where it landed. He pushed the weapon into the rear waistband of his trousers, the bullets were thrust into his pocket. Then he helped Fraser to the ground and took a look at the knife wound.

Nobody said a word as they waited, knowing that someone would have dialled 999. There was nothing to be said. Fraser stared at the body under the jacket and wept quietly. Donovan knelt by his side, a reassuring hand on the man's shoulder, but there was nothing he could do or say to make it better. Even Rab looked pale, his eyes shifting as he waited, nervous because he was involved in something he really shouldn't be anywhere near.

Davie felt his eyes smart. He was staring at the dead body of the woman he loved and he felt the tightness in his chest and the bitter constriction of his throat, but the tears still would not come. He doubted they ever would.

They were taken first to the small police office in Girvan then up the A77 to the larger headquarters at Ayr. A doctor was called to treat Davie's wounds, the cut on his chest was superficial but the slash on his cheek and the one to his thigh both needed stitches, so he was taken to hospital before being returned to the police station. Les Fraser's wound was more serious, although not life-threatening, so he was kept in.

There were questions, of course, and they all answered truthfully, although neither Rab nor Davie mentioned Liam Mulvey, opting instead for the fiction that Danny McCall had revealed his location to his son. No-one would ever be the wiser. And if Mulvey's body ever surfaced, which Rab fervently hoped would never happen, there would be nothing to connect him to it.

In the end, only Les Fraser would face any music. At the very least, his career was over. He had shot a man after all, albeit the bastard who had stabbed him, murdered his wife and was responsible for other deaths. They would never know for certain how many deaths could be laid at Danny McCall's feet, for there was nothing to link him to the three down south or even to the murders of Lomas and Harris. But Davie knew. And Donovan knew, although it wouldn't do him much good. A shadow would hang over him from now on, because he should have prevented the events at Ballantrae from happening.

But it wasn't Donovan's fault. Davie should never have allowed Fraser to come with him. He should not have hesitated when faced with his father. He should have gone for him immediately, surprised him. But instead he froze and gave Danny McCall the chance to take someone else away from him. Audrey had been right to silently accuse him. Les Fraser had been right. Davie had killed Audrey, sure as if he had wielded the blade himself. He had allowed his feelings for her to keep her close. He had ignored the creature within him, the one he had inherited from Danny McCall, and had failed to act.

And as he sat silently, watching the girl sleep, he vowed it would never happen again.

35

LUCA SAW THE young man come in and sensed his nervousness, but thought little of it. He was used to jittery young men in the café and knew he was in many ways responsible. This boy was clearly a junkie mired deeply in his addiction. His face was pale, shining with sweat despite the low mercury reading outside and when he spoke his voice had the distinctive choked sound of the seasoned user. His body shook as he asked for a cup of coffee. The boy dropped some coins with trembling fingers onto the counter top and then shuffled to a table, his hand vibrating so badly he spilled some of the liquid onto the floor. Luca sighed, knowing he'd have to clean that up.

It was a quiet night, with rain rattling against the café windows and only two other customers, a middle-aged couple Luca knew lived round the corner. Enrico had gone but Joe was there, the first time he'd made an appearance in days. He sat in his booth, watching Luca work. Luca ignored him.

The couple left, the man giving him a nod of farewell, the woman shooting him a little smile. He knew them, they were regulars, and sometimes he thought they came to his small café just to pass the time. They always ordered the same thing, a pot of tea for two and a brace of cheese toasties. It was hardly going to make him a millionaire but hell, he didn't need their cash. He didn't mind them nursing their tea for half an hour or so. They were a nice couple and it was good to have regulars.

He stepped into the small kitchen to fetch the mop and bucket in order to clean up the spilled coffee. When he moved back out, the boy was standing at the counter, his body pressed hard against the wood, as if it was holding him up. 'What can I get you, kid?' Luca asked. The boy watched him with such intensity that Luca thought, *Jesus, this kid's gonna try to rob me.* He glanced at the pickaxe handle lying on its shelf just under the counter and edged closer. He couldn't believe it, did he not know who he was? 'You want something else?'

He laid his hand on the solid wood of the handle just as the boy raised his arm and aimed a gun directly at him. The muzzle juddered as the hand that held it shivered feverishly and Luca stepped back, his arms outstretched as if he could catch the bullet he knew was coming his way. The boy said nothing as he pulled the trigger and Luca's chest caught fire as he jerked back, slamming into the mirrored wall behind him. The gun bucked again as the boy fired a second time and Luca felt the round slam into him, twisting his torso round. The third bullet ploughed into his back and then Luca was falling backwards, his head striking the edge of the sink below the counter. He lay on his back, hearing the boy's footsteps, then the door opening and closing. He closed his eyes, listening to the rain lashing against the windows and wishing he was out there, just to feel its touch one last time. He felt as if he was drifting, floating free, no pain, no sensation, nothing but the sound of the rain. He opened his eyes and saw Joe looking down at him.

'I'll be with you soon, Joe,' Luca said.

But Joe shook his head, almost sadly, then straightened and as he did so began to fade until there was nothing left but his voice. *No, my friend, you will never see me again.*

So Luca closed his eyes and listened to the rain until he floated off and he heard no more.

* * *

Bernadette McClymont lay on her back in bed, listening to her husband snoring at her side. She had grown used to the sound, could even sleep through it, but tonight she was awake, her mind filled with the events of the past few days. She knew everything about Rab's business, he often discussed it with her beforehand, and she actively promoted some of his actions. She was not the sweet Irish colleen she pretended to be. She was tough – she'd had to be, growing up in her father's household, with four brothers, every one of them as crooked as a mountain road. She knew the score, as they said in Glasgow. Her dad doted on her but had questioned her choice of man. He thought Rab was nothing but muscle – and a Prod, too. But she knew Rab had greatness in him. She loved him, would never allow anything to harm him. She wanted him to be top dog in the city, even if it meant getting her own hands dirty in the process.

Rab had been right in having Luca done. The old man had become nothing more than a parasite. He hadn't contributed to the business for some time, he'd merely sat in that café of his and leeched off the hard work of others. Rab knew all that was needed about the business now. He'd been correct in having Mulvery taken out, too. He would just have come back again, wiser, stronger. Stringer would have to be watched, though. He'd turned on one boss, he could easily turn on another.

And then there was Davie.

She knew her husband had grassed his old mate and she knew the guilt weighed heavily upon him. She also knew that a part of him feared Davie McCall, and from what Bernadette had learned, he had good reason. She feared what McCall would do if he ever found out about Rab's arrangement with the Black Knight.

That was why, through contacts of her father, she had arranged the attacks in prison.

He had proved his mettle by surviving every attempt. She liked that. It impressed her. But he remained a danger. Even so, she could not risk another bid. Luca was gone, Danny McCall was gone, and Davie remained convinced it was one or the other behind the attacks. No – she would keep him on side her own way now. She would keep him off balance by flirting with him, for that was his Achilles Heel. Oh yes, she had his measure. Others thought he was unbeatable, that he was a hardcase to his very core. Bernadette saw him differently. Old Joe had taught him well, too well. Never hurt women, children or animals. It was his weak spot.

Some day, it would be his downfall.

Author's Note

This is a work of fiction. The events, characters, situations described here are not based on any in real-life. The places mentioned exist, of course, but what occurs in these pages is, well, fictional.

There is no fisherman's shed on the beach at Ballantrae, so don't go looking for it, although there are sheds at the harbour. None of them have ever been owned by Danny McCall.

Some other books published by **LUATH** PRESS

Death of a Chief

Douglas Watt
ISBN 978-1-906817-31-2 PBK £6.99

The year is 1686. Sir Lachlan MacLean, chief of a proud but poverty-striken Highland clan, has met with a macabre death in his Edinburgh lodgings. With a history of bad debts, family quarrels, and some very shady associates, Sir Lachlan had many enemies. But while motives are not hard to find, evidence is another thing entirely. It falls to lawyer John MacKenzie and his scribe Davie Scougall to investigate the mystery surrounding the death of the chief, but among the endless possibilities, can Reason prevail in a time of witchcraft, superstition and religious turmoil?

This thrilling tale of suspense plays out against a wonderfully realised backdrop of pre-Enlightenment Scotland, a country on the brink of financial ruin, ruled from London, a country divided politically by religion and geography. The first in the series featuring investigative advocate John MacKenzie, *Death of a Chief* comes from a time long before police detectives existed.

Move over Rebus. There's a new – or should that be old – detective in town.
I-ON EDINBURGH

the author vividly brings to life late 17th century Edinburgh.
JOURNAL OF THE LAW SOCIETY OF SCOTLAND

Testament of a Witch

Douglas Watt
ISBN 978-1-908373-21-2 PBK £7.99

I confess that I am a witch. I have sold myself body and soul unto Satan. My mother took me to the Blinkbonny Woods where we met other witches. I put a hand on the crown of my head and the other on the sole of my foot. I gave everything between unto him.

Scotland, late seventeenth century. A young woman is accused of witchcraft. Tortured with pins and sleep deprivation, she is using all of her strength to resist confessing...

In the wake of the Scottish Parliament's Witchcraft Act, the Scottish witch-hunt began. Probably more than a thousand men and women were executed for witchcraft before the frenzy died down.

When Edinburgh-based Advocate John MacKenzie and his assistant Davie Scougall investigate the suspicious death of a woman denounced as a witch, they find themselves in a village overwhelmed by superstition, resentment and puritanical religion. In a time of spiritual, political and social upheaval, will reason allow MacKenzie to reveal the true evil lurking in the town, before the witch-hunt claims yet another victim?

Stealing God

James Green
ISBN 978-1-906817-47-3 PBK £6.99

Jimmy Costello, last seen at the epicentre of a murder investigation and a gangland turf war, is now a student priest in Rome. Driven to atone for his past sins, Jimmy is trying to leave the hardbitten cop behind him, but the Church has a use for the old Jimmy.

When a visiting Archbishop dies in mysterious circumstances, Jimmy is hand-picked to look into the case. With local copper Inspector Ricci, Jimmy follows the trail from the streets of the Holy City via Glasgow and back to Rome, where they stumble on dark forces that threaten everything Jimmy hopes for. But who is really behind their investigation – and are they supposed to uncover the truth, or is their mission altogether more sinister?

An explosive sequel to *Bad Catholics*, the first in the Jimmy Costello series.

Yesterday's Sins

James Green
ISBN 978-1-906817-39-8 PBK £9.99

Deliver us from evil…

Why would anyone put a bomb in the car of a retired USAF Major who writes cookery books in a small Danish town? Charlie Bronski has a past and it looks like it's catching up with him.

Charlie recognises the bomb attempt as professional and he should know because it used to be his line of work. When Charlie asks for help from the people who provided him with his new life and identity they ask him for a favour. It shouldn't be too hard, just to kill a middle-aged widower who's doing a placement as a Catholic priest. Name of Costello, Jimmy Costello.

A race against time begins. Can he get Costello before somebody gets him?

The third in the compelling Jimmy Costello series.

An intelligent and well-written thriller.
THE HERALD

Eye for an Eye

Frank Muir

ISBN 978-1-905222-56-8 PBK £9.99

One psychopath. One killer. The Stabber.

Six victims. Six wife abusers. Each stabbed to death through their left eye.

The cobbled lanes and back streets of St Andrews provide the setting for these brutal killings. But six unsolved murders and mounting censure from the media force Detective Inspector Andy Gilchrist off the case. Driven by his fear of failure, desperate to redeem his career and reputation, Gilchrist vows to catch The Stabber alone.

What is the significance of the left eye? How does an old photograph of an injured cat link the past to the present? And what exactly is our little group? Digging deeper into the world of a psychopath, Gilchrist fears he is up against the worst kind of murderer – a serial killer on the verge of mental collapse.

Everything I look for in a crime novel.
LOUISE WELSH

Rebus did it for Edinburgh. Laidlaw did it for Glasgow. Gilchrist might just be the bloke to put St Andrews on the crime fiction map.
DAILY RECORD

Hand for a Hand

Frank Muir

ISBN 978-1906817-51-0 PBK £6.99

A bright new recruit to the swelling army of Scots crime writers.
QUINTIN JARDINE

An amputated hand is found in a bunker, its lifeless fingers clutching a note addressed to DCI Andy Gilchrist. The note bears only one word: Murder.

When other body parts with messages attached are discovered, Gilchrist finds himself living every policeman's worst nightmare – with a sadistic killer out for revenge.

Forced to confront the ghosts of his past, Gilchrist must solve the cryptic clues and find the murderer before the next victim, whose life means more to Gilchrist that his own, is served up piece by slaughtered piece.

Hand for a Hand is the second in Frank Muir's DI Gilchrist series.

Luath Press Limited

committed to publishing well written books worth reading

LUATH PRESS takes its name from Robert Burns, whose little collie Luath (*Gael.*, swift or nimble) tripped up Jean Armour at a wedding and gave him the chance to speak to the woman who was to be his wife and the abiding love of his life. Burns called one of 'The Twa Dogs' Luath after Cuchullin's hunting dog in Ossian's *Fingal*. Luath Press was established in 1981 in the heart of Burns country, and now resides a few steps up the road from Burns' first lodgings on Edinburgh's Royal Mile.

Luath offers you distinctive writing with a hint of unexpected pleasures.

Most bookshops in the UK, the US, Canada, Australia, New Zealand and parts of Europe either carry our books in stock or can order them for you. To order direct from us, please send a £sterling cheque, postal order, international money order or your credit card details (number, address of cardholder and expiry date) to us at the address below. Please add post and packing as follows: UK – £1.00 per delivery address; overseas surface mail – £2.50 per delivery address; overseas airmail – £3.50 for the first book to each delivery address, plus £1.00 for each additional book by airmail to the same address. If your order is a gift, we will happily enclose your card or message at no extra charge.

Luath Press Limited
543/2 Castlehill
The Royal Mile
Edinburgh EH1 2ND
Scotland
Telephone: 0131 225 4326 (24 hours)
email: sales@luath.co.uk
Website: www.luath.co.uk